CORNER BLITZ

Books by David Chill

CORNER BLITZ

A Novel By

DAVID CHILL

Cover art photography provided by Jennifer Nicolaisen

For Dann Collins

One

The governor of California does not typically meet with people like me. But the governor of California does not typically have his teenage daughter go missing.

Governor Rex Palmer was a handsome man, tall and slim, with a square jaw and a distinguished face. He had a head full of black hair that was graying at the temples. His voice was a deep baritone, normally dynamic and upbeat, but now somber and subdued. The agonizing thought that he might not see his only child again was apparent. We were sitting around a conference room table; the governor, myself, and two members of his staff, one flanked on either side of him.

"She was supposed to appear at a campaign event with me on Saturday night," he said, gripping the armrests of his chair tightly. "But she was a no-show. And my wife told me she didn't come home that night. Or last night either."

"Has there been any communication from her at all?" I asked.

A few long seconds went by. "No," he finally managed. "I don't know who to turn to, Mr. Burnside."

"The police would normally be a good start," I suggested. "Or the FBI."

"Not with an election coming up," said the professional-looking woman to his right. "There's too much at stake here."

"And the last thing we need to do is involve the Federal Bureau of Incompetence," growled the tough looking man on his left.

The tough looking aide was Bill Thorn, the person in charge of the governor's security detail. The professional looking woman was Shelly Busch, who was managing the governor's campaign. The election was two weeks away and it had turned into a nasty race. Politics could be an ugly business, but never more so than at the end of a campaign. In this race, Governor Palmer, a moderate Republican, was running against State Assemblyman Justin Woo, a moderate Democrat. They were both centrists, which meant they agreed on more things than they disagreed. And when two candidates' political stances are similar, the campaign is bound to get personal. There's not much else to quibble about.

"Well, I'm impressed someone would rank my talents above an entire federal agency," I said to Thorn and then turned diplomatically back to Governor Palmer. "But I understand your concern."

In fact, I did not understand this at all. When children go missing, the natural reaction for most parents would be to hunt tirelessly for them. Most parents would look to any and every law enforcement arm at their disposal. But most parents did not have a high-profile career that now stood at a critical juncture.

"This is a sensitive issue, Burnside," said Thorn, eyeing me carefully.

"That's good," I answered. "I'm a sensitive guy."

He didn't reply and was now eyeing me even more carefully. I responded by pretending not to notice.

"You come highly recommended," the governor finally said. "Jeremy Hoffman was very lavish in his praise. He said you were the best."

I nodded appreciatively. My USC connections were coming into play once again. Jeremy Hoffman served on the Coliseum Commission, as well as on various committees at the university. He had been a fixture at USC long before I played football there. And that was a few decades ago.

"I'll thank him for the referral. His offices are just down the street."

"Yes," Palmer continued, "Jeremy is an old friend of the family. And as much as I respect Bill here, we need an outsider looking into this. I don't want this to be part of the campaign. It has to be a stealth investigation. This can't go public."

"Why not?" I asked.

An uneasy silence hung over the room like a cloud. The three of them looked down at the table. The governor finally spoke. "There are elements of my family life that just need to be kept private."

"All right," I said, not liking that a piece of information was being withheld. "Maybe you can provide some background on your daughter."

He sighed, stole a glance at his watch, and turned to his left. "Bill, could you share the particulars? The debate's tomorrow and I need to prepare and focus. This is the most important event of the campaign. The election may hang in the balance."

"Of course," he said.

Rex Palmer rose and turned to me before he left. "Mr. Burnside, my staff is at your complete disposal. Bill Thorn is a consummate law enforcement professional, please work with him. And keep us informed. But above all else, be discreet."

I stood up also and shook his hand. It was big and soft and warm. A politician's handshake. As he walked out, I looked over at his two associates and sat back down. Without the governor, it felt as if the molecules around us had changed. Another awkward moment of silence filled the room.

"So. How did you two come to know the governor?" I asked, more because I didn't know where else to begin.

Bill Thorn spoke first. "I was a captain in the Sacramento PD. Got to know the governor when he was the state treasurer. Sacramento's a small place. But Shelly's been with him a lot longer."

"Oh, yes," Shelly said in a knowing voice. "Rex and I go way back, college at Stanford. In fact, my husband, Land, ran against him for class president our senior year. Of course, Land wasn't my husband back then."

"Land?"

"Landon Busch. He's a state senator now."

"Ah."

Shelly continued. "I was actually a math major at Stanford and got interested in political polling when I graduated. That led me into managing campaigns. I directed Rex's campaign four years ago," she said, adding with a hint of pride, "I helped put Rex in the governor's mansion."

"Why aren't you managing your husband's campaign?"

"He was just elected two years ago, and his term in office is four years. So he's not up for re-election this year. If he was," she said with a sly smile, "I'd have a tough time choosing which campaign to work on."

"So who won class president?" I asked.

"Rex did," she laughed. "And Land resented him a little. Rex had advantages that Land didn't. When your father's a former governor, it paves the way. Politics was the family business for him, and Buster Palmer provided Rex with name recognition. My husband had to practically claw his way into elective office."

"That's not such a bad way to go," I commented. "You have to work harder, but you learn more. And you know you've made it because of your own efforts. Not someone else's."

Shelly considered this. "I suppose."

"So tell me about the daughter," I said. "What's her name?"

Bill Thorn spoke, clearing his throat first. "Her name's Molly."

"All right. And when was she last seen?"

"Two days ago. At the Coliseum. The USC-Oregon

State game. I suppose part of the reason the governor chose you was because of your USC background."

"Mmm. Who was Molly with?" I asked.

"A few kids from her school. Stone Canyon. It's a private school over in Bel-Air."

"Got any names?"

"Riley Joyner, Molly's best friend, is one. Connor Pierce and Alex Gateley were with them. Molly and Riley play together on the school volleyball team. I think Molly used to go out with Connor. Maybe Alex as well. But there's another kid who's involved here. Name's Diego Garcia."

"Was he at the game?"

"Yes," Thorn said. "But not as a spectator."

I frowned. The name didn't ring a bell. "Is he a football player?"

"No, he's a vendor. You know. Walks around selling peanuts and ice cream, stuff like that."

"Yeah, I know what a vendor does," I said, starting to frown. In fact, I knew all about that type of job. For a few summers during high school, I had worked as a vendor at Dodger Stadium. It was physically demanding, lots of heavy lifting, but it paid more money than working for minimum wage at a Burger King. Another big plus was I would sometimes stop in the 7th inning and watch the end of the ballgame. Usually in a box seat someone had vacated early to get a jump on post-game traffic.

"You look a little puzzled," Shelly said.

"What I don't get is how a stadium vendor would come to know the daughter of a sitting governor."

"They go to school together," she responded.

I frowned harder. "Private school tuition can be very high. Staggering even. If a kid needs to be working part-time as a vendor, how does he wind up at a school like Stone Canyon?"

"Diego's on scholarship. But the reason his name comes up is that Molly and Diego have been spending a lot of time together lately."

"Rich girl, poor boy," I mused. "Opposites attract."

"Yes," Shelly said. "Classic tale."

"So do you think foul play's involved?"

"I don't want to think that," she replied. "But I also know that neither Molly nor Diego showed up at school today. We can't ignore the possibility Molly may have been taken against her will. We just don't know."

Something didn't add up here. The USC-Oregon State game ended less than 48 hours ago. When a person goes missing, time is crucial. If they're not found within a day, the odds they met with tragic circumstances increase exponentially. That a parent would wait this long to start looking into a disappearance was unusual to say the least. Even if they had more important things on their plate. Like running for governor.

"Has anyone had any contact with Molly since the game?" I asked. "Have you checked the kids' Facebook and Instagram accounts?"

"Of course," Thorn said, "and there's been no activity. We've checked with airports, bus and train stations, hotels. We got nada. I've spoken to the kids who went with her to the game. They say Molly left to use the rest room in the 4th quarter and never came back."

"Okay."

"The only one we haven't talked with is Diego. We can't get a hold of him. Or his family. No one picks up the phone and no one answers the door."

"And that's where I come in."

"Uh-huh. At this point we need an outsider to step in."

I allowed for a pregnant pause. "You're aware of my fee."

"Yes, a thousand dollars a day."

"Plus expenses," I said. "And I'll need a week's retainer before I leave." No sense pussyfooting around this subject. I was keenly aware that it didn't matter how wealthy a candidate was. Political campaigns usually operated in the red, and it could take years before they retired their debt. And that's if the candidate won.

"I don't know if we can pay for a week up front," Shelly said.

"I don't work for free," I answered and started to get up.

"Wait," she said. "Look. Rex wants you. I'll make the arrangements."

"Okay," I said and sat back down. "Now I need to get a few things straight here. The daughter of a major public figure is missing. She's savvy enough to know if her disappearance was intentional it might adversely affect her father's career. If she was taken against her will, however, that's another issue entirely. But the idea a teenage girl could be abducted in a crowd of 90,000 people at a major sporting event is a little unlikely."

Bill and Shelly looked at each other, turned back to me, and shrugged in agreement.

"Okay," I said. "I'll need a way to get in touch with the kids she went with, and I'll need Diego's contact info, too. If you have photos of them, even better."

"We have a copy of the Stone Canyon School yearbook around here somewhere. it has pictures of every kid. You can have it."

"There's something else," I pointed out. "It's curious you haven't mentioned her mother. I'll need to speak with her, too."

Thorn nodded slowly. "We've spoken with Molly's mother. Her name's Nicole. She doesn't know any more than we do. You don't need to speak with her."

"Really?" I asked, my eyebrows shooting up. "A mother typically knows more about her kids than anyone else. Primary caregiver and all."

Shelly looked at me oddly. "This is not a typical case, I can assure you. And Molly's relationship with her mother is, oh, complicated."

"She's a teenager. It's supposed to be complicated. This is the time they separate and start forming their own selves."

"Are you a psychologist?" she said sarcastically.

"No. I'm just a student of human nature."

"Any children yourself, Mr. Burnside?" she asked.

"Not yet," I said, deciding not to push on speaking with the mother right now. "But my wife's expecting. She's due right around Christmas. Should be a great present."

"Congratulations. But you know, first babies are

usually late. I have three sisters, same thing happened with all of them."

"Good to know. Do you have kids?"

"No children myself," she added hastily. "Haven't had the time."

I knew the feeling. Shelly appeared to be about my age, and I was over 40. I always assumed I would have children, but it took a long time to meet the right girl. And my demanding career never relented. Then Gail Pepper entered my life, and things changed quickly. We hadn't spoken about having kids until she informed me she was pregnant on the day of our wedding. But since then, we shared so much excitement about our impending addition that it seemed as if we didn't talk about much else.

"They say kids change your life," I remarked.

"They do for a fact," Thorn broke in. "I've got three grown ones. Trying to kick the last one out of the house now."

"Sounds like he's not going willingly."

"Oh, he'll go. I may have to invoke the sink-or-swim method. Worked for me when my old man tossed me into the street."

I looked hard at Thorn. He was in his mid-50s, solidly built, with graying hair, a graying mustache and a sour expression. He reminded me of some of the older cops I knew when I was on the police force. The ones who punched the clock, waiting for their 20 years to kick in so they could collect a pension and go find another job they didn't like. They took their ire out on suspects, and sometimes on their own families.

"My guess is your kid won't go to bed thinking kind thoughts about you."

"He'll understand one day," Thorn declared. "Life is tough and you have to deal with it. Just like in politics."

"Not something I recall my political science professors saying."

Shelly gave me a bored look. "You know something about politics, do you?"

"Just enough to be dangerous," I said.

"Well, politics is a full-contact sport these days."

I laughed out loud. "Try watching a football game from the sidelines. You might not use that metaphor again."

"Oh, that's right. You played football at SC. I'd invite you to the debate tomorrow but it's at Royce Hall. Your rival's campus."

"I don't mind going to UCLA," I said slowly. "It's a nice enough place to visit. In fact, a debate might be a good event for me to attend. You never know who you'll meet or what they'll say. Might learn something pertinent to this case."

"I doubt that," she said, and then hesitated. "You mean you'd really like to go?"

"Sure. Would love to."

"Hmmm. All right. I'm sure I can wrangle you a seat."

"Can you make it two?" I asked. "My wife's a lawyer with the city attorney's office. She's interested in these things."

Shelly leaned back in her chair and sighed. There were dark circles under her eyes. She lit a cigarette and blew the smoke straight up toward the ceiling. "Fine. Why not."

"Thanks. I don't mean to make extra work for you. I'm sure you're swamped."

She reached over and absently tapped the cigarette near a round golden ash tray. She missed by two inches and didn't seem to notice. "This has been a tough campaign. Justin Woo has been hammering us continuously."

"Is it working?"

She waved her hand as if to feign ignorance, but unfortunately this time it pushed a plume of smoke with it. I tilted my head to avoid the trajectory. "We're still leading in the polls, but it's close. What we really want to do now is draw a clear distinction between the governor and his opponent. Rex spent his whole life in California. He has California's best interests at heart. Justin Woo is smart, but he came from somewhere else and can't even speak proper English."

"Let me ask you something. Would Rex Palmer have gotten elected if his name were John Smith?"

She glared at me and spoke in an annoyed voice. "His last name carries some weight around here. But it hasn't been as easy as people think. The reality of politics is Rex inherited half his father's friends and all of his enemies. Boy, you sure were right about one thing, though."

"What's that?" I asked.

"You do know enough to be dangerous. Or at least to be a royal pain in the ass."

I smiled my best smile. She had no idea.

Two

Rex Palmer's campaign headquarters were located along Wilshire Boulevard in downtown Los Angeles. Unlike the downtown LA of a few years ago, this was now an area replete with grandiose office towers, espresso bars, and sidewalks that were swept regularly. And the campaign was conveniently situated down the block from the law offices of Jeremy Hoffman, who had taken it upon himself to bring me into this case.

I zipped my jacket as I walked outside. It was October and the sky was overcast; a cool breeze was blowing and the temperature was a brisk 55 degrees. This was about as cold a day as we get in the City of Angels. Why people lived in frigid climates was beyond me. The fall colors could be very pretty back east, but they also signaled cold weather was coming. Parts of Los Angeles had some maple trees whose leaves changed colors as well, but that usually didn't happen until January. And cold weather never followed.

I strode into One Wilshire, the glass and steel high-rise overlooking the Harbor Freeway, and took the elevator up to Jeremy's 22nd floor office. His receptionist had me wait close to half an hour before ushering me in for an audience with Mr. Hoffman. He was already standing as I entered the plush, spacious suite with a panoramic view of the city. On a nice day, you could see forever; today you could barely see the La Brea Tar Pits.

"And a good morning to you, Burnside!" he exclaimed. "I had a funny feeling you might swing by!"

Jeremy Hoffman was tall and debonair. He had a tanned face that bespoke many hours on the golf course. Jeremy had been a successful attorney for decades and had the type of reputation that made many high-profile clients seek him out. Independently wealthy, he was in the unique position of picking and choosing the work he did. And it was hard to walk into his office without feeling just a little bit envious.

"I was in the neighborhood."

"Yes, I would imagine. Rex called me last night, under the auspices of discussing Coliseum renovations for the hundredth time. He weaved in that he needed a good private investigator. That revealed the true purpose of his call."

"Is the Coliseum ever going to be renovated?"

"Sure, as soon as SC takes it over and we get the government out of the way. The Coliseum Commission has lost nearly every major sports team in this town over the years, from the Raiders and Rams to our charming UCLA friends. Not to mention driving the Lakers and Clippers into building their own arena. The commission's been wildly successful at one thing: alienating every single tenant. Except for our alma mater of course."

"You've chaired that commission, haven't you?" I poked at him.

Jeremy Hoffman smiled a rich man's smile. It was the smile of confidence and relaxation and cosmetic dentistry.

Despite a busy law practice, Jeremy also managed to find time to serve on various boards and foundations. His energy was boundless and his enthusiasm infectious.

"Indeed," he acknowledged. "And I've had to deal with every incompetent politician who's held office around here. You know, there are times you have to be stuck in the mud for a while before anything can move forward. The failure to upgrade the Coliseum since the '84 Olympics has finally gotten everyone totally frustrated. Enough to hand day-to-day responsibilities over to USC."

"And let me guess. You're on the SC planning board that will oversee the renovation."

"That would be a conflict of interest, sir," he said. "However, one of my junior partners happens to be serving on that board."

I shook my head. "No footprints. You'll have influence without being obvious."

"Sometimes the best way to get things done is to avoid taking any credit."

"Speaking of the Coliseum," I said.

"Yes, sir."

"Who's in charge of concessions there?"

"Why that would be the Barry M. Steele Company," he said.

"Who's in charge over at Barry M. Steele now?"

Jeremy sorted through a very large Rolodex sitting on the credenza behind his desk. He pulled out a small card. "The Chief Executive Officer is Tony Longley. Not a real savory guy, not the type you'd expect to find as CEO. Has a police record too, if I remember correctly."

The name brought back a flood of memories. Before today, I hadn't thought much of my own days as a vendor, or about Dodger Stadium or Tony Longley in quite a while. The memories were bittersweet, maybe more bitter than sweet, and I didn't like dwelling on them.

"Thanks. So you know about the governor's daughter."

"I do. I've known the Palmer family for a long time, Buster and I go way back, we've done a few real estate deals together. So I guess Rex felt he could confide in me. In fact, my granddaughter was a year ahead of Molly at Stone Canyon. We helped get Molly accepted into the school. Very disturbing situation. I hope you can find her."

"I hope so, too. But I'm curious about what you just said. I didn't think the governor would need any help getting his daughter accepted into a private school."

Jeremy shrugged. "Some schools don't want that responsibility. Or the publicity. It's a double-edged sword with celebrity kids. The media circus can be a problem. But the family wanted Molly to go there. It's got a good reputation and it's not far from their home. So I put in a good word with Loretta Moss, the Head of School."

"I'm sure your word carries a lot of weight."

"Yes. Being a big donor affords me that luxury. But getting back to your other question. Why the focus on the concessions people?"

"One of Molly's friends works at the Coliseum as a vendor. Molly was last seen at the game on Saturday. I'm just following up on leads."

"I see," Jeremy nodded, waiting to see if I would say more.

"At this point, that's all I know," I told him. "But I thank you very much for the referral. I can always use the business."

"Happy to help out a fellow Trojan," he beamed. "You know, there's one other thing I was hoping to discuss with you."

"There always is."

"Yes," he agreed and took a deep breath. His smile vanished. "It's related to the football team. One of Johnny's players was picked up by the police late last week."

I sat back and crossed my legs. Now I knew why my name was passed along to the governor. Tit for tat. It was what greased the wheels in Jeremy's world. He started by doing me a favor. When I was on the job with the LAPD, we called that doing someone a solid. But accepting a favor often came with a price.

"Tell me about it," I said.

"Xavier Bishop. The police brought him in after his girlfriend was assaulted. That's why he didn't play on Saturday. That's why Norris Colby started at right corner."

"It was announced Xavier had severe migraines."

"Um, yes. A little white lie to divert the media. Johnny doesn't like to do that, but he obviously couldn't let on what was happening to X yet. Not until we know more anyway."

Johnny Cleary was the head football coach at USC, and a former teammate. We had been good friends for more than 20 years. I was brought in occasionally to help when players got into trouble. As was Jeremy.

"Xavier's absence was noticed. All-America players usually find a way to play in most games, even if they're hurting. Migraines can be a big problem. But you do what you have to do," I said, thinking back many years ago to when I was a player on the Trojan football team. Getting an injection with a painkiller, strapping yourself to an IV at halftime, fighting through injuries. Those were just a few of the rigors a player went through to make sure he got into a game.

"Yes, well, I'd rather not hear all the details about that," Jeremy said, looking down at his desk. "Sometimes the less an attorney knows about certain things, the better."

"So how can I help here?" I asked.

"Xavier was overheard having a loud argument with his girlfriend in her apartment. It sounded like there was a ruckus. And the girlfriend wound up with a swollen jaw and needed medical attention. She said Xavier hit her. When the paramedics heard this, they alerted the police."

"And what's his version?"

"He says he didn't hit her."

"Tough one," I observed. "It becomes a he-said-she-said thing. But nine out of ten times, the girl is telling the truth."

"Maybe. I'll admit things don't look good for him. If this case goes to trial, Xavier could get jail time. And see his prospects as a pro football player go up in smoke. The NFL is taking a big stance against domestic violence now. Xavier's in his junior year. That means he could enter the NFL draft after this season. Bad timing."

"Never a good time for this to happen," I pointed out. "You think he was planning to forego his senior year in school?"

"Probably. He was a lock to be a first-round draft pick. The agents are starting to circle, they smell money. And the type of money he stands to make is hard to pass up."

"So what's his explanation for what happened?" I asked.

Jeremy grimaced. "He won't tell me. Xavier had a swollen hand, but he's adamant he didn't hit her. There's obviously something more going on here. But for whatever his reasons, he's keeping it to himself."

"And you want me to find out what really happened."

"Look. We both bleed cardinal and gold. We want the best for USC. And for the kids who play football. They're helping the university, we try to help them. If it weren't for the football team, USC would have a much lower profile nationally."

"Sure," I agreed. "So would a lot of schools. A good football team is good for PR. Also good for bringing out the big donors writing checks to the university."

"That's how it works. And the team is having problems. They're thin at cornerback now. Lots of injuries. But we still have a shot at the Rose Bowl. I'd like to see Xavier back in a Trojan uniform in Pasadena come New Year's Day. Obviously so would Johnny."

"You sound like you belong on the coaching staff."

Jeremy sighed. "You know the old line. Trojan family. This is when we pull together, when things get tough. Whatever you can do to help out would be appreciated.

Technically I'm not hiring you, but I'll see to it you're compensated for your time. The governor's daughter comes first, that's certainly far more urgent. But I'd like you to look into this."

"Johnny knows you're talking to me?"

"Oh, sure," he acknowledged. "Johnny knows pretty much everything regarding his players. The head coach is always in the loop."

*

The business offices for the Los Angeles Coliseum were located inside a decrepit venue called the LA Sports Arena, south of the USC campus. At one time, the Sports Arena was home to everyone from the Lakers and Clippers to the Trojan basketball team. All had subsequently left for nicer digs. In my four years as a college student, I went to exactly one game there, and only then because one of my football teammates was moonlighting on the SC basketball team. On my way out after that game, I noticed a small rat crawling next to a trash bin. I hadn't been back since. The surroundings did not look like they had improved much.

The Barry M. Steele Company ran concessions in most of the local stadiums, and was headed by a knucklehead named Tony Longley. He was gruff, overweight, and always in need of a shave. On certain men, a little facial stubble was cool; on Tony it just looked slovenly. His assistant, a bored-looking woman with a weight problem herself, shrugged when I asked to meet with Big Tony. She directed me toward his office by jerking a thumb over her shoulder, before going back to chewing her gum and looking down at her phone. I thanked her for not bothering to get up. I yanked open a brown plywood door that and entered the office of the CEO.

"Mr. Longley, I presume."

"Who the hell are you?" he asked bluntly.

"Name's Burnside," I answered, and pulled out my wallet. Flashing my P.I. license, I told him I was doing background work on an investigation. He stared at me.

"Lemme see that ID again."

"I already showed it to you," I told him, and slowly pulled my jacket back to reveal the .38 special tucked into the nylon ballistic holster under my armpit. People like Tony Longley sometimes needed a strong message to get them to cooperate.

"How about I show you this?" I said.

Longley stared at me for a long moment. "Okay," he said. "Have a seat."

I glanced uneasily at a pair of faded orange cloth chairs facing his desk. They might have been in style 40 years ago. Or they might have appeared as cheap and tacky as they did right now. The chairs had stains on them and looked as if they might collapse under too much weight. Above us was a ceiling light fixture that had about 50 dead flies resting in it.

"I'll stand."

"Suit yourself," he said, eyeing me closer now. "You seem familiar. I don't know why."

"I get that a lot."

"No, there's something about you."

"I used to work for you," I told him. "Long time ago. You were running concessions at Dodger Stadium."

Longley leaned back into an overstuffed chair, the belly fat oozing over his belt. He studied me closer, and a glint of recognition appeared. "That was a million years ago. Lots happened."

"Yeah. You're now in charge of the whole operation. The Coliseum, Dodger Stadium, Staples Center. You're big-time."

"I am."

"You should get a nicer office," I remarked, looking around. "Or at least clean it once in a while."

Longley emitted a dry laugh. He was a man who could laugh without smiling. He didn't seem happy and he didn't seem to care. "I think I remember you now. Burnside. You were one of the big mouths."

"Sounds like me."

"I remember one time you were messing around. Stopped working your shift, sat down behind the dugout to watch the game."

"That's right. But it wasn't like I was hurting anyone."

"It was against company policy."

"I didn't know you had any policies. Except for the ones you made up on the spot."

"We had a business to run," he scowled. "We couldn't have vendors sitting in the season boxes acting like they owned the place."

"You didn't need to send your goons around to try and rough me up."

"Talking to you didn't work. But those were a couple of big fellas you took on. They needed three or four stadium cops to break it up. The whole stadium was watching. Even some of the Dodger players saw it."

"I wasn't about to just stand there and let them attack me," I said. "They picked the wrong guy to mess with. And the wrong time as well."

"You're lucky I didn't have you arrested."

"And you're lucky I didn't tell your boss you were skimming off the top."

We stared at each other. I didn't want to relive these memories, because the further back we went, the more painful they would be. The summer before I started at USC was one of the hardest and most awful periods of my life. Everything was shattered, in ways I could not have ever imagined.

"You were quick at picking up on things," he said slowly. "Guess that's why you're a cop. Or whatever it is that badge says you are."

I eyed him warily. There was no point in pretending any more. Longley knew something was suspicious, and it wouldn't take him long to find out. "I was a cop for 13 years," I told him. "LAPD. Been on my own for a while now. Private investigator."

"So if you're not a cop why should I pay any attention to you?"

"I still have a lot of friends on the job."

Longley considered this. "So what the hell do you want?"

"I need information about one of your employees."

"Who's in trouble now?"

"Look, I just need to find out a few things. It's about Diego Garcia. He's a vendor at the Coliseum."

"Name doesn't ring a bell," Longley shrugged. "But I don't know a lot of the guys working there these days. I moved up awhile ago."

"Were you at the game on Saturday?"

"Sure. I always go to the SC games. I get there early, show my face. Make sure my crew knows the boss is looking over their shoulder. I yell at a few people to get their attention. Then I go watch the game."

"You ever yell at Diego Garcia?" I asked.

"Probably. I yell at a lot of people."

I guess everyone has their own management style and Tony Longley was no exception. I wouldn't say it was a good management style, but given the type of people who worked concessions, it was probably still effective. Decades ago, this was called Theory X. It said managers should never trust their employees, and they should provide negative reinforcement to inspire fear and hard work. That management style had largely disappeared with the emergence of a new demographic. People today respond better to feel-good managers who allow employees a certain amount of latitude. But in the rough-and-tumble blue-collar world in which Tony Longley lived, you never gave employees an inch.

"Close game on Saturday," I said.

Longley shrugged. "I bet on SC and gave the points. They won the game but didn't cover the spread. I lost a few hundred."

"That's a crying shame," I said with a straight face and very little sympathy. The only people who came out on top in sports betting were invariably the bookmakers and the casinos. Gambling on sports was a sucker's bet.

"Yeah, well, the upside was the game wasn't decided until the last minute. It's always good for the concessions business when things go down to the wire. Most people stay to the end and keep buying things."

"So you don't know Diego Garcia."

"Nope."

"Can you find out if he was working Saturday?"

Longley turned toward his computer, an old desktop dinosaur with a bulky monitor that was outdated 15 years ago. The unit had coffee stains on the top and had a fan that made a whirring sound when he clicked the mouse. Everything about this office, including Longley, made me want to go take a shower afterwards. And I hadn't even touched anything.

"Yeah," he finally said, scanning the flickering screen. "Garcia worked the Oregon State game. Sold peanuts. Did a good job."

"Anything else you can tell me. What time he clocked out? Who his friends are here?"

"We don't have vendors punch a clock any more. They're just paid on commission now. And like I say, I don't know the kid."

"Can I get his contact info?" I asked, knowing the campaign staff had provided me with something, but I also knew that people moved and changed phone numbers.

Longley looked over at me. "I'm not authorized to give that out."

I pulled the jacket back again to show him the .38 special. "Now you're authorized," I said.

Longley gave me a dirty look, but finally decided he had little to gain by digging his heels in, and everything to gain by getting me out of his office. He jotted a street address and a phone number onto a slip of memo paper that had curled in one corner. The phone number matched what the campaign had provided, but the address was different. This one was about a block away.

"Thanks. Appreciate your cooperation."

Longley nodded cautiously. "Let me know if this kid Garcia is in any hot water. I don't want any troublemakers on my payroll. The last thing I need is a bunch of real cops sniffing around here."

I took another look at his surroundings. "They probably wouldn't like that, either," I said, and then I walked out of his very dirty office as fast as I could.

Three

It was a little past 5:00 p.m. when I reached 9th and Alvarado. This was an impoverished area just west of downtown LA, a neighborhood that better resembled a Third World country, than a community adjacent to a shiny, new urban enclave. It was situated near the heart of one of the most prosperous areas in the world, but most of the people who lived here did not share in that wealth.

The addresses I had for Diego Garcia were apartment buildings located near each other. They were close to MacArthur Park, a grassy area immortalized years ago in a song chronicling the end of a love affair. This was once a nice neighborhood, a place where people could take rowboats and drift out onto a small pond. Or lounge around on a beautiful green lawn. I suppose a few people still did that, but the neighborhood was no longer serene. It had changed drastically over the years and not for the better. Largely gang-infested, these were the mean streets I would frequently visit when I was an LAPD officer. The people who lived here were poor, and they stayed here because this was all they could afford. There were few ways out.

The campaign staff had provided me with a Stone Canyon yearbook from the previous academic year, so I knew what Diego looked like. But when I knocked on the doors at both addresses, there was no answer at either. My guess was the parents might still be at work, so I decided to walk around the neighborhood for a while. I passed a variety of shops hawking cheap phones, cheap toys and cheap food. A number of check-cashing outlets were nearby. A law office promoting immigration services had a large and prominent neon sign. Mexican *Ranchera* music blasted from speakers jerry-rigged next to the sidewalk. Nobody seemed to pay much attention to me, but I still didn't feel comfortable. I was glad I had my .38, but would have felt more secure wearing a uniform and a badge. And having a partner nearby.

As I wandered along Alvarado Street, I came across an attraction I had forgotten about. Many years ago, in a different era with different residents, Langer's Deli had flourished. The neighborhood eventually declined and business trailed off. It seemed the restaurant would likely go under. But a few years back, the city completed an initial section of the Metro Rail train line, connecting this neighborhood with the downtown business district. All of a sudden, Langer's was a five-minute train ride away for many office workers, and business steadily picked back up. It was often packed at lunch. Even now, close to dinner hour, the place was doing a brisk business. And with good reason. Langer's was considered the best place in the city for a pastrami sandwich, and foodies had declared it among the best pastrami in the world. I was a frequent patron as a patrol officer and decided now would be a good time to revisit old memories.

I took a seat at the counter, but before I ordered, I called Gail and asked if she wanted me to bring her home anything. She worked near downtown and was quite aware of Langer's. Yes, she said. Absolutely. A No. 19, please.

"Sounds like you know the menu," I said.

"I just know what I like."

"Is this what they call a craving?"

"Maybe," she said, "But I think I'd want one even if I weren't seven months pregnant."

"How are you feeling today?"

"Fat and ugly."

"You will never be ugly," I smiled into the phone. "Never, ever, ever."

"You're sweet," she said.

"I know."

"Do me a favor?"

"What's that?"

"Don't take all night to bring my sandwich home."

I laughed and said I'd try, knowing it might be a little while because I was working. I told her I needed to make some headway on finding Diego and his family.

A waitress in her mid-50s with bleached blonde hair stopped in front of me and asked what I'd like. She wore a harvest gold apron with a nametag that said "Maggie." I ordered two No. 19s, one for here, one wrapped to go. She wrote it down and smiled.

"Midnight snack, hon?" she asked.

"No, the other sandwich is for my wife."

Maggie pursed her lips, seemingly impressed. "You're a good husband."

"Happy wife, happy life."

"This is the way to do it. My ex-husband would order two of these and go eat 'em both himself."

A few minutes later I was diving into a big pastrami sandwich on soft rye bread, loaded with coleslaw, Swiss cheese and Russian dressing. The flavors co-mingled wonderfully. After I finished, I sat back and relaxed. The waitress sauntered back over.

"Hit the spot, didn't it?"

"It did."

"I used to think that was a crazy combination for a sandwich. Then I tried it. Amazing. You just never know."

"Helps to keep an open mind," I said.

"It does," she said and started to clear the dishes.

"Can I ask you something?"

"Sure, hon."

I took out the Stone Canyon yearbook and opened it to a page of student photos. I pointed to the one for Diego Garcia and asked if he looked familiar. She studied it for a long minute and then spoke.

"Yeah, I've seen him around the neighborhood. He was actually in here last week. Why?"

"I'm just doing a background check. But you say he was in here?"

"Yeah. A little unusual for a neighborhood kid, but what was really unusual was who he was with. A nicely dressed couple. Business suits, very professional. They were having a what seemed like a stern conversation. The kid didn't look too happy."

"Any idea what they might have been discussing?"

"No. I try not to listen in on people's private

conversations. When I first started waitressing I did. But I quickly found out most of these conversations are pretty darned boring."

"Anything else you can tell me about this young man?"

"Not really. I live up in the Valley. My only contact with this neighborhood is when I walk from my car to the restaurant. But I think I've seen him working at one of the stores down the street."

"Anything else?"

"Seems like a good kid. Never hassled me. I think he's got a couple of brothers though, or maybe they're just older friends I've seen him with. They're a little scary."

"How so?"

"Rough-looking guys. Shaved heads, arms all inked up. Always making comments when they see me. They're more the norm around here. That kid," she said, pointing to Diego, "is an exception."

I flipped a page and pointed to a photo of Molly. She had long, curly blonde hair and an upturned nose. "How about her. Ever seen her in the neighborhood? Maybe recently?"

She glanced at it and shook her head. "Never seen her before."

"Are you sure?"

"I'd know if I saw her. Especially in this area. Talk about someone who would stand out."

I thanked her, left a five dollar tip, and took Gail's sandwich with me as I walked outside. Stopping at my black Pathfinder, I placed it under the back seat, and demonstrably pressed the remote to make sure I locked the door and set the alarm. A couple of street kids sat on a fire hydrant and stared at me. I made eye contact briefly and then walked back down the block. I strode back into the address Tony Longley provided, and walked up four flights of stairs. The interior smelled musty with a slight hint of urine. Graffiti lined the staircase walls.

This time, when I knocked on Diego Garcia's door, it opened a few moments later. A short woman wearing a tired expression looked up at me.

"Mrs. Garcia?"

"*Sí?*"

"*Habla Inglés?*" I asked hopefully.

"Yes."

"Good. Are you Diego's mother?"

She nodded her head yes, eyeing me cautiously.

"My name's Burnside," I said and handed her my card. "I'm an investigator. I'd like to talk to you for a moment."

"All right."

"May I come in?"

She took a glimpse behind her before turning back to me. "I ... I don't think ... "

I waved my hand. "It's all right. I'm working for someone at your son's school. Stone Canyon."

A curious expression formed on her face. She said nothing.

"May I talk to your son?" I asked.

"He not home."

"Where is he?"

She hesitated. "I don't know. He may be around. In neighborhood."

I opened the yearbook to Molly's photo. "Have you ever seen this girl?"

The woman stared at the photo and her eyes widened. "*Si, señor*. Molly. She friends with Diego. Just friends."

"Uh-huh. When was the last time you saw her?" I asked.

She looked down and shook her head. "I don't know."

I sighed. I was learning things, but not exactly what I needed. Mrs. Garcia didn't know me, didn't trust me, and I didn't blame her. I was keenly aware that in her world, there were a lot of hidden dangers in cooperating with any authority figure. I didn't know if I could bridge the trust barrier, but I wasn't getting anywhere this way.

"Look," I started. "I don't think Diego is in any trouble. And I'm not looking to get him into trouble. I just need to find this girl. Her father is very worried. You're a parent, so I think you can understand. Diego and Molly didn't show up at school today. So I'm sure someone from Stone Canyon is going to be calling you, too. If they haven't already."

She considered this. "Diego with his father today. Down at the store. He say he could take day off from school and could work if we need. And we need money."

"Okay. But you look worried. Is there something else?"

She shook her head no. I tried a new tactic.

"What about the girl?" I asked. "Was she here this weekend?"

The woman's eyes got even wider. She opened her mouth for a moment and then thought better of it.

"If she's in trouble," I continued, "Diego could be in trouble. I can help you. I can help Diego. But you have to trust me. Just a little bit."

She looked into my eyes, seemingly trying to read what was behind them. She had no reason to confide in me. But Diego's mother was conflicted about something, and I needed to gain her trust somehow.

"When you have a problem" I said. "It helps to talk about it. Things aren't always as bad as they might appear."

"I never met you before," she managed.

"But you know there's a problem. And you know it's not going away by itself. I'm sure you'd want to help Diego if you could."

"Diego is good boy. He is different."

"I'm sure he is."

"And he is smart. Very smart."

"I don't doubt it. If he got into Stone Canyon School, I'm sure they saw something in him."

"Yes," she said. "But he was accepted because of my employer. The Gobay family. I work at their home. Many years. In Bel-Air, near the school. Sometimes I bring Diego with me, they have boy his age. They became friends. The family thought Diego should have a good education. They placed him in Stone Canyon. They have ... how would you say? Influence?"

"Yes. That's often how things happen," I agreed. No doubt the Gobay family was a big donor to the school. I waited for Mrs. Garcia to say more.

"I don't want to see Diego in trouble," she said. "And that girl is trouble."

"How so?"

"She and Diego. They don't belong together. They are from different worlds. They have different goals. Their future. It is not with each other."

"Maybe I can help," I said.

She looked down and said nothing.

"Mrs. Garcia, I'm going to find Diego eventually. It's what I do for a living. And if he's in trouble, I'll try to help him."

She thought about this for a minute, and a modicum of trust finally began to sink in. "All right," she finally said. "He is at the Grande Mart. Alvarado between 7th and 8th. This side of street. His father work there. Diego helps him."

"And the girl?" I asked.

She shook her head. I waited again. "She is gone," his mother finally said. "And she no coming back."

*

The Grande Mart wasn't so grand, and it wasn't much of a mart. It was a storefront that was shoehorned in the middle of a dozen other storefronts, all hawking cheap merchandise to customers who didn't have a lot of discretionary money. I wondered how many of these shops could stay in business for the long haul, and I had a funny feeling many of them didn't.

There were a few customers in the Grande Mart, mostly young men in their early 20s, all with tattoos and shaved heads. They milled about, picking up merchandise, looking at it and absently putting it back in a different place. Behind the counter was a 40-ish man and a teenage boy. Using the experience of my many years as an investigator, I deduced that the teenager was Diego. He was a slender, good-looking kid with black hair, slicked straight back. He wore a black t-shirt that said *L.A. Galaxy* in gold lettering. I walked to the counter and picked up a portable CD player that cost under $20. I got the feeling it might last a week. If it worked at all.

"*Hola,*" the young man said.

"You're Diego," I told him, not giving him the opportunity to think about it.

He stared at me for a moment, confused, and spoke slowly. "What can I do for you?"

I handed him my business card. No sense scaring him into silence by flashing a fake badge. "I understand you go to school at Stone Canyon."

He fingered my card. "Yes, I do," he said. "What is this about?"

"Molly Palmer. You're friends with her."

Diego Garcia turned away and didn't respond. The 40-ish man behind him looked at us for a moment, and then went about pretending to straighten things up as he listened in on our conversation.

"Molly hasn't been home in two days," I said. "Her father is concerned."

The young man processed this for a moment. "I'm

surprised he even knows she's gone."

"Why do you say that?"

He shrugged. "He's not very involved in her life. Neither her mother nor her father. They let her do almost anything she wants."

"Her father's an important man. You know that."

"Yes. Very important. But Molly's not important to him."

"She's told you that?"

"In a way she has. Lots of kids at school wish they could get away with what she gets away with. Can stay out all night, no curfew. Studies when she feels like it. Knows she's getting into a good college because of her family."

"Sounds like that bothers you a little."

"It bothers me because I know she's capable of more. She's smart. In her own way. She picks up on things fast. There's book-smart and there's people-smart. She's the latter."

"Which one are you?" I asked.

He gave a small smile. "I'm more book-smart. But around here, you have to know how to deal with people. It's the only thing that matters in this neighborhood."

No doubt about that, I thought. "Are you going to college?"

"Maybe. If I can get a scholarship. My parents have no money to help me. And the days of working your way through school are over. It's just too expensive. Even at a Cal State school. Without financial aid, I'd have to take out loans."

"They're available."

"I know. But I've seen people get loans, finish college and then not find a job. They come back here and just hang."

What he said made some sense, but it was also true people can choose their own paths. People who go to college with a definite purpose and study things with the intent of getting a specific job usually do all right. Business, math, engineering, teaching, and nursing, were all marketable areas of study. The people who had trouble finding work often studied something that didn't lead directly to an employable profession. Anthropology and philosophy majors were not high on most employers' lists of potential hires.

"So I have to ask you more about Molly," I continued. "Whatever you might think of her parents, you should know her father did hire me to find her. And to make sure she's okay. Do you know where she is?"

"No."

"Did you see her this weekend?"

He hesitated for a moment and licked his lips. "Yes."

"When was the last time you saw her?"

Diego tapped his fingers on the counter. "I saw her at the Coliseum on Saturday."

I had an uneasy feeling about what he said. And what he didn't say. Some people were bad liars. "It feels as if there's more to this," I commented.

The 40-ish man standing behind Diego now approached the counter. The man had a swarthy complexion and wore a thick black mustache. On the heavy side, with wide features, he was wearing a tan dress shirt, the type that wasn't meant to be tucked inside the trousers. I noticed something stuffed in his back pocket that appeared to be a leather sap. A sap had one basic purpose: to incapacitate an adversary.

"What's going on here?" he asked.

I held up my hands. "Just having a conversation. One of Diego's classmates has gone missing. Her parents hired me to find her."

"Who is that?" he asked.

"Molly Palmer," I said, handing him a business card. "Do you know her?"

"Of course," he said.

"Dad!"

The man turned to Diego. "Listen, *hijo*. When parents are trying to find a missing child, you help them. *Entiendes*?"

Diego rolled his eyes in exasperation. His father turned back to me. "She was here this weekend. She told me she and Diego had a class project they had to work on. She came back from the Coliseum with Diego. She spent the night."

I stared at him and said nothing. Sensing an important detail had been left out, he added, "Diego slept on the couch. She slept in his room."

"Is Molly still here?"

"No," his father said, glancing at Diego. "She left last night. Very quickly I might add."

"Do you know where she is now?" I asked.

His father looked at Diego. Diego said no.

"Okay," I answered. "Thanks. You have my card.

Please call me if you see her. Or if you hear of anything. Or remember anything. Anything at all."

I walked back out onto the street and started toward my Pathfinder. I sensed I was being followed. Rather than turn around, I slipped into a small market that had a rack of fruits and vegetables out front. I walked around the store for a minute and then walked back outside. Diego's father was waiting for me.

"Mr. Garcia," I said, and waited for him to respond.

He motioned for me to follow him into an alley. I took a glimpse behind me, but no one was joining us. We walked into a small dark area. I put my hands on my .38 and watched his hands to see if they moved toward the leather sap.

"No, no, *señor*," he protested, as he raised his hands. "It is nothing like that."

"Then what is it?" I demanded.

"I didn't want Diego to hear me say this. Or anyone else for that matter."

"Hear what?"

"That blonde girl you're looking for? That Molly?"

"Uh-huh."

"She will not be back here."

"Why not?"

"She was scared off."

"By you?"

"No. Of course not. Diego's friends are my friends."

"Then who?"

He took a breath. "By Diego's girlfriend. Sofia."

"Go on," I said.

"Yes. Sofia heard that Molly spent the night and she was extremely upset. She confronted them outside our building yesterday. Sofia told Diego if he kept seeing her, she would, well, help him go from rooster to hen, if you know what I mean."

I didn't need or want any further detail on that subject. "Diego was going out with Sofia for how long?"

"I do not know for sure," his father shrugged. "Two years, maybe three. But I've seen this pattern with other kids here. They may be doing that on and off forever."

"And this girlfriend scared Molly off."

"Yes. Sofia told her if she ever came around here again, she'd slit her throat. Called her a chalk outline waiting to happen. Sofia, she is a very passionate young woman. And she gets this wild look in her eyes at times. That blonde girl, you could just see she was shaking. After that, Molly, she got out of here in a big hurry."

I peered at him. "And how do you know all this?"

He shrugged. "I just know. And I can't say anything more. But I thought I should say something. I don't want anyone to get hurt. But I can only control so much."

"Were Diego and Molly in a romantic relationship?"

The father shrugged. "Not exactly. But they might have been headed in that direction."

I chewed on this for a moment and then asked what else he could tell me. Diego's father shook his head. He didn't look happy. He said he was worried for his son, worried for Molly. He looked just plain worried.

"You have my card," I said. "Don't hesitate to contact me if anything comes up. Or if there's anything more you want to share."

He said okay, we shook hands, walked out of the alley and then headed in opposite directions. It took a couple of minutes to reach my Pathfinder. Someone had left an empty can of beer on the hood. I took the can, walked down the block and placed it onto an overflowing trash bin. When I unlocked my vehicle and climbed inside, the first thing that struck me was the warm, pungent aroma of pastrami.

I turned over the engine and headed back to my world.

Four

Given my schedule and my general forgetfulness of events such as birthdays and anniversaries, I may never be the model husband. I did, however, receive a very warm welcome from the two loves of my life as I walked into our apartment. My wife, Gail, greeted me with a very big hug and then relieved me of the bag containing the No. 19 sandwich from Langer's. Our black cocker spaniel, Chewy, jumped up on me a number of times before realizing Gail had taken the sandwich. She quickly scampered away from me, and did what all dogs are prone to do. Follow the food.

"So how was your day, sweetie?" she asked, unwrapping her dinner.

"Quite good," I replied. "And I did get to meet the governor, albeit briefly."

Gail nodded, impressed. "And are you going to vote for him now?' she asked.

I shrugged. "I don't know. I'm a little skeptical of all politicians. But Rex Palmer is a client, and it helps to have friends in high places."

"So how did this new case come about?"

"Jeremy Hoffman recommended me to the governor. His daughter has gone missing and he wants someone to find her."

"Interesting," she said, taking a bite of her sandwich

and smiling approvingly. "And how did all this lead you down to Langer's?"

"A friend of the daughter's lives nearby. She was last seen with him. He goes to the same school, Stone Canyon, and also works as a vendor at the Coliseum. Brought back a few memories for me."

"Really?"

"I'll tell you about it another time. This needs more detail than I have the energy to expend right now. But it dates back to when I was a vendor. I was about this kid's age. Around the time my mother got sick."

Gail put her sandwich down and reached over to squeeze my hand. "You don't talk about your parents much. I know it's painful."

"It is. Made me grow up a lot quicker than I should have. Made me take things more seriously. It taught me you had to play the hand you're dealt."

"You've done all right," Gail said as she glanced at an eager Chewy, who was busy pawing her leg. When Chewy wanted something, she was not shy about letting us know, although she thankfully didn't bark. I wasn't even sure she knew how. Gail pulled off a small piece of pastrami and fed it to her. "That's all you get," she said. "This isn't the healthiest thing for me, so it can't be at all healthy for you."

"She'll have a big backyard to run around in soon," I said, feeling better as I watched my two favorite girls. "Any word from the bank on our mortgage?"

"The loan officer called again this morning. Wanted more documents. We're supposed to close in a few weeks and they can't figure out what they need."

"These things get worked out," I said. "Focus on how nice it will be to own a home. Our little family will soon have our very own place."

"Mr. Positive," she smiled. "I like that new persona."

"I'm going to miss living in Santa Monica. It's been a long time here for me. We're in a great neighborhood."

"I know. We just can't afford to own here. Yet."

"Maybe when my wife, the successful attorney, starts her own practice we can move back here. Or when I win the lottery."

"You never know," she said.

"We won't be far away. Mar Vista's nice. You know it means 'view of the sea' in Spanish."

"That's good," she said. "But the only water view we'll actually have is of our neighbor's kiddie pool."

"Funny. Oh, and I have an invitation you may like. Would you be interested in accompanying me to the gubernatorial debate tomorrow night?"

Gail put her sandwich down and smiled that megawatt smile. "Why, I would be delighted to. The governor gave you a few passes?"

"His campaign manager, actually. For you, it will be entertainment. For me, it'll be work."

"You think you'll find out something about his daughter there?"

"You never know. Put enough puzzle pieces on the table, and I can usually connect them into something meaningful."

"You know, you may not be the only member of this

family working tomorrow night."

"Oh?"

"I'm sure the city attorney will be at the debate. Can't hurt to say hello to him. You know I sometimes wonder about politics as a career. I might want to run for office. Down the road maybe. One day."

I took this in. "Politics is a tricky business. Everything you do is open to public scrutiny. Along with everything I do."

"If I worried about you doing anything morally wrong, I wouldn't have married you."

"My job occasionally requires me to take, ah, a few liberties with the law," I reminded her.

"Nothing I can't handle."

"You're great," I said. "And I think you'd make a fine public figure one day."

"Perhaps," Gail said, looking down at her tummy once more. "But in the short term I'll settle for getting my old private figure back."

*

The next morning came early as usual. My neighbor, Ms. Linzmeier, was now starting each morning by watching one of those religious shows on TV. Today, the Southern preacher was talking about how you get two lives, the one you're born into and the one you choose. I glanced over at the clock which read 5:30 a.m. and then over at Gail, who dozed happily, oblivious to any outside noise. I then felt a cold, wet object on my fingers.

Apparently Chewy was up early too, and wanted to go for a walk. After taking our little dog out to do her business, I drank my usual pot of French roast coffee, read the local news online, and then headed out into the day.

Summer had effectively ended in Santa Monica. The morning was cool and foggy. But Santa Monica was often a good bit cooler than the rest of the LA basin. As I made my way downtown to the LAPD's Rampart Station, the fog had mostly dissipated. I liked the fog. I thought it added character to the day, and I hoped that living in Mar Vista wouldn't take that from us. It was only a couple of miles from the coast, but in LA, that could mean a world of difference in terms of climate.

My drive took all of 20 minutes. If you can get on the freeway before 7:00 a.m., traveling in LA is not so bad. It also helps when you're going to see someone whose morning shift starts at dawn. And Juan Saavedra's new job not only had him up early, it kept him staying late as well.

The Rampart station was not on Rampart Boulevard, but rather along 6th Street, about halfway between the Harbor Freeway and MacArthur Park. The police station was housed in a building with a nice glass design facing the street, and a not-so-attractive white stucco and red brick exterior on the other three walls.

As I walked inside the building, I asked one of the uniforms where I could find the captain's office. Naturally, I was directed to corner office in the far reaches of the building. An assistant normally sat at a desk nearby, but she was nowhere to be seen. I took that as an open invitation to walk right in.

"Captain Saavedra."

Juan Saavedra was sitting at his desk reviewing a stack of reports, a pair of bifocals perched at the edge of his nose. His close-cropped silver hair and ruddy features gave him a distinguished look. He was a stocky man, and I noticed the start of a pot belly, something that hadn't been there before. Yet on his desk was a glass, filled to the rim with what looked like a chocolate milk shake. A white plastic straw rose out at an angle.

"Oh, looky here," he crowed. "If it isn't the president of the LAPD alumni association. Sorry, but I don't plan on joining for a few more years."

"I don't blame you. You're moving up the ranks quickly. I may come visit you in the chief's office one day."

"Unlikely," he said. "I prefer police work over politics. The chief's job requires a different set of skills."

"And maybe someone who makes healthier breakfast choices."

"I will have you know," he said as he lifted the glass, "that this shake has all of 90 calories. Part of a weight loss plan. It's not what it looks like."

"Glad to hear you're avoiding desserts for breakfast. How does it taste?"

Juan shrugged as he took a sip from the straw. "Not bad, not great. Healthier than doughnuts."

"Heck of an example you're setting for your men," I said. "A captain who doesn't eat doughnuts and doesn't wear a mustache. You're breaking protocol."

"Oh, just what I need today. A critique on how to be a

cop. Dare I review your history?"

I sat down. "Maybe not. I wasn't the model officer. Especially near the end."

"I'm well aware. Now you're getting high profile clients, you're raking in the big bucks, you have a Barbie doll wife and a perfect kid on the way. Sounds like things worked out for you."

"It's been a good year," I admitted. "Although I don't know about the big bucks. We're buying a house on the Westside, but it means moving out of Santa Monica."

"My sympathies. I have a nice place now, but it's down in Mission Viejo. South Orange County. Took me an hour to get in this morning. With no traffic."

"Must be nice to get out of the urban sprawl of LA though. Better place to raise your kids."

Juan shrugged. "I don't know about that. The schools down there might be a little better, but every place has its problems. At least my kids have a chance to play on a good high school football team."

"It's one of the best programs," I said.

"Indeed. So what brings you out here on this fine morning?" he asked. "I assume you need a favor."

I jerked my head back feigning shock. "Juan. I'm surprised at you. Can't I stop by and see an old friend and shoot the breeze for a little while?"

"You could, but you don't. I imagine there's something you want."

"And I imagine you'll have a price for me to pay," I countered.

"Look. You know the drill. That's what makes the

world go 'round. What's up?"

"Couple of things. I wanted to ask what you know about Xavier Bishop."

"Heck of a cornerback. He's done a great job at your alma mater. He'll be playing on Sundays."

"C'mon Juan."

"C'mon what? You think you can waltz in here and get confidential police info?"

"Yes."

"Cripes, Burnsy. Some things are off limits," he said, the slightest hint of a smile crossing his face.

I sighed. "Okay. Pair of tickets to the USC-Stanford game?"

"Atta boy. You haven't forgotten the wheels of justice can turn fast or slow. Depends on who's at the controls."

"I see getting promoted hasn't changed you."

"I am who I am. And I think I do my job damn well. I just want to get a little piece of the pie."

"Understood."

"So," Juan said, typing a few items into his computer. "Xavier Bishop, alias X, X-Man, X Island, and Granite."

"Granite?"

"Hey, I don't make this stuff up. Assume it has something to do with his physique. Let's see here. Picked up last week for assault on a one Desiree Brown. His girlfriend, I gather. Maybe former girlfriend by now. Over at Robinson Garden, on Ellendale Place. A few blocks north of the SC campus. Looks like it's not student housing, but the building is all students. Funny how landlords work things, huh?"

"Rich college kids pay their rent on time."

"More like their parents do. Anyways, the call was made at around 10:00 p.m. last Thursday night. Uniforms responded and found the victim had bruises on her face. She identified Bishop. All she said was they had an argument and he hit her. We picked up the suspect the next day and his hand was wrapped in a bandage."

"Okay," I said. "Anything else you can share on that case?"

"That about does it. Xavier was questioned and released, pending results of DNA testing. The media got it right. They called him a person of interest."

"Okay. Let me ask you about another topic."

"Sure," Juan said, rolling his eyes. "I've got nothing else to do today. Providing you with unauthorized police intel just makes me feel good about myself."

"Ah, Juan. I'm just trying to make your job easier."

"Why doesn't it usually work out that way?"

"I'll ignore that," I grinned. "What do you know about the Stone Canyon School?"

"The one in Bel-Air? Great school if you have the money. It's a 7 through 12 program, middle and high schools. You and Gail are quite a few years away from applying."

"I wasn't exactly thinking of us."

"You working on something?"

"Yeah. Anything ever require police attention over there? Any students in trouble?"

Juan shrugged and scanned the computer again. "Nothing out of the ordinary. Couple of kids got popped for DUI last year. Another got taken in for possession of weed. Nothing different from any other school. Except maybe the parents have an easier time getting them off."

"That's it?"

"Pretty much. Funny you mentioned Stone Canyon. When Rafael was in 5th grade, we were getting concerned about our local middle school in Reseda. Not a great place. So we took a tour of a few private schools and one of them was Stone Canyon. Unbelievable campus. Felt like we had entered another world. The school presented a perfect environment. Made it sound like anyone who didn't want to send their kids there would be shirking their parental duties."

"Did you apply there?"

"Nope. Their annual tuition is about double what we pay on our mortgage. I may be a captain, but I'm still on a government salary. That's why we moved to Orange County. Bigger house, get the kids out of the LA Unified School District. Our local elementary school was actually pretty good. But once they hit middle and high school age, the options in L.A. get bleak."

"I'll keep that in mind for the future."

Juan nodded. "You'll be fine until 6th grade. But that's 10 years away. At that point you'll have some decisions to make. Public schools in this town are a mess. When you and I were growing up, California had the best schools in the country. Now we have the worst. Thank Proposition 13 for that. They cut taxes and guess what. They wound up with a lot less money to put into schools. Kids paid the price."

"Some people might say there are other reasons our schools are in trouble. Sub-par teachers. And that Prop. 13 cut out some bureaucratic waste."

"Spoken like a true USC guy. Your heroes are Ronald Reagan and Buster Palmer. Anti-government Republicans from way back."

I didn't say anything right away, as Rex asked me to be discreet. Now wasn't the time to let Juan know my new client was Buster Palmer's son, and that I was looking for his missing granddaughter. I was suddenly reminded of a directive an aging partner had made when I first joined the LAPD. He was a year away from retirement and told me he'd rather I do nothing than make a mistake. Applied judiciously, it wasn't the worst advice, but he was full of these gems and was all too eager to impart them to his rookie partner. We lasted about three weeks before I asked to be reassigned. But that little tidbit stayed with me. There were times when it was indeed best to say as little as possible.

"Well," I said, "my opportunity to be a room parent is a long ways off."

"Trust me. It will happen. Sooner than you might think. Time moves quickly. I remember when our kids were in diapers. Didn't seem that long ago. But with kids, it's really like they say. The days go by slow and the years go by fast."

"Interesting."

"You've waited a while to become a father. It's a little tougher when you do it late in life."

"Sure," I said. "I'm a real old man. Next year at this

time, the baby will be more thrilled with his dad walking a few steps than vice versa."

Juan chuckled and then peered at me. "So what's the case you're working on with Stone Canyon?"

I held up my hands. "Can't tell you just yet. Confidential. You know."

Juan shook his head. "Ah, Burnsy. That may cost you."

"How so?"

"I think maybe now I'll be looking for three tickets to the Stanford game."

*

I spent the rest of the day trying to hunt down Xavier Bishop, Desiree Brown or any of Desiree's neighbors who might be able to tell me something. It was all in vain, as everyone was either in class or not answering their door. I drove to the Stone Canyon School, but noticed they had a security gate with a guard standing watch. I tried calling the other students who were at the Coliseum with Molly, but none answered and none returned my calls. Given the governor's specific request for discretion, it seemed as if I was reaching a dead end today.

I picked Gail up in the late afternoon and we drove over to Westwood. We stopped for a quick dinner before the debate, Gail deciding she wanted a falafel. In addition to cradling the UCLA campus inside its hillsides, Westwood was also known as the Persian capital of Los Angeles and had an abundance of Middle Eastern restaurants. Having done her undergraduate work nearby, Gail knew the terrain. The falafels were delicious, and not surprisingly, nobody else in the restaurant was over the age of 22. As we were eating, I pointed out falafels actually originated in Egypt. Gail acknowledged this with a perfunctory nod, before she went back to focusing on her dinner and taking another bite.

We made our way to Royce Hall, and once I gave my name in at Will Call, we were ushered to seats in the front row. This time, Gail was duly impressed.

"You have clout here," she cooed. "I like the extra leg room."

"How are you feeling?"

She took a deep breath. "Like I can't wait to have this baby and get the pregnancy over with. I once heard a girlfriend call her pregnancy a ball and chain. I didn't like that remark and still don't. But at least I understand it better now."

"It'll be over soon," I reminded her.

A few minutes later, the moderator stood up and addressed the audience. She was a bubbly, young anchor for one of the local news shows, and she began by reminding everyone the debate would be broadcast throughout California. Asking the audience to please be respectful of the candidates, she wanted the debate to be a civil and objective discussion of the issues. A number of students sitting in the back of the auditorium began to boo. The young woman looked a little flustered, repeated her request, and then sat back down.

"Were you this way in college?" I asked, pointing to

the back of the auditorium.

"What do you think?" she said with a slight glower.

"I'd think probably not."

"My biggest act of rebellion was eating extra spicy hot wings."

"You sound like you were a good girl."

She gave me another look. "Still am."

I laughed and put my arm around her. At that point, a young Asian man sat down on the other side of me and we introduced ourselves. He was Arthur Woo, the brother of Justin Woo, one of the candidates. He was excited about the debate, the campaign, and the prospect of the first Korean-American getting elected to the statehouse.

"This is amazing," he said with a slight accent. "I have to pinch myself every day."

"Are you involved in the campaign?" I asked.

"Oh, yes. Our whole family is going non-stop, every day. Rex Palmer is weak. He's a dinosaur. We have a real shot at unseating him."

"Well, good luck," I said.

"Who's your candidate?" he peered at me.

"I don't have one yet. I'll see how this debate unfolds first."

"Are you with the media? Local news outlet?"

"Nope, not me."

"So you're not part of a campaign, and you're not covering the debate as a journalist. Just how did you get seats like these, Mr. Burnside?"

I smiled. "You ask a lot of questions, Mr. Woo."

Arthur Woo didn't smile back. "You are an interesting

man. You don't give too much away."

"Perhaps."

He sniffed. "Tonight will be a very memorable night. Maybe historical."

"Do you mind if I ask you a personal question?"

"You may ask," he said cautiously.

"I detect an accent. Did you grow up here?"

"My family moved here from South Korea when I was a young boy. It's hard to fully shake your accent. Why do you ask?"

I shrugged, thinking back to my first conversation with the Palmer campaign. "I'm just a curious guy. I'm interested in people."

"Understanding people is critical in politics," Woo said in a manner that sounded almost mechanical. But then he turned to Gail and gave her a long look. "I'm sure you're going to have a beautiful baby."

Gail grinned in appreciation. "Thank you. Sounds like you may be running for office one day."

Arthur Woo gave the slightest hint of a smile. "Perhaps," he said.

The lights dimmed and the debate soon began. It started with introductions, not unlike a sporting event. I couldn't get away from the similarities between political campaign and ballgames. There were winners and losers, statistics, and rabid fans on both sides. And as the candidates took the stage, they each evoked wild applause and derisive yells. So much for civility. The two politicians were both dressed predictably in navy blue suits, white shirts and red and blue ties. They actually looked like they were on the same team.

The moderator began by asking the governor a question about his biggest accomplishments. Rex Palmer moved into actor mode, deftly detailing how he had cut wasteful spending in Sacramento, toughened the laws against violent criminals, and stopped tuition increases at all California colleges and universities. The last line brought a big cheer from the audience in the back of the auditorium. The moderator reminded the crowd to be impartial and the students responded with another round of boos.

"Typical UCLA crowd," I whispered to Gail. She responded by giving me an elbow in the ribs, maybe a little harder than I'd have liked.

The moderator then asked Justin Woo to assess the governor's term in office, and he took the opportunity to lay into Rex Palmer, calling his administration, among other things, a failure, a disaster, and the worst thing to hit California since the devastating earthquakes a few decades ago. Woo was scathing in his attack, accusing his opponent of neglecting the state's economy and allowing large corporations to move their headquarters to other states. Then Woo touted his business degree from Harvard and his experience working for startup companies in the Silicon Valley. He was a sharp speaker, and you could tell he was getting the audience's attention.

I noticed Justin Woo spoke with the same accent his brother did. Only Justin's accent was a little heavier. It was a clipped way of speaking and had a staccato ring to it. He would pronounce certain words with a little difficulty, one being California, which he pronounced, "Cal-phone-ya." And apparently I wasn't the only one who noticed. Whenever Woo spoke, Governor Palmer was scribbling notes. And about three-quarters of the way into the debate, the governor took an opportunity to bring this issue to the surface. And he did it in a way he would likely regret forever.

Politicians should avoid making jokes in public. Many are awkward at delivering punch lines and little good can come of it. I was a social science major at USC, which meant I took a lot of courses in psychology and political science. I'm not sure where I learned this bit of wisdom, it might have been in a political communications course. But it stayed with me. And when Rex Palmer went down this path, I knew immediately it would come back to bite him and bite him hard.

"Justin Woo," he said, "talks about California as if he is an expert. And yet he's only lived here less than half of his life. We should honor the fact that he has accomplished a lot in his brief tenure here. He came to America from a foreign country and he earned both a college degree and an MBA from a very good out-of-state school. I, on the other hand, went to college at Stanford and law school at Berkeley. I have lived in California all my life, and so have my parents and their parents before them."

The governor paused for a moment and smiled before turning to Woo and dropping his bombshell. "But if someone is looking to become governor of California, the least you could expect from them is to learn how to pronounce it correctly."

The large auditorium became very quiet, very quickly. The only sound audible was that of a few people gasping. Without waiting for the moderator to signify it was his turn to speak, Justin Woo turned to Rex Palmer and went after him.

"Governor, that is a most despicable and insulting thing you just said. I don't think I have ever heard any public figure say anything so nasty and bigoted. I think you owe an apology, not only to me, but to the millions of immigrants in this state. Your comments are reprehensible. And I wonder, and I think every voter should wonder, what kind of a man insults one-third of his state's residents and then thinks he deserves to lead them. How is that even possible? You do not deserve to lead them, sir. No, you do not deserve that at all."

The governor tried to respond, but he began to stammer. He knew he had slipped badly and didn't know how to recover. And he was all alone on the stage. Justin Woo did the smart thing, which is not interrupt and let his opponent keep babbling. When a politician is self-destructing, the best course of action is to stay out of his way. Rex Palmer did not exactly apologize but he tried to laugh it off as a joke, which may have made matters worse. And for the rest of the debate, Justin Woo hammered home the point that Governor Palmer was out of touch with the people of California and should not be awarded a second term.

When the debate ended, an excited Arthur Woo shook our hands and moved onto the stage to give his brother a hug. Gail and I started to move toward the exit when a familiar face approached. As thrilled as Arthur Woo was, Bill Thorn appeared equally dour.

"You need to stick around. Shelly would like to speak with you."

"Sure," I said. "Any other orders?"

"This isn't a good night to get cute with me," he snapped.

"Fine, I'm sure there'll be other opportunities."

"You don't know when to turn off that charm."

I shrugged. Actually I did. "Where is she?"

"She'll be in the spin room," Thorn said.

"Spin room?"

"Uh, yeah. That's where the media will be. Post-debate quotes. Follow-ups. Things like that," he said and pointed toward a door. "Go through there. At the end of the hallway is another room. Can't miss it. Unless you're an idiot."

We followed a group of important-looking people down the hall. They were dressed smartly in expensive business suits, and chattering non-stop as we entered a brightly lit ballroom. It was loaded with a variety of local luminaries, not just the on-air media and the candidates' staff, but virtually every politician looking to get his or her face on the 10:00 p.m. news.

As we moved into the spin room, there was a bevy of activity. Shelly Busch was nearby, already in full disaster mode. She downplayed the governor's flub, and tried to highlight a few of Justin Woo's shortcomings. Across the room, a number of outraged members of Justin Woo's campaign were rehashing how Rex Palmer was unfit to lead California.

I turned to Gail. "So you mentioned an interest in getting into politics one day?"

"I did."

"This is what you have to look forward to do," I said. "Arguing the issues of the day has taken a back seat to destroying an opponent or conducting damage control."

Gail sighed. "I know. It's the world in which we live."

"I suppose if you move forward with becoming a public figure one day, I'll be part of this world, too."

"I'm not worried about you, sweetie," she smiled at me.

"Good. I'll be worried enough for the both of us," I said, fully aware my witty rejoinders often had a biting edge to them.

"You know," Gail said, "while you're chatting up the staff, I think I'll go say hello to the city attorney. Can't hurt to get a little face time with the boss."

"With a face like yours, I'm sure you'll get his undivided attention."

Gail kissed my cheek and walked off to engage in some office politics. I began to walk toward Shelly, when an old acquaintance stepped in front of me and blocked my path. His large, round body and Cheshire cat grin was impossible to miss.

"Now I didn't think I'd be seeing you here," said Virgil Hairston. "Have you traded in your P.I. license for a job as a political operative?"

"Not exactly," I said. "But I didn't think the local Santa

Monica paper would be sending journalists to a gubernatorial debate."

"They probably didn't. But I'm not with the *Outlook* any more. Moved over to the *Times* earlier this year. A bump up."

I shook his hand warmly. "Good for you, Virgil. Glad to hear it. Although in some circles, working for the *Times* isn't exactly taking a step up. My SC friends like to call your paper the Fish Wrap."

Virgil Hairston was a reporter I had met a couple of years ago. He was covering a case I was working on at the time, the murder of my friend Wayne Fairborn. Virgil and I developed a nice rapport and were able to help each other do our jobs a little better. Virgil was an excellent journalist, someone I had wanted to stay in touch with. Like a lot of people. But then Gail came back into my life, work intensified, and time began to slip away. It had been a couple of years since we had last spoken.

"Yes, I'm aware my paper probably doesn't sit favorably in the minds of your Trojan buddies. But I'm sure you'll agree it's nice to have a wider audience," he said. "So just what brings you here?"

"The usual," I replied. "Business."

"Ah," he said. "Sounds intriguing. We should get together soon and talk. Catch up. Maybe lunch?"

"I'd like that," I said. "As long as I pick the place. Fried chicken and bacon cheeseburgers aren't part of my regular diet."

"Ha! You have a good memory. All right. Let's do it. Very soon. And maybe you'll be more forthcoming about your case here. I always love a good story. And I still haven't forgotten about doing a piece on a model LAPD officer turned rogue private eye. Might help build readership."

"I don't know about helping you on that one," I said. Some people think any publicity is good publicity. I wasn't so sure.

Shelly Busch had finished providing her take on the debate, and the bright lights surrounding her had dimmed for a moment. Virgil and I parted, and I approached Shelly. Her facial expression was tight, and she did not look happy.

"I guess this isn't a good night for you," I said, providing as much of an understatement as I could.

"Full blown catastrophe," she said. "We'll be in the field tonight with polling, and tomorrow I'll have a better idea of how bad this really is."

"I don't think this gaffe is going away."

"No. Woo isn't going to let it. Best we can do is just highlight Rex making an innocent joke and paint Woo as an intransigent with no sense of humor."

"Oh," I said, wondering about the wisdom of taking that stand. "What about making an apology?"

"I don't think so," she said. "The governor doesn't like to apologize. He learned it from his father. Buster says it shows weakness. He goes by the Henry Ford motto: never complain, never explain."

"I don't think that works so great in the 21st century."

Shelly looked like she needed a cigarette. Or a stiff drink. "In the end, the boss has the final say. I just give advice. I'm not the decider."

I nodded. "Understood."

"So where are we on our little girl lost?" she said, the night's events obviously weighing on her diplomacy and tact, revealing a side of Shelly that I did not like.

"I found Diego," I said. "But not Molly. They left the Coliseum together and I gather they both spent Saturday night at his parents' apartment. But she left there on Sunday. Rather quickly, too. I'm still trying to pick up her trail. Unless the governor eases up on his request to be discreet, I won't be able to move forward here. This is important. She may be in some danger. I'll need to talk to her friends at school, maybe her teachers, too. I'll need access."

"Let me speak with Rex tomorrow and I'll let you know," she said. "There are some issues. And he obviously has other things on his mind right now."

I stared at her. The idea that someone's daughter might be in trouble was not sinking in. I thought of Gail, her interest in politics and our impending arrival in late December. I began to feel my skin crawl.

"Of course," I said, dryly. "Let me know."

I walked over to Gail and waited patiently as she kibitzed and talked and buttered up the city attorney. There was a group around him, but he seemed more focused on Gail. I didn't really blame him. I was, too.

After a few minutes of standing in the background, I moved next to her and cleared my throat. Gail noticed me, picked up my signal and immediately made introductions. At that point, Gail gracefully told everyone we needed to go. When you have a husband with a big mouth, leaving the scene quickly is a wise move. We walked outside and headed toward the parking structure. I took Gail's hand, partly because it was cold outside, and partly because I liked doing it.

"Quite a night," I said, as we strolled across a darkened, empty lawn. I recalled something one of my professors told me when I was a student. He had taught at USC for 20 years, working in that not-so-great part of inner-city LA. Every night, he would walk from his classroom to the garage, often after 10:00 p.m. Despite the dreary neighborhood surrounding USC, he never had an incident. Yet one evening he had attended a symposium here at UCLA, nestled between the wealthy communities of Bel-Air and Westwood. And as he entered the parking structure, he was robbed at gunpoint. They took his wallet and his watch, possessions that were easily replaced. But they also changed his perspective. That the nicest parts of LA were not necessarily the safest. Things could jump out at you when you least expected them to.

And at that point, my cell phone rang. The number was blocked, but I decided to answer it anyway. Receiving an ungodly number of telemarketing calls had made me skeptical of always picking up, but tonight was different. Maybe something had just happened back at Royce Hall, maybe the governor wanted a word with me. This seemed like a night I should not let a call go unanswered. It turned out to be a wise move.

"Burnside," came a familiar voice on the other end.

"Hi Juan," I said. "You're working late."

"I am indeed. And I'd like to talk with you."

"What's up?" I asked.

"You were asking me about Stone Canyon School this morning. You wouldn't say much about it, but we're dealing with a homicide now. So you'll need to come over here and be a lot more forthcoming."

"Okay," I said, my stomach getting tense. "What can you tell me right now?"

"Oh, I can tell you something," Juan replied tersely. "Details will follow when you get over here. But the homicide involves a Stone Canyon student. Turns out you were looking into them."

I closed my eyes. "Go on," I said grimly.

"Everyone was shocked. No gang ties, that's for sure, but you never know how these things escalate. Victim took two in the head. Close range. Suspect drove off quickly. Could have been a drive-by, could have been premeditated. We got no license plate, no nothing. Just one dead kid. Name's Diego Garcia."

Five

I dropped Gail at home, taking a few minutes to escort her up to our apartment. She kept insisting she was fine, and reminded me she had once worked as a campus security officer. I reminded her that a woman who is seven months pregnant is in no condition to deal with adverse situations. And after Juan's phone call, I was taking no chances with whatever evil was lurking in the world.

The crime scene was across the street from MacArthur Park. It was past 10:00 p.m. by now and the night had turned cold, or whatever passed for cold in Los Angeles. Across the street, a crew from one of the local news trucks was setting up a shoot. I slipped under the yellow-and-black striped police tape and found Juan Saavedra giving directives to a pair of young, uniformed officers.

"No one from the media enters the area. No one. They stay over there in the park," he said, pointing a finger at them for emphasis.

One of the uniforms noticed me. "Should I get rid of this one, captain?"

Juan turned and looked at me. "Nah, he's not media. He's not a cop either. I don't quite know what the hell he is."

"That's quite an introduction, Juan," I said.

"Best I can do at this hour," he said, dismissing the uniforms. "Rookies. Got to start someplace."

"I remember my first day on patrol. My partner had been on the job for almost 20 years. He gave me an interesting piece of advice."

"What was that?"

"He told me whatever my instincts were, to stop and do the opposite. That's how you become a good cop."

Juan shook his head. "Old-school thinking."

He motioned to a detective, and the three of us walked to a more private area of a not-so-private crime scene. The detective seemed close to my age, 40-something, but he was short and squat. He wore a black windbreaker that was two sizes too big and had shaved his head to divert attention from male-pattern baldness. His name was Dennis Lally.

A sheet had been thrown over the body, and more than a few uniformed and plainclothes officers were milling about. When a shooting happens, there are plenty of things to do, but a show of numbers also serves to try and put the community at ease.

"So I understand you were down here last night," Juan said. "And you met with the victim."

"You do good police work," I remarked.

"Jeepers, thanks. I live for your approval."

"How did you find this out?"

"Look, we talked to the parents. But they only told us so much, they were just overwhelmed by all this. Weren't too forthcoming. They're scared about something else. Thought you might fill in the details."

"They told you I was down here?"

"Yeah, but not until we asked them specifically. We

found your card in Diego's pocket."

"Ah."

"So what do you know?"

I thought for a moment. Rex Palmer was a client, and he had asked me to be discreet. But now a murder had been committed, and his daughter, like it or not, had become a part of the investigation. And keeping details from the police was not always such a good idea.

"You've heard the name Molly Palmer?" I asked.

"Governor's daughter," Juan said. "Go on."

"She's a student at Stone Canyon, too. Been missing for three days. Rumor has it she and Diego had a thing going. Maybe yes, maybe no. But she was here on Sunday. There was a confrontation with another girl and Molly left."

"And you didn't think to mention that to me yesterday when you dropped by," Juan remarked.

I shrugged. "Who knew it would turn into this?"

Juan stared off in the distance for a moment and then focused on Lally. "This case just got escalated," he said.

"What does that mean?" Lally asked.

"It means," Juan said, "This may be front page news soon. Despite how it may look, I don't think we can conclude this is just a random drive-by. It also means you need to tread very carefully with the media. Someone's bound to pick this up. We don't know the daughter's involvement yet. But you have to be careful about what you say."

"What's this guy's role?" he asked, pointing in my direction.

"He doesn't have an official role. Burnside's a P.I., used to be on the job. He can be helpful. He can also be a pain the ass. See if you can figure out a way to coexist."

"Captain," Lally protested. "This is an official police investigation. Last time we let one of these jokers help out, the evidence was thrown out of court and the perp walked. What do we need with a private dick muddying up the waters?"

"I prefer private investigator," I pointed out. "Private dick is so 20th-century."

"Just stay out of my way," Lally said.

"You following that with an 'or else'?" I asked politely.

Juan raised his hands. "Stop. Look, Dennis, even if I told Burnside to stay out of this, he wouldn't, okay? Following orders just isn't in his genetic makeup. That's why he's not on the job any more. And that case you're referring to was two years ago, and that P.I. never wore a badge. Figure out something where two plus two equals five, okay?"

I grinned. "The public and private sector working as one."

Lally glared at me. "You find out something, I want to be the first to know."

"Sure. Same here."

Lally stared at me and said nothing. Something told me there might be a few road bumps ahead.

I spent the next few hours shadowing Lally, overhearing conversations the police were having with the medical examiners and with various people in the neighborhood. I didn't say much, just listened. Diego

Garcia had been engaged in a heated conversation with someone in a car parked near 8th and Alvarado. The car was silver and nondescript, and of course nobody got the license plate.

Diego had been leaning forward to speak with whomever was driving the silver car, when two pops were heard by people throughout the block. Diego fell to the ground and the car sped away. But according to another witness, a pair of neighborhood guys had been watching nearby, most likely because they had nothing else to do. They were too far away to hear the conversation, but close enough to take action when they saw Diego get shot. Both drew weapons and fired repeatedly at the fleeing car. They evidently didn't hit their target, because the car pulled a quick right turn onto Wilshire and kept going. They did however, shatter the windows of a different car that had the misfortune to be parked nearby, and pieces of glass were strewn about the street.

The pair of local guys denied any involvement, and when the police arrived they mysteriously didn't have any firearms on them. What they did have though, were rap sheets a mile long, and the police decided a night in the can might help jog their memories. It wouldn't of course, it would just make them look harder for the person in the neighborhood who ratted them out.

I pointed this out to Lally. He told me the police knew what they were doing. As usual, I had my doubts.

*

I left the crime scene at about 1:00 a.m., and briefly considered buying a pastrami sandwich at Langer's, but getting some sleep was preferable to a decadent snack. Gail was up early the next morning, and by default, so was I. The *Times* website contained nothing about the shooting. I received a text from Virgil Hairston suggesting lunch today, and I responded by asking if we could find middle ground on a restaurant. Maybe one that offered both healthy and unhealthy choices. After a few back-and-forths we settled on an old favorite downtown. It turned out the timing would work out perfectly. My phone rang a few minutes later, and it was an unexpected caller. Xavier Bishop also asked if we could talk this morning.

For a change, the morning was warm and sunny. I brewed a small pot of French roast to get me going before heading back downtown. Fortunately, we weren't meeting until 10:30 a.m., which meant I had an easy drive ahead of me. If I left Santa Monica at 8:00 a.m. on a weekday morning, it would take an hour to get downtown. Leaving at 10:00 a.m. meant it would take 20 minutes. Remove the traffic congestion and LA could be a much more livable place.

Many years ago, the city fathers devised a plan to rebuild downtown Los Angeles. It started with a few new office buildings, included the addition of nice hotels and condos, and the development of a theater district. A small group of urban pioneers moved in briefly, but a series of economic downturns stopped the regentrification in its tracks. A number of large companies departed LA due to corporate takeovers or better tax deals in other states. The upshot was that for many years, downtown remained a mecca for only the homeless and the destitute, rather than for young professionals. The tide finally turned a few years ago with the development of L.A. Live, a large plaza rimmed with a concert hall, a sports arena, hotels, restaurants and movie theaters. The Emmy Awards and Grammy Awards were held here, and a day rarely went by without a noteworthy event taking place.

I parked in the West garage about a block from L.A. Live and walked over to a Starbucks that was tucked between a Wolfgang Puck's Cafe and a sports bar that changed names every couple of years. Even though it was mid-morning, there were plenty of people milling about. Some wore Kings jerseys, which told me there was a hockey game that night. As I approached the Starbucks, I saw a young, muscular African-American kid who looked like he could be in college. He was at an outdoor table, sitting under an umbrella that blocked the sun. He was nursing what might have been a milk shake anywhere else, but was more likely an iced Frappucino here. He had dreadlocks that hung down past his shoulders, and his massive biceps bulged from inside a tight gray t-shirt. A black baseball cap was pulled down low and he had a stoic expression on his face.

"Xavier?" I said. "I'm Burnside."

"Hey," he said, getting up and shaking my hand.

"You picked a very public spot to meet. Maybe we should go inside."

"Okay," he said and followed me in. "I figured this would be convenient. Got a radio interview in a little while. Upstairs."

I frowned as I got in line to order a very large, very strong cup of black coffee. "Why are you doing an interview?"

"Some, uh, people thought it would be a good idea to get out in front of this situation. Let everyone know my side of what happened."

"I take it these people aren't associated with the university. The school probably wants as little publicity about this as possible."

"I guess," he said. "I'm trying to figure out what to do here. Getting a lot of advice from a lot of sources. It's tough to figure it all out and know what the right thing is."

It took five minutes before I got to the front of the line and placed my order. Oddly, the barista didn't ask for any money, she just smiled, handed me my drink and told me to have a nice day. We found an open table and sat down.

"Where are you getting this advice from?"

Xavier shrugged. "Not supposed to say."

"Okay," I said, knowing he was most likely talking with an agent, something college athletes should clearly not be doing. "Just make sure you don't sign anything yet. You're thinking of going into the NFL after this season?"

"I guess," he said. "Some people say I've got to. They think I'll be a first round draft pick. If I pass that up and stay in school, I may lose out. Millions. Even one year can make a difference. Got to take that stuff seriously."

It wasn't an unrealistic concern. College football players who pass up the chance to go into the NFL after their junior season could see their market value decline if they don't have a good senior year. Or if they get injured. Or if there are better players at their position the following year. Players who had a great junior year were often advised to enter the NFL draft and forego their senior year of college. And Xavier Bishop was correct on one point. These contracts could be worth millions.

"So how can I help you?" I asked.

"I guess you know my attorney, Mr. Hoffman. He said you were like a cop or something."

"Something like that," I said.

"He also said you were a football player."

"At one time. Coach Cleary and I played in the same secondary."

Xavier's face brightened for a moment. "Hey, he didn't tell me about that."

"I played free safety. Johnny was a cornerback. We were together for two years."

"Wow. You play in the league?"

"Nope. Messed up my knee before the draft. Torn ACL. Back then they didn't have the procedures they have today. I moved into a different career."

Xavier frowned, the pained expression returning to his face. "Sorry to hear. But that's a concern of mine, too. Injuries are part of the game. You never know when it might happen. That's why staying in school is a risk."

"Guys today get insurance policies to cover that. You have options. And in the long run, there's value to earning a college degree. It helps if you want to go into coaching one day. Or maybe some other career."

He shook his head. "I know. It's all been explained.

And I'll have to make my decision in January. But I feel real bad about letting my boys down. We should have beat Oregon State easily the other day, but it was close. Too close. My not being in there hurt the team. I'd like to be back for them. If not this Saturday, at least for the Stanford game next week. It'd be nice to play in the Rose Bowl again."

"So you want to be reinstated."

"Uh-huh."

"And that can't happen until these assault charges go away."

"Right. You get the picture."

"So tell me what happened with your girlfriend. Her name is Desiree?"

Xavier said yes. He sat back in his chair and took a sip on what was no longer an icy drink. He drummed his fingers on the wooden table. A few people sauntered by and took long glances at him, their faces conveying the sense they had seen him before, but couldn't quite place where. It was a phenomenon unique to LA. The guy you recognized as you were walking down the street might work in your building. Or you might have seen him on an episode of *CSI*.

"It's not quite what you think," he said.

"It never is."

"I didn't punch Desiree."

"But you punched someone," I said.

Xavier looked me dead in the eyes for a long moment. "Why'd you say that?"

"Your knuckles are still nicked up," I said, pointing

down at his right hand. He stopped for a moment before raising his hand to eye level and pretending to examine it.

"I'm not sure how they got this way," he said, shaking his head. "I could have dinged my hand during practice. It happens."

"But that's not what happened here. Not unless you punched someone in the helmet, and we both know that's a dumb thing to do. And All-American players don't normally do dumb things on the field."

Xavier took a breath. "Let's just say I got into a scuffle after practice."

"Any witnesses?" I asked.

"No. It was private. And that's the God's honest truth."

"Maybe it is," I said. "But it makes it pretty hard for me to help you."

"What if you could talk to Desiree for me? Might help to find the guy who really hit her. The police aren't going to do any more. They think they got the right guy. But they're wrong."

I frowned. Relationship management wasn't part of my skill set. "You've tried talking with her since this happened?"

"Like I say, it's complicated."

"How long have you been together?"

"Over two years. Was getting serious. Met her family and everything."

"How'd that go?" I asked.

Xavier shrugged. "Okay, I guess. She's from a different world. Grew up just over in Baldwin Hills. They like to call that the black Beverly Hills. It's a nice area."

"Where did you grow up?"

"The CPT. Can't get more different from Baldwin Hills."

The CPT was slang for Compton, which was one of the roughest places in the LA area. Low income, high crime, lots of gang activity. The type of place you tried hard to get out of. And not a place you'd want to go back to.

"I didn't know people still called it the CPT."

"Some do. My mama listened to a lot of NWA. I guess I picked it up from her."

"Did your mom approve of Desiree?"

Xavier peered at me. "Why you asking that?"

"Just trying to sort things out. Wondering if there was an issue."

"Not exactly. My mama liked that Desiree was smart and pretty and all. Thought she would be good for me. But mama also warned me. She said there will always be girls who want you for the money and the fame. I guess I figured since Desiree's family had made it, that wouldn't be an issue."

"That she'd like you for who you are."

"Yeah. But mama said it didn't matter. Women are women."

"Was she right in this case?"

Xavier didn't answer and I didn't push him. He might not have had an answer and could possibly be searching for one. He kept a pained expression on his face and didn't say anything.

"Okay" I finally said, getting back to the matter at

hand. "Look. If you didn't hit Desiree, who do you think did?"

Xavier shook his head. "That's what I need you to find out. All I know is it wasn't me. I went over to her place, we had an argument and then I left."

"What'd you argue about?"

He shrugged. "Stuff."

"You're not giving me much to go on here," I told him.

"Yeah, I know. But I heard you're good."

Sitting back in my chair, I took a long drink of strong coffee. It had a nice bite to it. The temperature had cooled sufficiently, hot enough to be satisfying, but not so hot that it burned going down the throat.

I considered Xavier's situation. Things weren't adding up here. People who came to me were all too eager to spill their guts and tell me about their problems. They often gave more information than I needed or wanted to hear. But for a young man facing expulsion from college, possible jail time, and a potential fortune hanging by a thread, Xavier Bishop was parsing his words far too carefully.

Suddenly things became even stranger. Xavier Bishop rose abruptly, shook my hand, and quickly said that any help I could provide him would be appreciated. He mumbled something about the radio interview and I watched him walk quickly out the door. Across the plaza I caught a glimpse of a familiar face, albeit not one I expected to see, nor was eager to see. But some things began to fall into place. After nodding ever so slightly at Xavier, the man strolled into the coffee house and approached my table.

"And isn't this a coincidence," said Cliff Roper, taking a look around the room before sitting down in the same chair Xavier had just occupied. "I was just thinking about you."

"That's funny," I said. "I haven't been thinking about you."

Cliff Roper pulled out his iPhone and did a quick scan of his messages before responding. "That's not a nice thing to say. Especially after I gave you such a generous bonus a few months ago."

"If I remember correctly," I said slowly, "I helped get you off on a double murder charge. I'm still waiting for a thank you."

Roper waved his hand. "Twenty grand should be plenty of thanks. You should stop being so sensitive."

I rubbed the bridge of my nose. Cliff Roper was a sports agent with whom I had had a number of interactions, and none were savory. He had hired me earlier this year to investigate the shooting of his business partner. Roper was the primary suspect in that case, which ultimately spiraled into a pair of murders. The year before, I needed to twist his arm to get him to stop pressuring a freshman football player into signing with his agency before he was eligible for the draft. Of all the coffee houses in LA, this is the one I had to be in this morning. But of course, it was hardly a coincidence. And it now explained why Xavier Bishop was talking with me, and why he was on his way to do an interview. As it always was with Cliff Roper, unanswered questions hovered close to the surface.

"So you've been advising Xavier on things," I said.

Cliff Roper shook his head. "Absolutely not. A college player working with an agent is a violation of NCAA rules. You ought to be ashamed of yourself for even thinking such a thing."

"I'll give myself a strong talking to later," I said dryly. "What are you doing here?"

"Me?" he asked, seemingly startled. "I'm just a guy getting a hot beverage. Saw an old friend and decided to sit down and have a chat with him."

"We're not old friends," I pointed out, "or even new ones."

"You need to relax," he said. "You're going to be a dad soon. Heard you slipped one past the goalie."

"You still have such a charming way with words."

"Incidentally," he continued, "Honey sends her regards. She says congratulations on your upcoming addition."

Honey was Cliff Roper's daughter, and probably the only thing in the world that kept him human. "Thanks," I said. "I guess she and Gail stay in touch."

"Your wife's a smart cookie that way. I know you have a thing for Honey. This helps remove any temptation you might have. You know the old saying: Keep your friends close and your enemies closer."

I shook my head. "Maybe Gail and Honey simply like each other. You have a warped way of looking at the world."

Roper narrowed his eyes. "It's worked for me. Damn

nicely, if I do say so myself."

At that point, a young woman wearing a green Starbucks apron came over and placed a cup of coffee down in front of Roper. He gave her an appreciative nod and took a small sip. I stared at him and shook my head.

"Most people have to pay for their own coffee," I remarked. "And also have to stand in line to get it."

"What can I say?" Roper responded with another wave of the hand. "People just like to do nice things for me. Which is why I'm glad I ran into you this morning. Coincidentally, of course."

"Go on," I said slowly, not entirely sure I wanted to hear what nice thing Cliff Roper might want from me. When I got the murder charges dropped earlier this year, he sent his appreciation in the form of a large check, with the vague hint he might ask for a favor one day. I guess that day had come.

"So here's what you need to do for me," he said, leaning forward and lowering his voice.

"I don't need to do anything for you," I said evenly.

"Sure you do. I'll explain that in a minute. You need to get rid of those charges. X didn't hit his girlfriend. Start by talking to her and push her to tell the truth. You're persuasive."

"No one's told me what the truth is. And I'm not pushing an assault victim to do anything. She's already given the police her story, which is that Xavier hit her."

"Look, you're good. If anyone can unravel this, you can. X wasn't the one. Trust me. "

"Trust you?" I asked. "You're as trustworthy as a three

dollar bill."

"Hey, hey, hey. Don't get smart with me," Roper said, pointing a finger in my face. "If you don't want to do it for me, do it for that USC family thing you Trojans like to brag about."

I stared at him with as much incredulity as I could muster. "That doesn't include twisting the arm of a young woman with a bruised jaw just so a kid can go off and make millions."

"Then do it because it's the right thing to do."

I shook my head. "And you know the right thing to do."

"Look, would a big-time attorney like Jeremy Hoffman be taking X on as a client if he thought he did it? Jeremy's not going to embarrass himself like that."

"You know Jeremy?" I asked, eyebrows raised.

"I know everyone in this town," he said. "Everyone who's worth knowing, that is. Who do you think steered Xavier to Jeremy? I know who the movers and shakers are around here."

I thought for a moment. "So that's how Jeremy came to call me."

"I knew you picked things up quick," Roper smiled, leaning back in his chair. "That's why I wanted you on my team. You'll get to the bottom of this. You're my go-to detective. You're my guy here."

"Your guy," I repeated. "Look. I'll see what I can do. But not because of you or Jeremy or even SC. When I joined the LAPD, one of the first things they taught us was it's just as important to exonerate an innocent person as it is to convict a guilty one."

Roper shrugged. "Hey, if that works for you, it works for me."

"I'll tell you something though. If Xavier's lying, I'll find that out, too. And no amount of money is going to get him off."

"Yeah, yeah, yeah," he said. "You know, for a former cop, you really don't know how the system works here."

"I know exactly how it works. I just don't like how it works. But before you run off, let me ask you one last thing. Xavier's going on the radio to discuss this incident. How does that help him at all?"

Roper shook his head as if he were speaking with a small child. "It'll help to get the NFL to take a more balanced view of things," he said slowly. "And we're playing the long game here. If you do your job, the charges will get dropped. If X does his job this morning, the public -- and therefore the NFL -- will turn a more sympathetic eye toward him. So he'll be back to playing football and all will be right with the world."

"And if you do your job, Xavier will get a multi-million dollar deal next year. For which you'll get a percentage."

Roper smiled broadly. "Everyone should be compensated for their work," he said as he rose and walked out of the coffee house. I stared out the window as he merged with the various people walking along the plaza of L.A. Live. So I was Cliff Roper's guy now. Lucky me.

I had 45 minutes before I needed to meet Virgil for lunch. Pulling out my iPad, I opened the online version of the *L.A. Times* and scanned it. I didn't expect to see any news about Xavier Bishop and none was there. But there was an article, buried down the local news page, near the bottom, written by a staff reporter named Adam Lazar. It told of what appeared to be a drive-by shooting in the Rampart district, possibly gang-related. A student at the prestigious Stone Canyon School had been murdered. No suspects. But at the end of the article was a note about the slain young man, Diego Garcia, being romantically linked with the daughter of a high profile public official.

Before I left, I walked back to the counter for a refill on coffee. I handed the barista a five, but she told me there was no charge.

"My lucky day?" I asked.

"Maybe, I guess," she said. "That gentleman you were sitting with gave me a $20 bill earlier and said your drinks were on him. Strange he didn't mention it to you."

Six

I took a walk around Staples Center and the Nokia Theatre before heading off to lunch. I thought about Xavier Bishop and his new friend, Cliff Roper. Nothing made sense here, except maybe Roper being involved in yet another distasteful situation. Xavier Bishop clearly punched someone, but wouldn't say who it was, only who it wasn't. On my drive over to lunch, I heard Xavier on the radio, saying largely the same thing he told me. The host pressed him about his scraped hand, but Xavier would only say it was an unrelated injury. I flicked the interview off after a few minutes.

My destination was on the edge of Chinatown, across the street from Union Station, and down the block from Olvera Street. Skid Row was not far away. I arrived at the restaurant a few minutes before noon, which meant the long lines were already forming. I found Virgil Hairston already waiting to place his order, and I apologized as I cut in front of a number of unhappy customers. At Philippe's, there was always a line and it always moved slowly. Their counter people also sliced the meat and assembled the sandwiches, and they were folks who had pride in their work. They took their time, but they served the best French-dipped sandwiches in town.

"I'm glad we could forge a compromise on lunch," I said.

"You have good taste," Virgil said. "Although I was more in the mood for a Hollenbeck burrito."

"You'll live longer eating here," I pointed out.

A short, chunky man standing next to Virgil spoke. He wore a plaid shirt with a black tie, had an olive complexion, and his brown eyes were deeply set. "I don't believe in all that. Mexican food is the best."

I glanced at the little man and then back at Virgil. "Friend of yours?"

"One of my reporters. Burnside, Adam Lazar. Adam Lazar, Burnside."

"Ah, I just read your article," I said as we shook hands. His handshake was limp and obligatory. "Good journalism. I can't wait to hear your sources."

"You won't," he snorted. "That's why they talk to me."

I turned back to Virgil and spoke. "I take it you brought him along to lighten the mood."

Virgil looked at us. "I thought you two might be a good match. He's a lot like you. Finds a way to piss people off and get them to say things they wouldn't ordinarily say."

"Just what the world needs," I observed wryly. "More people like me."

I ordered a French-dipped beef sandwich and a baked apple. Same thing I had been ordering since my USC days. Virgil ordered a lamb sandwich, a beef sandwich and a number of side dishes. Lazar asked for a side of coleslaw and two orders of pickled pig's feet.

"You don't see that everywhere," I remarked as we found space at a communal table in the back. "In fact, I don't think I've ever seen another restaurant that serves pig's feet. Or anyone here who's ever ordered it."

"See," Virgil pointed at him. "He's like you. Old school. Just like this place."

Old-school certainly described Philippe's, an LA institution that had been operating for over 100 years. They claimed to have invented the French-dipped sandwich by accident. As the legend goes, when a police officer stopped by for a roast beef sandwich on a roll, the counter man accidentally dropped the roll into a pan of beef drippings. The officer said not to bother making a new sandwich, he'd take it that way. The next day he went back and specifically asked for the roll to be dunked in the drippings again. The idea caught on, and the sandwich soon became the biggest seller at Philippe's. Oddly, another restaurant nearby also claimed to have invented the French dip. The truth, like so many things in life, was buried a long time ago.

"So tell me about your new job," I said to Virgil in between bites of my sandwich. It was moist and warm and good.

"Political editor for the *Times*," Virgil responded. "My dream job. I oversee everything about state and local politics, including campaigns. Especially campaigns."

"You've got a good one going now," I said. "The gubernatorial race is getting very interesting."

"Last night's debate was a godsend for the media. The polls are close, but when a politician sticks his foot in his mouth, things get ramped up in a hurry. Justin Woo's already cutting an ad featuring Rex Palmer mimicking the way he pronounces California. The next two weeks are going to be vicious."

"I'm sure you'll be busy," I said and turned to Lazar, who had picked up a pig's foot with his hands and was busy gnawing away at it. "How's that thing taste?"

"Very good. But it's the texture I like. Nice and chewy. Want one?"

"No, I think I'd prefer to watch you enjoy it. From a distance."

"You have no idea what you're missing," Lazar declared and looked up at me. "None whatsoever."

"Ignorance is bliss," I said. "Especially here."

"Suit yourself."

"So tell me about Diego Garcia."

"You tell me," Lazar responded. "You were one of the last people to have talked with him."

I turned to Virgil. "This might not go as swimmingly as you had hoped."

Virgil shrugged, finished his first sandwich and glanced to his left. A grubby man with a tattered beard sat down at our table, his tray holding only a cup of hot coffee. The coffee here still cost just a dime. He carefully poured a generous amount of cream in and added two spoonfuls of sugar before stirring it for a good five seconds. He took a sip and smacked his lips satisfactorily.

I turned back to Lazar. "Your story mentioned the daughter of a high profile public official. I take it you know who that is."

"Of course I do," Lazar said as he continued to gnaw on the pig's foot, trying to get every speck of meat he could reach. "I'm not releasing that morsel yet. Saving it for a little while. The governor is making all the news we need right now."

"Not a shining moment for him last night," I remarked.

"Rex Palmer is an idiot. He doesn't deserve to be in office. He got there through his family name and family money."

"That describes half the politicians in America," I scoffed, starting to get annoyed. "So who do you like, Justin Woo?"

The young man stopped eating and put what was left of the pig's foot down. "I don't like either of them. They pander to Latinos. Every four years they come and ask us for our vote. Then they forget about us. I would have loved for a serious Latino candidate to be in this race."

"You're Latino?"

"Yes. Why?"

"Lazar's not a Latino name, is it?"

He smiled for a brief moment. Very brief. And it wasn't really much of a smile. "My family name was originally Salazar, but my father changed it. He earned a college degree, but nobody would hire him. Wouldn't even give him an interview. When he changed the name to Lazar, doors started to open. He wound up being director of marketing for a large toy company."

"The world's different now," I offered.

"Not so much."

"Have you experienced the type of prejudice your father did?"

"Oh, yes."

"How so?"

"I grew up in the Valley. Van Nuys. Played soccer in high school. We'd sometimes have games with private schools. Played Stone Canyon in fact. I got a few red cards."

"You were ejected from soccer games?"

"Yeah. Those kids called us everything from beaners to wetbacks to spics. They didn't like us and we didn't like them. I kicked a few of those snooty, rich kids in the nuts. The refs told me to knock it off. I told them I just had bad aim."

"You've still got a lot of anger in you."

"I call it passion."

"The same type of passion Diego Garcia had?" I asked pointedly.

He gave me a blank look. "What do you mean?"

"Diego struck me as a passionate guy. Think that's what got him killed?"

Lazar eyed his pickled pig's feet for a long moment. "You raise an interesting question."

"You think Diego's death was a random drive-by?" I asked. "Gang-related?"

He took a long breath. "I don't know. You can't rule it out. But I think the campaign played a role here. There's no other explanation. Not with Molly involved. Too coincidental."

Now it was my turn to take a long breath. "That's quite a leap. Why would the campaign want to kill a teenage kid?"

"It's an angle I've been thinking about. That may find its way into my next article."

"Maybe you should think harder."

Virgil wiped his mouth carefully with a napkin. "Now this is what I hoped for. Progress. I was wondering the same thing. We heard Diego had been approached recently by people from the Palmer campaign. But we can't run with hasty conclusions, Adam. I need more substance before this gets into print."

"What are you suggesting?" Adam asked.

"I'm suggesting maybe the two of you take a drive up to Stone Canyon together. Poke around. I'll try and set up something with the Head of School there. You'd probably want to talk with her anyway, about Molly. You should try and find out more about Diego. The two of you might work great as a team, synergy and all that."

Lazar scowled. "I work better alone."

"Me, too," I added, although the idea was not totally unappealing. As annoying as Lazar was, he seemed bright and knew how to yank people's chains. I knew from personal experience that could be a blessing or a curse. "But I might be up for giving it a shot."

"I don't know about this, Virgil," he said.

"Do it as a favor to me. You might be surprised at what happens."

I thought for a moment. Between LAPD Detective Dennis Lally and *Times* Reporter Adam Lazar, I was getting my share of partners assigned to me. For someone who had left the LAPD to start my own agency, this wasn't quite what I had planned.

*

Adam Lazar said he'd meet me at the Stone Canyon School at 3:00 p.m.. I had a few hours to kill, so I tried Desiree Brown's apartment north of the USC campus, but she was still out. The apartment manager, a gruff man with a Deputy Dog accent, said it was hard to catch her, he only saw her periodically. The building was mostly students, he drawled, so in the early afternoon it was mostly empty. It took about 15 minutes of listening to him babble to come away with this information.

I began a slow, meandering drive along Sunset Boulevard, starting at the Harbor Freeway near downtown. The route snaked past the Echo Park bars near Dodger Stadium and wound its way through Silver Lake and Hollywood. When I worked plainclothes for the LAPD this was part of my territory. Over the years, some of these dilapidated neighborhoods had sprung back and began to regentrify, adding trendy shops and eateries. But sections of East Hollywood still had a ways to go. Eventually I passed the stately mansions of Beverly Hills and turned into the hills of Bel-Air. A few minutes later I made a right turn onto a private road that slithered upward for a quarter of a mile before opening into a sprawling, picturesque campus.

I managed to arrive at the Stone Canyon entrance about 30 minutes before I was supposed to meet Adam Lazar. Stopping at the guard station, I gave a friendly smile and a wave to the security officer on duty. He was wearing a dark green rent-a-cop uniform, wire-rimmed sunglasses, and looked professional and polished.

"Hello sir," he smiled. "You know, pickup isn't until 3:30 today."

I smiled back. "Yes, yes, I know," I said in my most jovial fatherly impersonation. In a few years I might have to actually embody this role. "My daughter forgot her sneakers. She has volleyball practice. Teenagers. You know."

The guard's smile continued. "Of course, sir," he said, and as he waved me in he added, "Your timing is perfect. The team starts practice in a few minutes. Big playoff game tomorrow."

I acknowledged this and drove down a smooth, jet black road, framed by perfectly mowed green grass on either side. The parking lot was almost full, but I noticed a black Toyota Prius pulling out of a space. The driver was in his late 50s and had a short white goatee. He waved and smiled. I waved and smiled. Everyone seemed so happy here.

The Stone Canyon campus was unlike any school I had ever visited. The buildings were new and the architecture was majestic. I wandered into the Oppenheim Theatre Complex and was treated to the sounds of about three dozen kids practicing for orchestra. The theater held around a thousand seats, all dark red and velvety. The walls and ceilings were painted black, and dramatic spotlights were shining directly on the young musicians. I spent a few minutes listening to a nice passage from Bach's Brandenburg Concertos before leaving them to their privacy.

Stepping outside, I asked a couple of polite kids where I could find the gym. They pointed me to an olive green structure, two buildings down. As I walked there, I passed a number of students. The girls were all dressed in tan skirts or shorts, with black tops, and the boys were all in tan khakis with black sweaters or golf shirts.

The Tucker Sports Complex had a plaque outside, honoring the family that had donated gobs of money toward building most of the athletic facilities. This included a gymnasium, which housed basketball and volleyball courts, as well as a gorgeous soccer field, an immaculate baseball diamond and an Olympic-size swimming pool. I walked into the gym and saw a group of about fifteen girls in black volleyball uniforms, tapping balls back and forth. I approached one of them.

"I'm looking for Riley Joyner," I said. "Would you mind pointing her out to me."

"Oh, sure," she said and extended her left arm in the direction of the far wall, where a couple of girls were doing their stretching. I approached and asked if one of them was Riley.

"That's me," said a tall girl with big brown eyes and a long, skinny nose. Her auburn hair was pulled back into a small ponytail.

"Can we talk for a moment?" I asked and motioned to the bleachers.

"I guess," she said, as she gave a questioning glance to the girl next to her.

"It's okay," I said and handed Riley my card. I didn't

want to arouse suspicion by flashing my P.I. license. While that usually got the attention of the person I was speaking with, people nearby often noticed it as well. In a place like Stone Canyon, I did not want to run the risk of getting a quick escort out.

"I'm an investigator working for the governor."

Riley's eyes widened. "I don't know anything."

"About what?" I peered at her.

"About ... whatever. Molly. You know."

"Anything you can tell me about where Molly is would help," I said, watching her carefully. "As well as anything about Diego. Maybe start with what happened at the Coliseum."

Her big brown eyes grew even wider. "Look. We went to a football game on Saturday. Molly hooked up with Diego. I went home afterwards. What more can I tell you?"

"Hooked up," I repeated, knowing this could mean just about anything. "Can you tell me more about that?"

"She liked him. And I think he liked her."

"Good match?" I asked.

"I dunno. I guess. The whole thing now is just so sad."

"Sure is. Did Diego ever indicate he was in trouble in any way?"

"No," she said, now with a trace of annoyance. "And neither did Molly."

"You know where Molly might be?"

"I dunno," she said, her voice trailing away, and her eyes looking past me.

"Is she safe?"

"I guess."

"You guess?" I asked, with more than a trace of annoyance rising from my own voice. I didn't want to bully her, but she obviously knew more than she was letting on. "Molly's been missing for five days. The guy she's been romantically linked to was shot dead last night. And all you can say is 'I guess'?!"

"Hey," she said, taking a step backward. "You can't talk to me like that."

"I can talk any way I want. And unless you want to get dragged down to the police station and get grilled by the cops, you had better start talking about what you know, rather than what you don't know. You can get into some big trouble here."

"What? Do you know who my father is? He's a major donor to this school."

"Do you know I really don't care? But if you're withholding evidence in a kidnapping or a murder case, all your father can do is provide you with a pricey lawyer. And visit you on weekends up at the state prison in Lompoc."

Riley's cheeks started to flush. "Look. Molly's had a crappy life. You wouldn't know it, nobody would. Everyone thinks it's easy being Rex Palmer's daughter. They have no idea what she's dealing with."

I looked at her and decided to push the needle a little further. "Daughter of a governor. Sure. She's had it rough. Rich, famous. Who would want that?"

Riley's mouth opened in anger and disbelief. "You don't know what you're talking about. Molly felt her life couldn't get any worse. Diego came from a different world, but at least he had a family around, and people who cared about him."

"Diego's world was different from hers all right."

"Oh, how would you know? How would anyone know?"

"I don't," I said, my voice softening. "I'm just trying to understand all of this. I'm trying to find Molly and I'm trying to find out more about what happened to Diego. Anything you might know could help out here."

Riley drew silent for a moment. "Look, I might know where Molly could be," she finally said. "Let me, uh, ask around. But Diego? I don't know what happened to him. He was nice, I guess. But he lived in a bad neighborhood. Stuff happens."

"Sure," I said. "Look, anything you can do to help locate Molly would be appreciated. And you may not think much of her family, but I'm sure you can imagine her father is worried."

A look of anger flashed across her face again. "I don't know about that. Her father's too busy running the state."

I thought of something. "What about her mother?"

"Her mother is too busy with her own life. Planning fundraisers. Getting her nails done. Whatever. I doubt her mother even cares where she is."

"Okay," I sighed. "One last thing. There were a couple of other kids at the game with you last week. Where can I find them? I think their names are Alex and Connor."

"Alex is probably at football practice," she said. "But Connor's right over there. Shooting baskets."

She pointed to a tall, lanky kid at the far end of the floor. Most of the backboards had been raised to the ceiling to make way for volleyball practice, but a couple remained down. I said goodbye to Riley and walked across the gym. As I approached the basket, Connor sunk a 20-foot set shot.

"Swish," I said, gathering up the ball and tossing it back to him. "Connor Pierce?"

"That's me," he said, catching the basketball and tossing another shot straight into the basket. I picked up the ball again, but this time didn't pass it back to him. "Got a minute?"

"Sure," he said and walked over. He stuck out his hand. "I guess you know who I am."

"Yup," I said, shaking hands. "My name's Burnside."

"Are you a college scout?"

"Not exactly," I said. "Are you expecting one?"

"Just kidding. I start for the varsity, but I'm not in line for a scholarship. I'm a 6'2" forward. If I had another six inches, every D-1 college would be all over me."

"Funny how that works. Where are you thinking of going after Stone Canyon?"

"I've applied to Stanford for early decision, but it's 50-50. After that, I'm looking at Duke and Northwestern. Maybe Amherst. And if all else fails," he laughed, "there's always USC."

"That's not such a bad choice," I remarked.

"Where'd you go to college?"

"USC."

He blinked for a moment and then held up his hands.

"Sorry man, no offense."

"None taken," I said. It's funny how one person's ceiling is another person's floor. USC was my only scholarship offer, and it was also my first choice. My mother had enough money saved to pay for the first two years at a state college. After that, I'd have needed student loans or financial aid. My mother said she'd help as much as she could, but that was before she got sick. When a scholarship offer came in from USC, it was one of the happiest days of my life.

"So I'm actually here on a different type of business," I said, handing him my business card.

"Wow," he said as he fondled the card. "An investigator? What's up?"

"I need to ask you about Diego Garcia. And Molly Palmer."

"Oh. Diego, yeah. That was awful. Really terrible."

"Did you know him well?" I asked.

"I guess. It's not a big school here. Everyone sort of knows everyone."

"Diego have any enemies?"

Connor shrugged. "Hey man, it's high school. No one gets out of here without pissing someone off along the way," he said and then stopped. "But Diego was a good guy. Everyone liked Diego."

"Apparently not everyone."

"Oh. Yeah. I dunno. I can't imagine who would do such a thing. I read the police think it was a random drive-by. That's the only thing that could ever make sense. The person who did this? They probably didn't know him."

"Maybe not," I said. "Were you and Diego friends?"

"Not friends exactly. We were into different things. And we're all real busy. Schoolwork, sports, clubs. Plus, Diego worked part-time. At the Coliseum, at his father's store. Real crazy place, that neighborhood down there."

"You've been there?"

"I've driven through it. You know. On the way downtown to Laker games and stuff. It's a little scary, no one speaks English there, all the signs are in Spanish. It's like being in Tijuana."

I nodded. Scary indeed. The neighborhoods surrounding downtown had a far greater share of violent crime than those on the Westside of LA. Separated by less than 10 miles, but a world apart.

"Think Molly had any connection with what happened to Diego?" I asked.

He shook his head. "I can't imagine. She seemed to really like him."

"Have you heard from Molly since Saturday? I heard you went to the SC game with her and a few friends."

"Yeah. She got up in the 4th quarter, said she was going to the restroom or something, and then she never came back. She texted Riley and said she had found Diego and was going to hang out with him."

"You didn't go to the Coliseum in her car?"

"No. Molly doesn't drive. Weird, huh? We all went in my Prius."

"And you haven't heard anything since?"

"No," he said with a shrug. "But that's not unusual. Molly comes and goes."

"Were you and Molly close?"

"We went out for a little while this year. Nothing serious. We're still friends."

"Who ended it?"

"I dunno. Mutual, I guess. We didn't really break up. It just sort of stopped."

At that point my phone rang. It was Adam Lazar. It turned out the security guard was unaware of an interview with Loretta Moss, the head of school. Lazar was fuming when he told me the school had a strict policy of limiting access to the media. He said he had a plan to get in and would meet me at Ms. Moss's office in 10 minutes. I turned back to Connor.

"Okay, look. If you hear from Molly or you think of anything else, please give me a call."

"Yeah," he said. "Hey, is Molly in any trouble?"

"I don't know. I hope not. But she hasn't been home since Saturday."

"Okay," he shrugged. "But I'm sure she'll turn up. She always does."

Connor gave me directions to the office of the Head of School. I waited outside the building for what was close to 30 minutes before a rumpled Adam Lazar showed up. He had grass stains on his pants and I told him to remove a couple of leaves from his hair.

"I hiked up through the back entrance," he panted. "Knew about that from when we played Stone Canyon in soccer and I saw some cross country runners. Nice place to go jogging if your parents can cough up $40,000 a year."

"What happened with security?"

"Oh, I don't know," he said. "Virgil said he set up the appointment but that Nazi at the gate likes to throw his weight around. I tried to argue, but it didn't work. Had to take the long way in."

"I admire your tenacity," I said, scanning his disheveled appearance, "but not much else."

"How'd you get past Security?"

"To be honest, I lied a little. Old detective's trick."

Lazar shook his head as we walked into the administrative building. A minute later we were ushered into the office of Loretta Moss. She was a handsome woman in her late 40s, wearing a gray, tailored business suit with a low cut top that did little to hide what was clearly an extremely attractive figure. Standing behind her desk, she had a cross look on her face. She didn't invite us to sit down.

"Ms. Moss," Lazar began, "I'm a reporter ... "

"I know who you are," she interrupted him. "What I don't know is how you got in here. I believe our security guard sent you away."

Lazar's face contorted in mock outrage. Possibly even real outrage. "I think the public deserves to hear more about Diego Garcia. It's not a school issue."

"No, it's not. It's a tragic situation. And I can't comment on a criminal investigation."

"I think you might want to get out in front of this," I offered, trying to soften the tone Lazar had set. Good cop, bad cop. "This way you can define Diego before the police do."

"What do you mean?"

"Right now he's just being considered the victim of a drive-by shooting. Gang-related. But he's a kid who was going to an elite prep school. It doesn't add up. None of this makes any sense. It won't make sense to the police. And it certainly won't make sense to the public."

Loretta Moss stared for a moment and finally motioned for us to sit. She plopped into a big overstuffed desk chair. "This is a terrible day for the school. Not to mention the family. Diego was not a typical Stone Canyon student, he was here on scholarship, and not an athletic scholarship. He was just someone in whom we saw potential, albeit with some risk."

"What do you mean you saw some risk?" Lazar asked.

"Every student we admit is thoroughly vetted. Academically, socially. They need to be a good fit for our program. We want our graduates to succeed once they leave Stone Canyon. It helps our reputation. We're like any other brand. We live and die by what we produce. And what we produce are successful students who turn into successful adults."

"I'm not sure I understand what you mean by brand here," I asked.

Loretta Moss considered this. "I ... I may have misspoken. It's been a tough day. We're like any other school. We want our students to do well."

It's interesting when people say they misspoke. They rarely do. Under stress, people sometimes reveal the unvarnished truth, and it's often inadvertent. According to Freud, there are no accidents, no slips of the tongue, just revelations that seep out. Stone Canyon was a brand all right. And a profit center. A student who makes the news for reasons other than athletic or academic achievement can adversely affect their business. And their brand.

With Lazar poking at her with more questions about Diego, Moss spoke glowingly about him. His fitting in, despite having a vastly different background from his classmates, was a testament to the school. After a few minutes of listening to this whitewash, I began to wonder if Loretta Moss should be running for political office herself; she seemed to know the drill. As she wound down her infomercial on how great a school Stone Canyon was, I decided to push on the other reason I was here.

"Tell me about Molly Palmer."

Moss froze. "What do you mean?"

"She's gone missing."

"I wasn't aware of any such thing."

"Really?" I asked, leaning forward. "The Head of School unaware the governor's daughter hasn't shown up for class in three days?"

"I'm aware," she said, a touch of condescension growing in her voice, "that her father's an elected official and is campaigning for governor. I'm sure she's helping him."

"But you don't know that for a fact."

She looked at me carefully. "I've been in touch with her mother. I know more than you think. I'm sure Molly is fine."

"So her father has no idea where she is, but her mother does," I said. "Do I have that straight?"

"I don't care to comment further on that," she said."We maintain a strict privacy policy at this school, especially when it comes to our families. There are numerous children of celebrities who attend here. It's how we maintain our reputation."

"Your reputation," I repeated. I thought of Gail and our baby. When he or she was ready for 7th grade, I got the feeling Stone Canyon would not be on our list of schools. I was equally sure our name would not be high on Stone Canyon's list of families granted preferential treatment for admission.

"Well it's good to know that Molly is safe," I said, recognizing we wouldn't be able to get much more out of her. "But the fact is she was one of the last people seen with Diego before he was killed. That is going to become very public, very soon."

Lazar shook his head in agreement. "We're going to get to the bottom of this. It's better if you cooperate."

"My goodness," she exclaimed, "you're not the police."

"No," said Lazar. "My paper is more important. We shape opinions."

Moss stared at Lazar in disbelief. So did I. And I knew what was coming next. The Head of School rose and walked toward the door.

"Thank you for your time, gentlemen," she said, holding the door open for us. "Good day."

Seven

As we made our way to the parking lot, Lazar whipped himself into a frenzy about the story he was going to write. He said he would decimate the school, and highlight any and every role it may have played in the demise of Diego Garcia. He asked me about the other kids who had been with Molly at the USC game. I doubted they'd reveal anything additional to him, and Adam Lazar struck me as a loose cannon. And while I didn't think too much of the staff right now, I also didn't believe the school deserved a hatchet job. Not wanting to give Lazar any more fodder, I didn't reveal more names to him. He sniffed and said he didn't need anyone's help. He'd go find them himself.

As Lazar stalked off to hunt for the students, I drove toward the edge of the campus, and got a final laugh as I exited. A dark sedan was stopped at the entrance. The security guard was arguing with a man who was pointing a threatening finger at him. As I cruised past them, I slowed down and gave Detective Lally a smile and a wave. He stopped arguing for a moment to watch me leave, his mouth open and his head shaking.

Loretta Moss had brought up something interesting. She indicated she had had contact with Molly's mother and that Molly was okay. Molly's father, ostensibly the most powerful man in the state, was somehow, inexplicably, unaware of this. Jeremy Hoffman had told me Molly lived near the school. I tried to get the address from Shelly Busch. but was told she was in conference and couldn't be disturbed. I placed a quick call to Juan Saavedra, and after providing assurances he would not regret it, Juan provided me with Rex Palmer's home address. He also cagily pointed out if I knew what I was doing, I could probably scrape this off the Internet. The Palmers' home was located adjacent to Beverly Glen, a short drive from Stone Canyon.

Beverly Glen Boulevard is one of those north-south arteries that connect the Westside with the San Fernando Valley. The road starts at the Rancho Park Golf Course and meanders up past Wilshire Boulevard into Holmby Hills, one of the many exclusive neighborhoods dotting the Westside. The Palmers lived two blocks away from a studio mogul who had built a 50,000 square foot palace, a massive structure that dwarfed even the most magnificent of homes in the area. It had cost tens of millions of dollars to construct. And yet the rumor was that when the mogul moved in he quickly wound up suing his contractor. Apparently, the roof leaked.

Rex and Nicole Palmer lived on a quiet street in a big, beautiful home, mostly hidden from the street behind large hedges. I pushed a button next to an iron gate, and was soon buzzed in. The house was white with black shutters, and was dramatically lit by a series of upward pointing spotlights. The large green lawn had a few leaves scattered about, giving it a New England feel. There were floodlights turned on in the backyard.

Wiping my feet on the welcome mat, I rang the

doorbell which set off a sequence of chimes that took a good five seconds to complete its progression. The door eventually opened and a housekeeper said hello. I flashed my P.I. license and told her I needed to speak with Nicole Palmer about an urgent matter. Her eyes widened and she told me to wait. A few minutes later, a tall, slender woman with ash blonde hair and pale blue eyes appeared before me. She was wearing a dark v-neck sweater with jeans, and she held a wine glass casually in her right hand. She swirled it absently.

"Mrs. Palmer?"

"Yes, that's me."

I handed her my card. "My name's Burnside. I work for your husband. Can I speak with you for a few minutes?"

"About what?" she asked, not bothering to look at my card.

"I'm a private investigator. Your husband asked me to look into finding your daughter."

"Really? That's interesting. I wasn't aware he had hired anyone to look for Molly."

I stared at her. "Her friends say they haven't seen Molly since Saturday."

"And which friends might those be?"

"Riley Joyner and Connor Pierce."

She thought about this for a moment. "All right, well it sounds like you're not a complete fraud."

"May I come in?" I asked.

Nicole Palmer shrugged and motioned me inside. As I entered, I noticed my business card had fluttered out of her hands and landed on the white carpet. She didn't bother to pick it up. Neither did I.

We walked through the spacious home, and she led me onto an outdoor patio. A pool and Jacuzzi were nearby, and the sparkling blue water of the pool shimmered amidst lights on the deck. The backyard was surrounded by a small redwood fence.

"Would you like a glass of wine?" she asked, picking up a bottle of Chardonnay.

I politely declined. Work and alcohol were never a good mix for me.

"So I'm surprised Rex even knew Molly was away," she said, pouring wine unevenly into the glass. "Or did some apple polisher in his campaign point it out?"

"Maybe a little of both. You don't seem too impressed with his staff."

"You think? Those toadies have one goal. To be in the governor's good graces. Whoever the governor winds up being. Trust me, if Rex loses, they'll have their resumes in front of Justin Woo the day after the election."

"You think he'll lose?"

She shrugged. "It was a close win last time."

"Were you involved in Rex's campaign four years ago?" I asked.

"Not so much," she said, taking another sip. "But that shouldn't be surprising. Spouses aren't usually a big part of a campaign, unless it's for president. First ladies matter there. Voters care about who a president is married to. But not a governor. It's just as well. If they knew what our marriage was like, I don't think he'd get many votes."

I took this in. Given the way she was drinking, I imagined his campaign had wanted to keep Nicole Palmer as far away from public view as possible. Her attention was riveted on her golden Chardonnay. She swirled the wine around, and held it up to see how it draped the glass.

"We all have our private lives," I finally said.

"Sure. And Rex's life is so private that I rarely see him these days. He's normally in Sacramento all week, and he flies home on weekends. But with the campaign in full swing, he's staying downtown at the Ritz-Carlton."

"What about Molly? You don't seem worried. Have you heard from her?"

"Oh, maybe," she said in a high-pitched voice, that was probably intended to make her sound playful, but only served to make her sound tipsy.

"That's an interesting answer," I mused.

"Thank you. Yes. I heard from her. She texted me on Saturday. She said she was staying with a friend after the game."

"Anything since?"

"No," she shrugged. "But Molly's 18 now. She's an adult. She can do what the hell she wants. She can go out with who she wants."

"Who's Molly going out with?"

"You mean this week or last week? Or the week before? I have trouble keeping up."

I shook my head. "Did you know she's missed school?"

"What are you, the truant officer?"

"No," I said, my patience rapidly disappearing. With parenthood a few months away, I was perhaps a little more sensitive to this topic than I might otherwise have been. "But I know parenting doesn't stop just because a child becomes an adult in the eyes of the law."

"Oh, and when does it stop, Mr. Expert?" she said, glaring at me. "When do I get to have my own life? On my own terms? When do I get to stop living my life through my child? Or through my husband? When is it my turn?"

"Sounds like I hit a sore subject," I commented, waiting for her to continue.

"You did all right. Ever since right after college, when I got knocked up by Rex. We decided to get married and have the baby. I thought, okay, there are worse things than being married to a wealthy guy, the son of a former governor. How bad could that be?"

I didn't bother to provide the answer, I knew the Chardonnay would bring it out of her.

"It was plenty bad. Sure, this house is lovely, my family is rich and famous, but let me tell you something, mister. My life is not my own. Everything I do comes under scrutiny. I can't even go out to lunch without someone tweeting about what I ordered. And I'm getting a little sick of it. This place is nothing more than the crown jewel in the California prison system."

"So you wouldn't be unhappy if your husband lost the election?" I observed.

"Take a guess."

With that, she slammed her glass down on the table, and it teetered for a moment before falling onto its side. The small amount of wine still left in it sloshed out and spilled onto the carefully tended grass. She stormed off, leaving me to gaze out at the shimmering pool and the steaming Jacuzzi. After a few minutes, when it became obvious Mrs. Palmer wasn't going to return, I got up and walked through the house. As I approached the front door, I noticed my business card on the white carpet. It was still there when I walked outside to my black Pathfinder.

*

When I arrived home, I smelled something very good. The kind of aroma that makes you hungry. But Gail was not in the kitchen, rather, she was sitting on the couch in the living room, curled up, reading a book. Chewy was curled up next to her.

"Taking a break from slaving over a hot stove?" I asked.

"Not at all, in fact the stove is cold. We're doing takeout tonight. I had a craving."

"I'm praying it's not pickles and ice cream."

"That's an old wives' tale. I can't imagine anyone having that kind of craving," she said. "Nope, I felt like Chinese. There's something about salty foods that I like right now. Pregnancy thing, I'm told."

"Speaking of which, how are you feeling?" I asked.

"Wonderful," she replied. "Except for all this extra weight I'm carrying around."

"All for a good purpose," I said, bending over and kissing her pouty lips. "How was your day?"

"Good, just winding down a few cases. I'll have to hand off everything next month. Doctor Habish said he wanted me at home in December. Bed rest. We're going to have quite a Christmas celebration."

"Indeed."

"I pulled a bottle of wine out for you," she said.

"That's thoughtful sweetheart, but I'm going to pass. It's been a rough day." I sighed, recalling Nicole Palmer's tipsiness and thinking maybe a clear head would be a better choice tonight.

"Goodness, do I dare ask? Most people think of winding down a rough day with a glass or two of something potent in their hand."

"You can't drown your problems," I said, recalling an old axiom I had picked up from a sergeant who went through AA. "They just learn to swim."

I eased onto the couch and slipped my arm around Gail. She responded by putting the book down and nuzzling closer to me. I stroked her chestnut brown hair and gazed into those lovely clear, gray eyes. Chewy looked up and then put her chin down on Gail's lap.

"Tell me about it," she said, stroking the back of Chewy's neck.

"So it's like this. The governor hires me to find his missing 18-year-old daughter. But he doesn't have enough time to spend with me. So he delegates it to his campaign staff, who act like they'd rather be doing just about anything else. The governor's wife says her daughter's disappearance is nothing out of the ordinary. The head of her school says largely the same thing. The girl's friends think she'd be better off staying away from her parents entirely. And all wrapped up in this is the shooting death of her classmate, Diego Garcia. Who she may have been romantically involved with. In fact, she's one of the last people to have been seen with Diego before he was killed."

"Interesting," Gail said. "The city attorney has gotten very intrigued by this case, too. Especially after that blurb in the *Times* today. They figured out it was Molly rather quickly. Speaking of the *Times*, did you have lunch with Virgil?"

"Yeah, we went to Philippe's."

"And?"

"Good French dip."

Gail poked me in the ribs. "And ... ?" she asked, raising the timbre of her voice.

"And I made a new friend today. The reporter who's covering that story. Name's Adam Lazar. Guy's a piece of work. Has a smartass answer for everything."

"Oh, really?" she asked, her eyes shining. "You know, sweetie, they say the things we dislike in other people are really the things we dislike in ourselves."

I chuckled. "That come from a psych class?"

"I think I heard it from one of those shrinks that used to be on talk radio."

"Ah."

"And so what do you think of the possibility that the campaign is somehow involved in Diego Garcia's murder?"

"Well, my dear assistant city attorney, I only have circumstantial evidence to tie them together. Not much, in fact. But Diego was identified as having a meal at Langer's recently with a couple of professional-looking folks in suits and ties. It's possible the suits were part of Rex Palmer's campaign. I'm not sure why they would be taking a poor kid in the neighborhood out for a $15 sandwich. But I think they did, and evidently the conversation became a little heated."

"Okay. But you're right. Very circumstantial."

"Anything the assistant city attorney would like to share?"

"Let's see," she said, pursing those pretty lips and wrinkling her brow to pretend she was deep in thought. "A murder investigation that might involve someone close to the governor of the largest state in the union. Sorry, sweetie. Some things I can't share. Other than to say it might be worth looking into."

"Rats. What's the point of sleeping with a beautiful ACA if all I get is great sex and a burgeoning family out of the deal?"

Gail kissed me on the cheek. "You also get Chinese food. Anything else you'd care to share with me about your day?"

"Hmmm," I managed, as we got up and moved six feet to the dining room table. I was clearly looking forward to having more room in our new house. "My other case. I had coffee with Xavier Bishop from SC. Wants me to find out who beat up his girlfriend."

Gail started to laugh as she opened the myriad of white food cartons, steam drifting out of them. "And what did you tell him?"

"I told him I'd try."

"You Trojans stick together. But that one's looking like

a slam dunk. A couple argues, an altercation ensues, a young woman gets assaulted and a young man has bruised knuckles."

"Glad you're at least sharing something with me. Are you working on that case?" I asked as I sat down and opened a container of velvet shrimp and spooned some onto my plate.

"No, one of my colleagues was yakking about it at lunch. I guess Xavier was on the radio this morning. Sports talk. Pleading his case to the court of public opinion. But my understanding is we're going to pursue this."

"The kid swears he didn't do it."

"Wouldn't be the first time an athlete lied about his behavior."

"You know," I said, piling white rice next to the velvet shrimp and then adding cashew chicken on top of it. "There will be times when our cases overlap and we wind up on opposing sides. We need to be able to deal with that."

"I can deal with it fine," Gail said, reaching for the velvet shrimp and glancing down into the carton to see how much was left. "But I'll tell you only what I'm at liberty to tell you."

"Sometimes that's enough," I answered, taking a bite of dinner and smiling. Chewy pawed my leg and I responded by shaking my head no. She gave me a disgusted look and turned her attention to Gail.

"There's something else I'm going to tell you," she said, carefully wiping the oil off a piece of chicken and slipping it to Chewy.

"What's that?"

"The velvet shrimp," she smiled. "I'm finishing it."

*

I woke up hearing someone speaking with a Southern twang, a happy voice extolling people to always give their best and let the Lord do the rest. I glanced at my Swiss Army watch and the glowing green hands told me it was 5:40. The pitch black room told me the sun had yet to rise. The only thing I didn't quite know was what day it was. Thanks to Ms. Linzmeier's DVR and her newfound devotion to religion, I got to hear the preacher's sermons on a daily basis. For me though, the only thing getting saved was the ability to get some extra sleep.

I took Chewy for a quick stroll, leading her back to the apartment right after she did her business, denying her a full walk. She gave me a disappointed look when I turned her around before we reached Palisades Park, as if to ask why we weren't going to look out at the ocean today. Maybe tomorrow, I told her. She walked slowly, maybe her way of telling me she didn't think too much of that idea. When we got home, I gave her a piece of rawhide to try and buy my way back into her good graces.

Skipping my normal pot of French roast, I took the opportunity to beat traffic going downtown and sat myself down at a Starbucks, this one across the street from USC. The sky was cloudy, so I missed out on seeing a sunrise. After downing a maple scone and spending a half-hour sipping on a *grande* Sumatra blend, I headed off to Ellendale Place, north of the campus. The apartment building was located just south of Adams, on a street mixed with student housing and local residences. One of my teammates lived on this block many years ago, and I remember hanging out with him one afternoon. An ice cream truck was parked across the street and it continuously played the first half of the tune of *Three Blind Mice*. The music would stop abruptly, wait four seconds, and then start playing again from the beginning. It took about a week to get that annoying sound out of my head, but more than 20 years later, I could still dredge it back up.

It was a little after 7:00 a.m. when I buzzed Desiree Brown's apartment from behind the security gate. No response. I buzzed three more times before a student on his way to class absently held the security door open, and allowed me in. I walked up to Desiree's apartment and knocked. No answer. I knocked a little louder. Maybe she had the same sleep patterns as Gail and was able to block out any and every noise. Finally, the next door neighbor opened her door to see what the racket was about.

"I'm sure she's not there," said a trim, bespectacled girl with straight brown hair that stopped just above her shoulders. She was wearing jeans and a sweatshirt, and she had that wide-awake look that told me she had been up for a while.

"Hi," I said, walking over and introducing myself. "Any idea where Desiree might be at this early hour?"

"Um, I don't know. Maybe in class. Her parents don't

live too far away, so she could be at home. Honestly, I have no idea. Desiree doesn't spend a lot of time here."

"So I've gathered. What's your name?"

"I'm Kristy. Can I help with something?"

I flashed my P.I. license. "I'm doing an investigation and I need to speak with her. Any way of knowing how to get in touch? Phone number maybe?"

"Ooooh," she said. "A real life private eye. That's so cool."

"Sometimes," I said. No sense clarifying things, and spoiling the image. "Can I talk with you for a few minutes?"

"Sure," she said and waved me into her apartment. I sat down. She left the front door partially open. Smart girl.

"I'm looking into what happened last week," I started. "With Desiree ... "

" ... and Xavier?" she quickly interjected.

I nodded. "Were you at home at the time?"

"I sure was."

"Did you hear anything?"

"Did I ever. Quite the soap opera," she said in a sing-song voice.

"How so?"

"The two of them fight all the time. They're like children."

"Has it ever gotten violent?"

"Not sure. But this was the first time the police showed up."

"So tell me what happened."

"Okay, so Xavier comes by and the two immediately

start yelling at each other. Mostly name calling. Then I heard what sounded like a fight. Didn't last long, maybe a few punches thrown. Then Desiree started yelling at him again, yelling at him to get out."

"Go on," I said.

"And then the door slams really hard and I thought Xavier had left. But I heard more yelling and arguing, and then the sound of another couple of punches thrown. Then the door slams again. This time I was sure he had left, there was no more noise coming out of Desiree's apartment. I was about to go over and see if she was all right, but then the cops showed up."

"Do you have any idea what they fight about?"

"I think they have expectations of how the other should behave. They both want to be the star of the relationship and they think the other should be there to support them. On the surface, you know, they make the perfect couple, the big, strong football hero and the beautiful princess. Once you get to know them a bit, you realize they're just not a match. Why they've stayed together is obvious. He'll be very rich soon and she makes great arm candy. Beyond that though, I can't see it lasting."

"If they fight a lot, it probably won't."

"Okay, no relationship is 50-50 all the time," she declared and began to speak extensively on the topic. "It's usually more like 70-30. In the better relationships, the couple just take turns who takes care of whom. But sometimes you have an unusual pairing that has unusual needs. Sometimes one person wants to be doing all the giving and the other just wants to take. It's not a bad thing, *per se*. If it works for those two people. It just isn't working here."

"You know a lot about relationships," I smiled. "You a psych major?"

"Oh, no," she said. "I think you need to be a little crazy to be a good psychologist."

I considered this. "Let me throw something out there. Xavier says he didn't hit Desiree. Do you believe him?"

She shook her head no. "That doesn't hold. I don't know the whole scenario obviously, but I know the sound of a punch landing."

"Do you?" I asked.

"Sure. I've seen about a million movies. That's where you learn about real life. It sounds like this," she said and drew back her right fist, smacking it loudly into her left palm.

"Fine," I laughed. "Glad you have some expertise on this subject."

"So, I'm actually a film major. Getting the sound right is critical, but fight scenes are really easy to stage. I'll tell you what, though. These two have given me great material for a script. In fact, I'm almost done with the first draft."

"My, you're ambitious," I said. "Do I dare ask who you plan to cast in it?"

Kristy grinned. "I'm keeping that to myself. I just need a good way to end it."

I hoped it would be a happy ending, but in cases like these, happy endings were infrequent. "I have to say something, Kristy. You've managed to hear quite a bit.

You're aware of some very intimate parts of their relationship. You know a lot about them. Are you and Desiree good friends?"

"No, like I said, I hardly ever see her. And when we speak, it's usually just to say hello in passing."

"Then how do you know all this stuff? Are the walls really that thin?"

"Noooo ... not exactly," she said, her smile getting a little devious. "I hold a glass up to the wall and put my ear against it. Saw that trick in an old spy movie, once. You know, it really does work."

Eight

Howard Jones Field was a short, five-minute drive from Ellendale Place. It was the football team's practice field, named after a legendary USC coach from the 1930s. I parked my Pathfinder in the lot adjacent to the McKay Center. There were 10 reserved parking spaces out front and all were taken. The slot marked with the number "one" was filled by a black Mercedes coupe. Not that I had any doubt he would own an impressive car, but it was nice to see Johnny Cleary was enjoying the fruits of his success. As the head coach of a team that was consistently ranked among the top 10 in college football, he had every right to do so.

I entered the practice field from the same pathway the team used as they made their way out of the locker room. Passing through Goux's Gate, I gave it a slap, just like the players still do today. Maintaining the tradition was important to me, even though nobody was there to see me do it.

On the field, I was approached by a team manager with a clipboard who informed me this was a closed practice. I told him I was a former player, and his eyes lit up. When I mentioned I played in the same defensive backfield as Johnny Cleary, he practically genuflected. He told me he'd let Coach know I was here, but I said not to bother him right now. His time with the team was precious. I'd collar him in a little while, after practice was over.

The practice was smooth and crisp and professional. Every 15 minutes or so, a horn blew and the players moved to a different part of the field, either to scrimmage or work with their position coaches. It was orderly and everyone knew what they were supposed to do. Along the sidelines, a few visitors like myself stood around observing.

Years ago, all football practice sessions were held in the afternoon, following classes. When Johnny took over, he instituted a change, deciding the players would be fresher in the morning. But afternoon practices had also become a real scene, with many dozens of people milling about. There were the usual fans and alumni, but there were also a growing number of agents and their runners. The goal was for the agents to ingratiate themselves with star players, to the extent of trying to arrange meetings, dinners, trips, or even blatantly slipping them money. Most players had the good sense to politely decline these gifts with their not-so-secret agendas attached to them, but when Johnny took over as head coach, he clamped down. Practices were now limited to a few observers. I noticed that after my conversation with the kid holding the clipboard, he went over and spoke to a man in a suit and tie, and pointed me out. Whoever he spoke with must have recognized me, as no one returned to escort me off the field.

When practice ended, I approached Johnny and walked him back to his office. He pushed a few pieces of memorabilia off his tan leather couch, tossed himself onto it and pointed to a soft recliner next to him.

"Have a seat, Burnsy," Johnny said as he stretched out across the couch.

"Your office is getting more cluttered," I observed. "Keep going to Rose Bowls and there won't be any room in here."

"A small price to pay," he said. "But I'm not looking toward the Rose Bowl just yet. We have to start by getting past Washington on Saturday and then Stanford. Would be easier if we had Xavier available."

"I got the call from Jeremy. Not sure if I can unravel this thing quickly."

"It's a tough one. We had to suspend Xavier pending the police investigation. Looks like he may get charged with assault. Until that's cleared up, he can't play. And if he's convicted, that may be the end of his football career."

I didn't bother to mention Xavier had been in contact with a sports agent, Cliff Roper, an indiscretion that could further jeopardize his college career. "I spoke to Xavier yesterday."

"What did he tell you?"

"He denied hitting his girlfriend. Swore up and down he didn't touch her. Said they just had an argument. Voices raised is all. But he couldn't explain the bruises on her face."

"This just doesn't sound good," Johnny said.

"I know. And I get the feeling there's more to the story. He wouldn't say what they argued about, other than it was about their relationship. Guys like Xavier have a shot at making serious money when they turn pro. And the girls all know that."

"Yeah, that's an interesting thing, too. Desiree's parents are professionals, father's an executive, I think her mother's a doctor. X just doesn't come from that world."

I considered this. "Okay. But even doctors don't earn anywhere near what a pro football star can. If Xavier makes it big in the NFL he can make millions every year. And there's also the fame that comes with being attached to someone in the spotlight."

"You're right," Johnny said. "But at this point the team has to plan on moving forward without him. It was tough against Oregon State, their receiver torched our backup corner for over 100 yards. Last year X held him to two catches for 20 yards."

"I believe Xavier's referred to as a shutdown corner."

"Yeah. We call him X Island. Put him out there and he can cover any receiver one-on-one. Frees up the rest of the defense, gives us a lot of options. And he's just so quick. Plenty of guys say they can run the 40 in 4.4, but he really can. Maybe even a shade faster. You just don't replace guys like X."

"I hear you."

"Unfortunately, things may even be worse against Washington this weekend. They're loaded at receiver. We've had a bunch of injuries this season and we're really in trouble at cornerback, our number two is actually a converted safety," Johnny said, and then gave a canny smile. "And you know safeties can't play cornerback."

I returned the smile. "Funny how some people think

that safety and corner are interchangeable. But I could never have done what you did at cornerback. My hips didn't swivel easily, I just didn't have that flexibility."

Johnny smiled back. "You weren't as fast as me either."

"True. But safeties usually tackle better. When I got a hold of a guy, he went down."

"I could wrap someone up when I had to."

"Sure," I acknowledged. "But that's not what makes a great cornerback. All of you guys get beat at some point. The good ones can make up the lost ground and break up the pass play. A safety's job is to prevent a touchdown when the corner gets beat. We're the last line of defense."

Johnny gave me a strange smile. "You haven't forgotten much."

"Some things stay with you forever."

"They sure do. Maybe you can try calling defensive schemes on Saturday. I remember when we were playing. You used to give the Bulldog suggestions. He sure loved that, didn't he?"

Gus "Bulldog" Martin was head coach at USC when Johnny and I played together. He was a gruff, no-nonsense drill sergeant of a coach. Smart as a whip and tough as nails. He got his nickname as a young man, when a very large, very angry, unleashed dog attacked him. Coach got hold of the dog by the scruff of his neck and wouldn't let him up until he started whimpering for mercy. Both survived unscathed, but Bulldog became his new name and it stuck forever.

"I recall giving the Bulldog some ideas on play

calling," I mused. "And I especially recall when I told him we should use the corner blitz more. Let you cornerbacks attack the offense for a change. Let the safeties cover the receivers. Not be so reactive all the time."

Johnny started to chuckle. "Yeah, I remember that one. Telling Coach to use the corner blitz. One of the riskiest plays in football."

"The Bulldog just stared at me," I laughed. "Didn't say a word for like 15 seconds. Talk about an intimidating moment. Coach finally jabbed a finger in my chest and told me to stick to playing safety. And to let him worry about calling the damn plays."

"I thought he was going to smack you for even suggesting it," Johnny said. "That play's great when it works, but it's a disaster when it doesn't."

"It takes special circumstances," I said. "And special players."

"You know, every once in a while I wonder how you'd do as a football coach. Given our pass defense lately, I may need someone to coach the defensive backs next year."

"You're kidding," I said.

"Not necessarily. And I remember that speech you gave to the team last year. It was a thing of beauty. The players were really fired up. You've got that touch with the kids."

Last year Johnny had invited me to address the team and lead them onto the field before the UCLA game. It was a wonderful moment for me. The fact that we won the game big made it even better. But I perceived that as a joyous one-time event, not a prelude to a full-time job.

"We've been through this before, Johnny. I get more satisfaction out of cracking a case."

"People change," he said. "Circumstances change. You're going to be a father soon. And a homeowner. With that new house comes a big mortgage. Private eyes only make so much. Assistant football coaches these days? Their salaries can go way into six figures."

I didn't know whether Johnny was serious or just exhibiting frustration over a sub-par game last week. But I had some other, very immediate and more pressing business to deal with. I needed to put this out of my mind for now. But I knew Johnny Cleary didn't become a major college head coach by taking no for an answer, and that this subject would rear its head again.

"Fine," I lied. "I'll give it some thought."

"Fair enough. How far along is Gail?"

"Seven months. Due around Christmas."

"Best present you could ever get."

"I think so, too."

Johnny leaned back. "You know, this is going to be a challenging time for you."

"How so?" I frowned.

"New moms focus all their attention on the baby. Not much time left over for dad. You may find yourself looking around. Maybe not seriously, but you'd be surprised at how one thing can lead to another. Keep that in mind. I've seen marriages break up this way. Might sound surprising, but it happens."

"I know I'm lucky to have what I have," I pointed out.

"Good to hear," he said.

"Look, I'm not 22 years old, Johnny. I like to think of myself as more mature than that."

"I know," he said. "But there's a saying that behind every successful man is a woman. And behind the fall of many successful men is usually another woman."

I thought back to my brief flirtation earlier this year with Cliff Roper's beautiful daughter, Honey. If I could resist her, I could resist anyone. But it also got me thinking about my cases. And I thought about something interesting. Maybe there was another angle I needed to look at.

*

It was getting close to lunchtime, and I grabbed a banana and a green apple at one of the kiosks near the Student Union. The off-campus fare was fine when I was a student, not so fine as a middle-aged man. My favorite meal back then was a unique creation called the Garbage Burrito that was only served at a local joint called El Rey's. Years later, I managed to talk my LAPD patrol partner into stopping there for lunch one day. What I had once recalled as a great mix of tasty ingredients, no longer felt so great. The football-sized burrito started with a king-sized flour tortilla and was loaded with ground beef, spices, rice, beans, vegetables and some other things I couldn't fully recognize. The outsized meal stayed with me all day and all night. After that, I let my partner pick the lunch spots.

When I arrived at Governor Palmer's campaign office,

the place was a whirlwind of nervous activity. I could feel the anxiety the moment I walked off the elevator, as staffers were darting around quickly, and shouting at each other down the hallway. No one bothered to ask who I was, so I sauntered in and found Shelly Busch sitting at her desk, clenching her phone tightly, and screaming into the mouthpiece.

"I don't care if you have to pay your programmers extra! I want another poll in and out of the field tonight. I want tabs in my inbox by 7:00 a.m. tomorrow ... So have him go buy another list, do I have to do everyone's job for them?! ... Yes, I wrote that questionnaire... Yes, I know what a push poll is, you moron ... That's the campaign's decision, not yours ... Look, if you want to see any more business, you better get this done!"

With that, Shelly slammed the phone back down on the set. It made a loud sound, but the person on the other end would never know that. To them it would just sound like she had hung up normally.

"Tough day?" I asked politely.

She glanced up at me and groaned. "Oh, not you. Not now. I have enough problems."

"It's so nice to feel appreciated. I figured you might want me to update you on my investigation."

"At this point, I could care less," she said and lit a cigarette. "If the governor's teenage daughter wants to run away, that's her business."

"Guess you have bigger problems," I mused, figuring she'd miss the sarcastic underpinnings.

"You betcha," she responded. "We went from being

ahead by four points a couple of days ago, to now being down by four. This is a nightmare scenario. We cut a new set of ads yesterday that begin airing this afternoon."

"Oh? How are you spinning this?"

"Well, mister political consultant, Politics 101 says when you make a mistake and your opponent attacks you on it, you focus on the opponent's aggressive tactics. We call it jiu-jitsu. Use the opposition's strength against him."

"Ah, clever. So you're painting the governor as the victim here."

"That's the plan," she said. "Unless you have a better idea, you being such a master of political strategy and all."

"I wouldn't dream of telling you how to run your campaign," I said.

Shelly Busch lit another cigarette. "I'm glad I won't have to listen to your opinions," she said. "I get enough amateur advice."

"But I do need to tell you. Things might get worse."

She stared at me. "Really?"

"Yes. I know a few reporters at the *Times*. They believe Molly was in a romantic relationship with Diego Garcia. It's just a matter of time before they run it. Thought you might want to know."

She expressed very little surprise at this nugget of information and tapped some ash into a nearby garbage pail. "Thanks. But a romance is not such a bad thing here."

"Oh?" I remarked. "Why's that?"

"Might improve Rex's standing with the Latino community. Couldn't get much worse right now."

I peered at her. "Anything to win an election. Even if it means pimping the governor's daughter?"

Shelly Busch took a long drag from her cigarette and blew the smoke directly at me. "I wouldn't put it that way. We're just trying to stem this tide. You've really got a vulgar way of describing things. It's very off-putting."

"Sure," I said. "When one kid gets murdered and another goes missing, I spend a lot of time worrying about what people think of me."

"Maybe you ought to."

"And maybe if you blow any more smoke in my face I'm going to shove that cancer stick up your nose. With the lit end first."

She stared at me, took another puff, and this time blew the smoke discreetly toward the ceiling. "I forgot. You're a tough guy. You hit women if you don't like what they do?"

"Not as a general rule," I said.

"How noble."

"*You* want to tell me about being noble?" I started, feeling the anger rising. "Someone whose interest in a missing teenage girl is grounded on whether you can use her as a campaign tool? That the girl's safety is secondary to getting your boss re-elected?"

"You've got a lot of stones, you know that? We're paying you to do a job, not lecture us on civic responsibilities."

"Tell me something. Why does the governor stay in a suite downtown rather than go home to his wife each night?"

She gave me a curious look before responding. "Because his time is valuable and he doesn't need to waste it driving back to that nut job he calls a wife. Whenever he spends the night at home, he comes back in a tizzy. We have less than two weeks in which to finish a campaign and every minute counts."

"Sounds like he's a real happily married man."

"And just what do you know about his marital life? You can't even do the simplest thing like find his daughter before she gets herself wrapped up in a murder investigation."

"Who's he sleeping with?"

The silence in the room seemed to last indefinitely. Shelly Busch looked at me and then out the window. An eternity seemed to go by before she started speaking again. I didn't push her. I simply waited. Me being so noble and all.

"I have no idea," she finally responded. "Why are you asking me that?"

"Because that's why men stay in hotels. Something's going on here. Campaign or not, happily married men normally want to be home in bed with their wives, if they have that option."

"My," she finally said, "you are quite the investigator. But I don't know every aspect of his life. Just who do you suspect?"

"I wouldn't know where to begin," I said. "And I'm not here to investigate the governor. But this all seems tied together. And after meeting his wife, I wouldn't be at all surprised their marriage is on the rocks. Or why the campaign is keeping her at arm's length. Nicole Palmer's like the crazy aunt a family keeps locked in the attic, hoping word won't leak out about her."

"What?! You met his wife?! What made you think you could do that?! You had no business approaching Nicole. That's outrageous. You should have vetted this with the campaign first. You've gone way beyond what you were hired to do."

"No, I'm doing exactly what I was hired to do."

"And just what did Nicole tell you?"

"Nothing that helps me find Molly. And frankly I'm not convinced anyone around here really cares if Molly's found or not."

"You can't continue with this," she said, pointing a finger at me. "We can't have you talking to whomever you want. You're dismissed. You can keep what's left of the retainer, but you're fired as of right now."

"Sorry. But my answer is no."

"No?!" she sputtered, her voice rising. "What the ... you don't get to say no! You're finished here! Get it? You're fired!"

"I don't think so. I was hired by the governor."

"I speak for the governor. You're fired."

"The governor's the only one who can request I stop the investigation."

"Request?!" she screamed. "What the hell are you saying here? Are you implying you'll continue this investigation even if the governor of California orders you to stop?!"

"I'll consider it," I said evenly. "And then I'll decide."

Shelly reached over and stabbed her cigarette in the ashtray a few times. She then reached into her purse, pulled out a fresh one and lit it.

"You have no idea what kind of shit storm is about to come down on you."

I shrugged. "I've dealt with worse. And for the record, I didn't start my own agency just so I could take orders from power-hungry egomaniacs that think they can push me around."

"Well," she said, glaring at me. "I'm generally good at sizing people up. But I was certainly wrong about you."

"How's that?"

"You're a far bigger pain in the ass than I could have ever imagined."

I smiled broadly and said nothing.

"You think that's funny?" she demanded.

"Yes. Very. I think It's terrific when someone finally gets me."

*

The cloudy sky had turned even more dark and ominous by the time I reached the Rampart station. A light rain began to fall on my drive over, and now started to increase in intensity. This was an unusual weather pattern we were having, some days warm, some days cool. But rain in October was very atypical for the Southland, and could presage a series of winter storms in the months ahead. After a long period of dry summer weather, rain was usually a good thing. Except when you were driving.

During the first rainstorm of the season, the dried oil on the streets became wet again, and the road conditions often became slick and treacherous.

I found Dennis Lally at his desk, his bulky frame crammed into a small chair, eating a foot-long sandwich from Subway. He was glancing through the sports section of the *Times*. A soft drink the size of a small bucket sat nearby.

"Sorry to interrupt your Code Seven, Detective," I said, making an LAPD reference to a lunch break.

Lally glanced at me and reached over to take a long pull from that sugar-sweetened swill. His lips tightened as he tugged on the straw. He swallowed, belched, and leaned back in his chair.

"I was wondering when you were going to make an appearance," he said, and wiped his mouth with the back of his hand. "Captain said you were cooperative with law enforcement. Hate to be questioning the top brass."

"Juan wasn't always in management," I observed. "And it wasn't that long ago he sat at a desk like yours. And he had the same healthy eating habits."

"I eat what I want."

"Good for you. Just don't be surprised if cardiac arrest is in your future."

"You sound like a college professor."

"You don't know any college professors."

"Smartass," he said. "You live up to your billing."

"That should be reassuring," I smiled. "You know what to expect from me. Any luck over at Stone Canyon?"

Lally snorted. "After I finally entered the campus,

yeah. When you drove by, I was about to cuff that security guard. Most people understand what a gold shield from the LAPD means."

I shook my head. "At places like Stone Canyon, a gold shield is trumped by gold itself."

"What does that mean?"

"I told the guard I was a parent. I guess they figure anyone who pays a bundle for tuition gets the white glove treatment. This is LA after all. Nothing speaks louder than money in this town."

"No argument there. So what'd you find out?" he asked.

"The governor's daughter is still missing. But my hunch is she's safe."

"Gee, that's wonderful. Warms my heart. How about the Garcia homicide? Learn anything?"

"Oh, nothing. How about you?"

"Cut the crap. I don't want you ruining my lunch."

"Wouldn't want to do that," I agreed. "Cost you what, five bucks?"

"Cost me nothing. I know the manager. Whaddya got?"

I shook my head. Cops weren't supposed to take free meals, but some of them never got the memo. "Diego Garcia was a good kid," I said. "Everyone liked him. No issues I could uncover. But one odd thing came up."

"Oh, yeah?"

"Diego was seen at Langer's a few days before the shooting."

"So? What's odd about that?"

"Mexican kid with very little money eating in a pricey deli. Strike you as unusual?"

"Maybe a few friends from that private school introduced him to the finer things in life."

"Like what? High-end pastrami? No, the odd thing was he was there with a couple of professional people, dressed in suits. They were having an intense conversation. Not sure who it was. May have had something to do with the governor's campaign staff. Just odd is all. May mean something, may mean nothing."

"Great," he shrugged. "Thanks for the insights. Anything else?"

"That's about it."

"Gee," he said. "You've been doing real yeoman's work the past few days. So glad you're helping us out."

"My pleasure. How'd you do with those two characters you picked up the other night? I take it they didn't identify who killed Diego."

"Nope. Just that the driver did the shooting. No one else was in the car," he said. "There was also one detail neither of them bothered to reveal at first. Turns out they were Garcia's brothers. Or half-brothers. Different name. I guess they were from the mother's first marriage. The parents finally told us."

"What do you make of it?"

"Despite what the captain thinks about the governor's daughter's involvement, this is still gang-related in my book. The brothers' role confirmed it for me. My guess is the Garcia shooting had something to do with the brothers' activities. Probably drugs. In that world, maybe a business acquaintance with a beef goes and drills a family member. Garcia's bad luck he was born into that life. Sucks, but it happens."

"So that's it. Case closed?" I asked.

"Got nothing else to run with here. Kid's gunned down by someone in a car, car disappears. Ballistics said he was shot with a 9 mm, but there are plenty of those in circulation. Can't find anyone in the neighborhood who knows anything. The guy who runs concessions at the Coliseum, Longley, he wasn't very helpful. No one at that school could provide much. So unless something else turns up, we got nothing. The Palmers haven't filed a missing persons report on their daughter, so that's not on our plate. But trust me, I got plenty to do."

And then it happened. The timing could not have been more propitious. Juan Saavedra approached the two of us, a piece of paper in his hand.

"Good to see the two of you are learning to work as a team," Juan said.

"We're the best of friends now," I smiled. Lally rolled his eyes.

"Wonderful. Hey, Burnsy, you making any progress for us?"

"For you? No. Not much for myself either. Or anyone else."

"Maybe this will give you something to chew on. Someone just called in a homicide. Body found in an alley off Alvarado. Close to where that Garcia kid got popped."

I took a breath. "Got a name?"

"Unidentified female. Teenager. You can follow

Detective Lally down there, just stay out of the way."

Lally didn't bother to look at me, but he did take one last bite of his foot-long and washed it down with his drink. He took the paper from Juan and headed out the door without me. I shrugged.

"Guess I'm not getting a ride with him."

"No, we're not a taxi service," Juan said. "But there's a few cruisers already there. You won't have any trouble finding the crime scene."

My mind raced as I drove slowly through the rain-drenched streets. When I reached Alvarado Street, I saw six LAPD patrol cars and a group of uniforms milling about, as well as a group of plainclothes officers. I caught up with Lally, but he wouldn't let me view the body. He told me police business meant just that.

I stood nearby and waited a few minutes. The rain eased up to a drizzle. Then I saw a pair of familiar faces. Sad faces, worried, despondent and anguished. I walked over to the parents of Diego Garcia.

"Hello," I began.

"*Señor* Detective," Mr. Garcia said. "This is so tragic. So bad."

"I'm sorry."

"It's awful. They found her body this morning. It may have happened last night, we can't be certain. We heard about it through a neighbor. We're all very scared."

I stared at him "Just what happened here?"

"I can't believe someone would do such a thing. Not to a young woman. Not to Sofia. But someone did. They shot her. They shot Diego's girlfriend. Many times."

Nine

When I was on the LAPD, I saw this tragic scene unfold far too often. Losing a child is a calamitous event, from which many parents never recover. It is catastrophic beyond anything imaginable. The world normally dictates that children are supposed to bury their parents, hopefully after a long life. When parents have to bury their child, they bury much of themselves as well.

The police interviewed Sofia's parents, and they wore the same heartsick look I had seen so many times in the past. The same look the Garcias had. They were in shock, they had no idea who would do such a thing. The locals weren't saying much, although various gang names came up as they always did. Bitter memories of scores not settled were bandied about by people in the neighborhood. They may or may not have been correct, but this kind of response would always be given. There were usually no eyewitnesses to the slaying, and the detectives were left without much to go on. Except in this case, the name Molly Palmer was now being openly discussed. Finally, Dennis Lally took me aside.

"Okay. Looks like your missing girl case is now priority one," he said.

"Sure," I said. "Everyone wants to talk to Molly now."

"Where do you think she is?"

"Gee, Detective, let me see. Hmmm. Does the phrase

'I don't know' work for you?"

"You're doing a real bang-up job here, Burnside. I'll bet the governor gives you a bonus soon for all your great work."

"If he's still governor, that is."

"Oh, now you're a political guru, huh? You just have so much to offer. Why don't you take off and go do whatever it is you do. Leave the police work to the pros."

"Sure, you're a pro all right. How much have you accomplished? You eat sandwiches with the best of them."

We stared hard at each other for a long minute before Lally turned and walked away. My connection with Juan Saavedra probably saved me from a physical altercation or being cuffed and driven over to lock-up. As I walked away, though, I heard my name being called out. I turned and saw Adam Lazar approaching.

"Hey, you learn anything here?" he asked.

"Just that the cops know as much as we do," I said. "Maybe less."

"Yeah, those guys keep things too close to the vest. Where you headed?"

"Haven't decided. You?"

"Stone Canyon," Lazar declared. "Time to turn that place upside down."

"With that attitude, I'm sure you'll be entering from the back way again. Your dry cleaner will become rich getting those grass stains off your pants."

"Uh, yeah. I thought maybe I could ride in with you. I think I burned my bridges with that security guard."

I looked at Lazar and sighed. He was a handful of

trouble, but I wasn't making much progress on my own.

"Why not," I said. "Park your car off of Beverly Glen, south of Sunset. There's a small street called Bainbridge Avenue. I'll pick you up over there."

The rain had stopped, but traffic was heavy as I made my way slowly out of downtown. While rush hour had yet to start, two cars got into a bad accident and everyone had to slow down to view the gruesome scene. One vehicle had overturned, and the other looked smashed beyond repair. It took 45 minutes, but I finally picked up Lazar, who had parked in front of a palatial estate. He was leaning on the fender of a rusty 20-year-old Toyota Tercel, looking down at his phone. The Tercel certainly didn't fit in with the BMWs and Mercedes parked nearby. Maybe the neighbors would figure it was owned by someone's housekeeper.

We drove up to the school's security gate and I told Lazar to let me do the talking. I handed him a white USC baseball cap, and instructed him to pull it down low and turn his face toward the passenger side window. Hopefully, the guard wouldn't recognize him from his obnoxious behavior the day before.

"Hello there," I beamed, smiling as close to a rich man's smile as I could muster. The guard beamed back.

"Daughter forget her sneakers again?"

"Nope," I said, the confident smile pasted on. "Big playoff game tonight. Want to make sure we get good seats."

"Sure. So what's your daughter's name again?"

I thought quickly. "Riley Joyner," I said.

The guard waved me through and even gave me a

small salute. I turned to Lazar. "I hope you're taking notes. Honey catching more flies than vinegar, and all that."

Lazar made a grunting noise. "You're giving me advice on how to talk pleasantly to people?"

"Um, okay. Fair enough."

We parked and walked over to the sports complex. Once inside, we sat down in the bleacher seats and watched the girls stretch and practice. Nearby, a man about my age sat and watched as well. After a few minutes, I walked over and sat down next to him.

"What do you think of the team's chances tonight?" I asked.

"Very good," he responded. "I don't think Brentwood can stay with us. Another win and we go to the regional semis."

"Big game," I agreed. "You have a daughter on the team?"

"Oh, I'm not a parent. I teach AP Math here. Couple of my students are playing. You?"

I shrugged. Lying was part of my job, and I was going at it pretty good this week. "I'm coaching at UC Santa Barbara. Looking at a few recruits here."

"You're probably after Riley Joyner then," he said with a knowing glance.

"Riley," I said slowly, noticing Lazar moving to the row in front of us and turning his head. "Riley Joyner. Yup, she's a heckuva player."

"You may have to hustle. I hear UCLA wants her bad. They need a big hitter who can get some kills."

"Yeah," I muttered, wondering where this lingo emanated from. Looking over at Lazar, I could see he was itching to pounce in with a myriad of questions. I gave him a subtle sign with my eyes to keep quiet, but I had no idea if it would register. This matter required delicacy, and while I was hardly light on my feet, I was a veritable *Baryshnikov* compared to my new journalist companion.

"Any other girls here I should keep my eye on?" I asked.

"Oh, there's a few, but Riley's the star."

"What about Molly?" I asked, watching him carefully. "Is she ever coming back to the team?"

He gave a shrug. "That one? Who knows. She's actually a decent player, she comes up with some good kills. When she shows up, that is. She comes and goes. Kids like her are part of the reason I'm leaving the school after this semester."

"How's that?"

"I'm a little frustrated. Teaching isn't what I expected it to be. Don't get me wrong. This is a good school, by and large."

"I understand a lot of kids here wind up at great colleges."

"Sure. But the smart ones would probably get into them anyway, no matter what high school they went to. The middling kids benefit the most, especially the ones whose parents are big donors. They'll go off to a top college because they're legacy. The parents went there and they have the Stone Canyon seal of approval. But mostly it's because their families can give a lot of money."

"Like Molly."

"Yup, like Molly. She puts in the bare minimum, but her family donates a lot. Grandfather, especially. She'll have her ticket punched to a great college. That's how it works."

I nodded. "If you don't mind my saying so, you sound quite cynical."

"Yeah, I probably am."

"Good idea to leave then," I commented. "Better to get fed up and leave than to get fed up and stay."

He looked at me thoughtfully. "Fair point."

"So what are you going to do now?"

He shrugged. "Back to the private sector. I have a job lined up running data analytics with one of the big tech companies in the Bay Area. Loretta wasn't too happy to hear about that. CEOs don't like replacing teachers in the middle of the year."

"What do you mean by CEO?"

"Oh, yeah, sorry. Ms. Moss. Our Head of School. She's more like a CEO. Steers the ship from a business point of view. She does a good job of bringing in wealthy parents and tapping into large donations. Ms. Moss is all about growing the greenbacks. Doesn't hurt she has quite a foxy body for a middle-aged broad. I think half the dads give extra money just to drool over her cleavage for a little while."

I laughed. "Whatever works."

"Yeah. I went to a private school like this maybe 20 years ago. It's changed a lot. The headmaster was more about the teaching. Here it's more about the money. And the reputation."

"I guess it takes a lot of dough to build a campus like this," I said, figuring I had gotten as much out of him as I could. I wished him good luck and walked off. Lazar didn't bother to wait two seconds before getting up and following me. I walked toward a group of students on the other side of the gym, Lazar was in back of me, but quickly breezed past and suddenly took the initiative.

"Hey, guys, you got a minute?" he asked a group of six students, half boys, half girls. He began to pepper them with questions ranging from Molly Palmer to Diego Garcia, to problems they had with Stone Canyon, as well as any racism they'd seen against Latinos. Whether he'd get these students to reveal anything more than annoyance was questionable.

I drifted away from them, suddenly wishing I could slip away and not have to escort Adam back to his car. Part of me thought of stranding him here anyway, which might have been a fitting end. Instead, I went back to the bleachers and sat down behind a trio of middle-aged women, most likely moms of the girls playing today. I listened to their banter for a few minutes. Most of it was just general gossip, but then one of them began to talk about Molly Palmer.

The conversation centered on when Molly would be back on the team, and meandered to when she would be back in school. There didn't seem to be any discussion questioning her whereabouts or of her being missing at all. It mostly focused around how her absence would affect the volleyball team. Finally, one of the women noticed my eavesdropping. She elbowed the others and they changed the conversation. One woman, 40-ish, with long blonde hair that looked unusually straight and golden, glanced up at me.

"You seem familiar," she said, her big brown eyes looking at me curiously.

I smiled. "I get that a lot."

"Are you an actor?"

"Only when I need to be," I said and gave a wink.

The blonde woman laughed. "You must be a Brentwood parent. We've been sending our kids here for years, and I've never seen you."

"A Brentwood parent," I nodded. "Yeah. Something like that."

"Oh, a spy! All right, we'll let you be secretive."

"So, do you think Stone Canyon will win today?" I asked. Burnside, the glib conversation maker. I guess if Gail and I ever managed to save enough money to send our child to a school like this, I'd need to hone the skills of small talk. And if Gail ever decided to run for political office, making friends with strangers would become a requirement. Gail would call these stretch projects for me.

"Oh, I think we'll win," she said, displaying a smile that were very even and very white. It was a pretty smile to look at. "You?"

I gazed out onto the court. The logo on the floor spelled out *Stone Canyon* in streaking letters, and also featured their nickname, the *Coyotes*, with a picture of a cuddly little predator, smiling happily.

"As long as Riley comes through," I said slowly, "I

think the Coyotes are probably going to the finals."

The blonde gave a puzzled expression. "You know about Riley?"

"Sure. I follow the game," I said, the wheels in my head spinning to remember my conversation with the departing math teacher. "She's headed to UCLA next year. At least that's the rumor."

"Goodness, you sure know a lot about things here. Did you know Riley's my daughter?"

I blinked. "Ah. Lucky you. She's very talented."

"She is."

"And she'll probably get a scholarship. A full ride will save you some money."

"Seriously, money's not an issue with us."

I kicked myself. Her comment served to remind me about the people I was dealing with here. To spend $40,000 a year on high school tuition meant they were paying a lot more now than they would pay at UCLA. Or at any other state university for that matter. Unlike for me, money was indeed not an issue for these folks. They had it, they spent it, they managed to get more.

"Sure," I said. "So do you work outside the home?"

"Oh, not any more. I used to be a drug rep. But I gave that up."

"Smuggler?" I joked.

She laughed. "No, I would call on doctors and talk to them about prescribing medications my company had on the market. Drug rep is a legitimate job. It's just developed a bad reputation lately."

Indeed it had. Drug reps were notorious for lavishing

gifts on physicians, not just taking them out to pricey lunches and sponsoring exotic vacations, but in a few cases, handing them envelopes of cash. Most doctors refused the direct bribes, but often accepted everything else. When I was working plainclothes with the LAPD, we did sting operations and made a number of arrests on bribery charges. One time I posed as an internist and an exceedingly attractive drug rep practically gave me a lap dance, along with a pitch to prescribe more of her Company's medications. She didn't offer me any money, and the lead detective decided there was no law against being shameless in making a sale.

"So you don't have to deal with doctors anymore. I imagine that's a relief."

"Hmmm. Not exactly."

"Oh?"

"I have to deal with a doctor all the time."

"Injury?"

"Oh no. Not at all. We're perfectly healthy."

I frowned and shook my head to communicate my lack of understanding.

"It's the reason I'm no longer a drug rep. I don't call on doctors anymore," she said, holding up her left hand and displaying a sparkling diamond ring. "I married one."

*

Stone Canyon won the first game by three points against Brentwood, although Riley Joyner did not play all that well. I wanted to stay for the rest of the match, but my new friend Adam Lazar was chomping at the bit to leave and write his story for tomorrow's edition of the *Times*. He wouldn't tell me what would be included, but promised it would be worth the read. I finally dropped Lazar off at his car and returned to Stone Canyon.

I waited in the parking lot until the volleyball match ended, whiling away the time listening to the radio. I couldn't find any shrinks on the air, so I alternated between sports talk, political commentary, and religious shows. After a half-hour of listening, I learned nothing new. USC would be in for a rough game tomorrow at Washington, Rex Palmer was in trouble with his re-election bid, and many people in L.A. were going to burn in hell. I finally switched to a music station.

It had grown dark by the time Riley Joyner and her mother arrived at the parking lot and got into a white Mercedes. They pulled swiftly out of the lot, and I followed them onto Sunset, and then up a side street that led into Tigertail Road. We drove for another half mile up Tigertail, before they pulled in front of a large home. Riley got out and waved to her mom, who sped off quickly. Instead of using a key to get in, she knocked on the front door, waited a minute before it opened, and went inside.

Pulling out my iPad, I cruised the Internet until I found a site that listed the property owner of each house on Tigertail Road. Most of the homes were owned by family trusts and interestingly, the assessed values of the homes varied wildly. Some were listed at over $15 million, others at the relatively paltry price of $500,000. In California, the price you paid for your home dictates the assessed value and therefore the property taxes you pay. It doesn't matter if your home was purchased over 30 years ago and the actual value has increased more than tenfold. This was all due to Proposition 13, the landmark tax bill that all but freezes property taxes until you sell or remodel your house. So two homeowners, owning identical properties side-by-side, might be paying wildly different amounts in taxes. It all depends on when the homes were purchased. And the home Riley Joyner walked into was purchased a good 45 years ago. The owner was Buster Palmer.

I let the Pathfinder idle as I pondered my next move. After 10 minutes of pondering, I turned off the engine. And then I waited. The vaunted life of a private eye actually meant spending long periods of time waiting for someone to do something. Anything. In this case though, I only had to wait another 20 minutes.

Two teenage guys walked out of the house. One was familiar, Connor Pierce, who I spoke with yesterday. The other was a bulky kid, not quite as tall, but with much wider, thicker, frame and carrying a good bit of belly fat. They walked toward a shiny new black Escalade with chrome molding, and unlocked the vehicle with a remote. I hopped out of my 10-year-old Pathfinder and jogged over before they could get in. Connor was at the passenger side door, the other guy was the driver.

"Hey fellas. Got a minute?"

A glint of recognition crossed Connor Pierce's face. "Oh, yeah. You're the detective. I spoke with you yesterday."

"You did what?!" the other kid exclaimed. "What did you go and do that for?!"

Connor shrugged. "It's not a big deal, Alex."

I walked over to the big guy. "Alex? Alex Gateley?"

He stared at me. "How do you know my name?"

"Like your friend said, I'm a detective." I took out my fake gold plastic shield and held it up briefly. A nearby street lamp provided enough light to suggest it was an important-looking badge, but not enough to actually discern anything.

"We got nothing to say," Alex sneered, before turning to get into the Escalade. "Fuck off."

I took hold of his left arm. "I'm looking for Molly. Is she in that house?"

The two of them glanced at each other and said nothing for a minute. Their silence told me what I needed to know. Molly Palmer was inside.

"We can't talk about it," Connor said, still standing on the other side of the vehicle.

"Maybe you guys ought to," I responded, tightening the grip on Alex Gateley's arm. I saw his face start to wince. "Maybe you should start talking before you get into any trouble."

"Maybe you should let go of my fucking arm before I kick your ass!" he responded.

"It doesn't work that way," I said. "Why is Molly in there?"

"Hey, man," Alex said. "Let go of me! You don't know who you're messing with. I'm a football player!"

I laughed in his face. "You'll have to do better than

that."

Alex Gateley tried to twist his arm free, and when that failed, he balled his right hand into a fist and threw a sweeping punch that I anticipated and easily ducked under. I slugged him hard in the solar plexus with my right hand and he doubled over in pain. Letting go of his left arm, I hit him in the face with a sharp left hook. He fell against the vehicle, breathing hard. I hit him again with a right cross and he began to slide down the side of the vehicle. At that point, I saw Connor Pierce move around the vehicle. Stepping back, I jerked my .38 out of the holster, pointed it at him and told him to freeze. Unlike his friend, Connor Pierce had the good sense to do what he was told. He also put his hands up.

"Whoa ..." he said.

"Tell me why Molly's in there," I demanded.

"She's with her grandfather."

"Is she being kept against her will?"

"No," Connor said. "Not at all. She's there by choice."

"Why?"

"Why what?" he asked.

I sighed. "Why is she choosing to be there instead of at home with her mother?"

"She's just in a messed up situation."

"What's messed up about it?"

"I can't talk about it."

"Hey," I said, waving the .38 back and forth. "I'm holding a gun here. That means you can talk about it."

"Are you going to shoot us if we don't?" Connor asked.

I stared at him for a moment. When I was a police

officer, we sometimes reminded each other that reacting with too much force was better than not reacting with enough. There is a wall in the LAPD offices where they hang photos of officers who were killed in the line of duty. The general presumption was that some of these officers might be alive today if they had been more aggressive. Even if it meant standing trial for their actions. The motto among officers was it was better to be judged by twelve, than to be carried by six. But that didn't seem to apply here. These were kids, not hardened criminals, and there was no reason to think they were armed.

I lowered my gun and began to wonder if I really would have pulled the trigger if he came at me. I had to fire my weapon twice when I was in uniform, but both were justified shootings. In those instances, I was engaged with dangerous felons who could have just as easily killed me. In this instance I was only dealing with a pair of teenagers who may or may not have been involved with a missing girl. No proof they were engaged in foul play. I was merely trying to diffuse a situation. In the wrong scenario, this could have culminated in tragic results.

"No," I said. "I'm not."

We looked at each other for a long minute, none of us entirely sure of what to say or do. Finally, Alex Gateley pulled himself off the ground and found his voice. "I think we're gonna go home."

I wanted to ask more questions. I knew they had a story they weren't telling. But it was plainly obvious I wasn't going to get any answers from them. At least not tonight. They silently climbed into the Escalade and slowly drove down Tigertail road. I watched the bright red taillights disappear around the bend. The street turned dark again as I looked over at Buster Palmer's house. There was no point in waiting any longer. If one of them hadn't texted Molly about what happened yet, they were bound to do so very soon.

Ten

I walked over to Buster Palmer's front door and rang the bell. We were in the hills above Brentwood, and there wasn't much of a front yard. It took a long minute, but finally a Hispanic woman in a black and white housekeeper's outfit opened the door. I handed her my business card and asked to speak with the former governor. No sense pretending with the fake shield. People like Buster Palmer weren't afraid of the police. In their minds, they owned the police. Buster Palmer was worth over $100 million and in that rarified air of money and power, the rules were simply different.

I half-expected the woman to come back and tell me to go away, but instead she opened the door and led me into what one might call a parlor. It was more like a sunken living room, down three steps, with soft blue carpet and a cathedral ceiling. A very husky man with a shock of white hair and a thick white mustache, sat in an easy chair. He had on a plaid shirt, gray trousers and camel-colored tasseled loafers. He didn't bother to get up, but since he was in his 80s, I didn't really blame him. And if I were worth $100 million, I wouldn't bother getting up for every visitor, especially one who arrived uninvited.

"Good evening, young man" he boomed, and pointed to the couch. I sat. It had been quite a while since anyone had called me a young man.

"Good evening to *you*, sir. Thank you for seeing me."

"Oh, I wouldn't have missed the opportunity. After I saw what you did to that big fellow out there, I figured I'd meet with you. I'm intrigued. Genuine tough guys don't come around here much. Not lately, that is."

"You mean they used to?" I asked, feeling a small grin start to take shape on my face.

"I once ran with a tough crowd. Gave as good as I got. But that was a long, long time ago. My only fights these days are with the little woman."

"You're safer that way."

"Don't be so sure about that."

I laughed. "My name's Burnside."

"I know who you are," he said. "I saw your card. I also know my son went and hired you."

"He did. And it turned out his daughter was here all the time. With her grandfather."

Buster Palmer nodded slowly. "Yes. She wasn't missing. That was a ruse. Kept her away from the parents, away from the campaign and away from any chance to do the damage that young people are prone to do. Which is to say, open up too much and say the wrong thing. That unfortunately runs in the family."

"Okay," I responded. "May I see Molly? Just to make sure she's really okay?"

Buster Palmer shook his head no. "Not at this point. I need to talk with her about a few things. I wasn't really expecting anyone to find her. But I should have known teenagers can't go long without texting their friends. And once they start texting each other, you might as well publish their every move in the newspaper. Which I know is coming tomorrow morning."

"You know about Adam Lazar?"

"Who?"

"A journalist. He works for the *Times*. He's writing a story about this. My sense is it's not about Molly *per se*, but she may get mentioned. And as the governor's daughter, that story will overshadow everything else."

"Your sense is correct. It's about that rotten business across town, those murders, but Molly will be collateral damage. I didn't know the writer's name. I was on the phone earlier with Harry Blumstein."

"The *Times* publisher."

"Yes, we go way back. He did me the courtesy of providing a head's up on the article."

"Nothing like having friends in high places."

"That's quite true."

"You know, about that business across town," I started. "The police are looking for Molly. They need to question her. Like it or not, she's involved. Even if she had nothing to do with those acts. Even if she wasn't there. The police still want to talk with her."

"I know. But you let me handle the police. I'll make arrangements. Just not yet."

I took a deep breath. You sometimes meet people who know how the world really works. Not how it's supposed to work. How it actually works. And with Buster Palmer, he was one of those who helped build this world. There was no point in pushing him. Being in his good graces was the only sensible option.

"So tell me something, Governor Palmer."

"Buster," he interjected. "Call me Buster. I stopped being governor decades ago. Nasty job. Your friends are disappointed when you can't do every favor for them. Your enemies just end up hating you even more. And your life's not your own. Even your own family can turn against you."

"But your son ran for governor, too. You didn't try to talk him out of it?"

"Do you have children, Mr. Burnside?"

"My wife is expecting. Our first."

Buster Palmer shook his head approvingly. "It's a joy and a heartache all wrapped together. But you'll find out quickly enough they have minds of their own. And after about age 10, they usually stop listening to you. Maybe age 13, if you're lucky."

"Does Molly listen to you?"

"Ah, grandchildren. They are a different story. There is a very special bond between grandparents and their grandchildren."

"How's that?"

"We have a common enemy," Buster Palmer said, giving a wink and a small chuckle.

I paused to think for a moment. Parents and children and politics. Buster Palmer was a rock-ribbed Republican, a supporter of conservative movements from the tax-cutting revolution to the John Birch society. But his son was none of those things. Rex was as middle-of-the-road as they come. A moderate, a consensus builder, a politician who was cautious in nearly all things that mattered. The only risk he ever took was making an off-color joke about his opponent's accent, an atrociously ill-timed comment that might cost him his career.

"Just what do you think of Rex's politics," I asked.

Buster looked past me, gazing off into the distance. He didn't speak for a while and neither did I. Finally he took a deep breath and let it out.

"Rex thinks we're living in a new era. Maybe we are, although things never really change much."

"Did you encourage him to enter politics?"

"Oh, no, I would never do that. He's the one who chose to run for public office, I certainly didn't push him into it. But once he entered the arena, I certainly bankrolled him."

"But you couldn't have been happy when he pursued a political agenda different from your own."

"You know something about politics, do you, young man?"

I shrugged. "Just what I get from the media. And what I cobble together."

"Never believe everything you read from journalists, Mr. Burnside. They just want to color your thinking and have you parrot their ideas. But you're right on point about my not being too happy with my son. Although maybe for different reasons."

"How's that?"

"Rex wasn't as conservative as I was. I could live with that. But he wasn't seizing control in the way he needed to. He wasn't getting anything of substance done. I spent eight years in office and left quite a legacy. Tax cuts, reducing that bloated infrastructure up in Sacramento. My terms in office meant something. For Rex, nothing he did will last. He missed the opportunity. He was too willing to please everyone. When you try to please everyone, you please no one."

"Well said."

"You've been asking a lot of questions. Let me ask you a few."

"All right," I said cautiously.

"Where'd you learn to be such a tough guy?"

I smiled, maybe a bit sadly. I tried not to think about certain things from my past too much. But hearing Buster Palmer talk about his son, and thinking about our baby coming in a few months had loosened me up. And aside from Gail, there weren't many people I felt I could open up to. I was a little puzzled as to why I felt so comfortable with Buster Palmer. Maybe he reminded me of the man I had dreamed my own father might have been.

"It's a long story," I said.

"I have plenty of time, Mr. Burnside. In fact, all I have is time. I'd say someone must have taught you a few good lessons about fighting. Your father?"

"No," I said. "I grew up the child of a single mother. But it's not quite what you think. My father died a few months before I was born. Car accident."

"I'm sorry to hear that," Buster said, leaning forward. "Tell me more."

"It was hit and run. The police never found out who did it, only that it was a rainy night in October, the streets were slick and it was a head-on collision. My father was driving a small car, the other driver was in a big pickup truck. The pickup was speeding, and a witness said it looked like he lost control of his truck. Probably alcohol was involved. After the accident, the other driver got out of the pickup and ran. He was never caught. And as it turns out, the truck was stolen, so there was no way to track the driver down."

"Go on."

"My mother was planning to be a stay-at-home mom. But that all changed. It had to. She went back to school and became a nurse. Worked in an ER for years, sometimes had to work the night shift. She wasn't always there for me. My grandparents took care of me for a while. But they passed away, and from an early age, I learned that I'd need to take care of myself."

"Very astute."

"It wasn't easy. I grew up in LA, Culver City actually. There was a Big Brothers program my mom enrolled me in. The man they assigned to me was a retired LAPD officer. He was a tough guy and he helped me. Taught me things about the world, some good, some not. He was a big reason I joined the LAPD. Before I met him, I thought I wanted to be a fireman."

"Both lines of work are dangerous," he mused.

"Sure. But he told me most firemen were thieves and psychopaths. That you had to be crazy to run into a burning building. And that firemen wore these oversized clothes so they could steal valuables and walk away with them undetected. I guess he arrested a couple of them once and concluded they all did it. Like I said, not everything he taught me was so great. Or accurate."

"But he did instruct you on how to take care of yourself."

"Yes, very true. One thing he taught me how to do was how to fight. In his world, it was a critical skill. And that later became my world."

"And it looks like he did a good job of it. Not too many people would even think to take on a brute like Alex Gateley and then knock him down."

I gave him a long look. "You saw all of that?"

"I did."

"But we were behind his Escalade. Even if you were peering out your kitchen window -- which I doubt you'd do -- you wouldn't have seen it."

Buster Palmer smiled. "Mr. Burnside. I am a wealthy man and a well-known man. I take precautions."

I nodded warily. "You had video cameras installed outside."

"They're almost everywhere. In and around the property. Even on the street lamps, although you're not supposed to do that. I got an exception from someone in the city. I still have pull in this town. And I must say, you pack quite a punch."

I shrugged. "I wish I didn't have to employ it so much. I'm getting older."

"Physical altercations are sometimes necessary. But you've got a ways to go before age will be an issue, I can assure you. And I appreciate your sharing that story with me. I'm sorry about your father. I'm sure you'll make it up to your child. We always try and give our children the things we didn't have."

"I appreciate hearing that," I said softly, and then tried to steer the conversation back to why I was here. "You know, I'm a little confused as to what to do next."

"About what?"

"About Molly. I was hired to find her. I guess I have, although I can't be fully certain."

"And I'll bet you're the type who doesn't like leaving jobs unfinished."

"That's right."

"I'm sorry, Mr. Burnside," he said. "I can't assist you any further right now. But I appreciate your diligence. And I can guarantee you good things come to people who work hard."

At that point, the housekeeper mysteriously appeared and said she'd show me out. I thanked Buster Palmer for his time. The only other person with whom I had shared my background in the last few years was Gail, and even then, I hadn't told her everything. Oddly, it felt good to talk about it with someone I barely knew. But people like Buster Palmer always had reasons for doing what they did. I just couldn't figure out what they were yet.

When I arrived home it was close to 10:00 p.m.. Gail warmed up some leftover pasta she had made for dinner, and we talked about my very long day. It had started by looking into Xavier Bishop's relationship with Desiree Brown, continued with a frustrating meeting with the governor's campaign chief, escalated into another murder along Alvarado, swept me back onto the campus of an exclusive private school, which led to some fisticuffs with a mouthy teenager, and finished with a sit down with one of the wealthiest men in the state. I had put in a full week's work in one day.

"I'd imagine you must be exhausted," Gail said.

"I am," I said, as I finished dinner. "You'll excuse me if I go straight to bed?"

"Of course. But you know there is an article in the *Times* you should read."

"It's out already?" I frowned. "Adam Lazar's piece?"

"It is."

"You think the world will be safe if I wait until tomorrow morning to read it?"

"I think so," she said, kissing me on the cheek, "And you should read it after a good night's sleep."

"That bad?"

"No. It's interesting. But get some rest."

I needed no further motivation. I think I actually fell asleep a few seconds after my head hit the pillow, and I managed to sleep through Ms. Linzmeier's daily sermon from the Southern preacher. Strands of sunlight were seeping through the blinds when I awoke. I felt rested, but only somewhat refreshed. I got the feeling that although my body was resting, my mind had still been active.

Gail had gotten up early and made coffee, but we did not share the same taste. Gail preferred a lighter, smoother coffee, one which did little for me. She was fortunately in the shower, sparing me the temptation of commenting on her choice of beverages. I got dressed, left a loving goodbye note and headed out the door. A quick stop at Starbucks yielded a more preferable Italian roast, along with a lemon scone. I had planned to eat it in my office, but the treat was gone by the time I pulled into my parking space. The coffee had just cooled to an acceptable level. I brushed some crumbs into my hand, deposited them into a trash bin and walked upstairs to my office.

I opened up my iPad and quickly brought up Adam Lazar's article. Although it was on page one and was seemingly a news story, it had all the earmarks of slanted piece which belonged on an op-ed page. I wasn't surprised at the tone, only that Virgil would allow the story to be published in the news section. After reading it, I drank some coffee, stared into space for a few minutes, and then read it again.

TWO FUNERALS AND AN ELECTION
by Adam Lazar

In the Rampart district, life is hard, and life can be short. This was demonstrated most presciently over the past few days with the murders of teenagers Diego Garcia and Sofia Rodriguez. They were not gang members, they were just kids who happened to live in the neighborhood. They were young lovers, but their murders came less than 48 hours apart. And they were both killed with the same weapon, which was a 9 mm handgun. In the case of Sofia, she was shot six times.

Diego Garcia was a star pupil at the exclusive Stone Canyon School in Bel-Air, a place where the children of the rich and powerful choose to matriculate. It is an exclusive school in many ways. And it was at this school that Garcia befriended Molly Palmer, daughter of the governor, an encounter which may have cost him his life.

A police investigation is ongoing, but it has turned up little thus far. It took a private investigator, hired by the Palmer family, to uncover the fact that Molly Palmer had accompanied Garcia back from a football game on Saturday. She apparently had spent the weekend with him. Efforts to find Ms. Palmer have been fruitless.

Sources at the Stone Canyon School have been mum about Ms. Palmer's whereabouts, other than to say she did not show up for classes this week. The Head of School, who is often dubbed "The CEO," would only provide glowing testimonials about her school, confusing an interview about two tragic murders with an opportunity to provide the public with a marketing message promoting Stone Canyon. She spent her time touting the benefits of applying to a private school with soaring tuition that is beyond the reach of most Angelenos. Her biggest concern seemed to be increasing the number of school applications so that Stone Canyon can turn down an even greater number of kids, thus crowning it as one of the most exclusive prep schools in the state, or perhaps even the country for that matter.

All of this comes on the heels of a rollicking gubernatorial election, which has seen Governor Rex Palmer's approval ratings drop precipitously this week. This is a direct result of his blatantly racist remarks about the manner in which immigrants speak, and his tepid response to the withering criticism. It is no surprise that Governor Palmer's standing in the polls has declined. The governor is a man who can't even account for the whereabouts of his own daughter. How he could possibly think he has earned the right to another four years as governor of California? This is perhaps the most confounding question in what has become a series of stunning questions that have emerged this week.

Very soon, the voters of California will provide an answer to who should lead them as their governor for the next four years. And hopefully the police will be able to provide some answers too, although I'm betting my money that the private investigator will uncover more evidence than the LAPD ever will. The families of Diego Garcia and Sofia Rodriguez deserve better. And so do all the citizens of California. Regardless of the way anyone pronounces it.

I was grateful Adam Lazar had chosen to omit my

name from this acid-laced article. But it didn't take long for those with even a tangential relationship to this story to begin leaving messages on my voice mail. By 8:00 a.m. I had over 35 messages waiting for me. I drank some more coffee, and looked out my office window for a while before deciding to listen to them. And just I as I was about to hit the *Play* button, an unexpected visitor knocked on my door.

"Mr. Burnside," he said. "You're a tough man to get a hold of."

"Not too tough, Arthur. You certainly managed to find me."

"Ah, you remember me. I knew you were a sharp man. From the moment I met you."

Arthur Woo walked in and sat down. I didn't invite him to sit down, but he didn't seem to care. He was wearing a dark blue suit and tie, and also wore a relaxed face that bespoke a man who was enjoying life very much these days. Not a surprise, of course. In a matter of 10 days, his brother had a very real chance to be elected governor of California.

"Well, Arthur, I understand your brother has taken a small lead in the polls. I'm sure you're thrilled."

"I am indeed, Mr. Burnside."

"So what brings you here?"

"A proposition, actually. I've been thinking about you."

"How flattering."

Arthur Woo smiled slightly. Very slightly. "I understand," he said. "You've been busy trying to find the governor's daughter."

I bowed my head slightly in acknowledgment. "You've obviously read the *Times* article."

"Oh, that just confirmed it. But after we met at the debate, I was curious and did a little research. I learned you are a private investigator. Why would a private investigator be at a political debate? And in the first row, no less. You weren't part of Justin's campaign, and you weren't part of the media, so you had to be working for Palmer. I had initially assumed you were digging up dirt on us, but yes, the *Times* article pointed to a very different assignment."

"All right. You get an 'A' for being assiduous. But I don't see how I can help you. Especially given the fact that I do work for your brother's opponent."

"You know, the campaign will end in 10 days. And then my brother will be the governor-elect. I'm in charge of the transition team, vetting people who can serve in the administration."

"Ah," I said. "But it sounds like you've shown up at the wrong office. My wife might be a better fit for a political appointment than I would."

"Your wife has a very good resume," he observed. "I looked into her, too. The city attorney's office is a good starting place. But for the time being, we're actually looking at you."

"Me?" I asked, eyes wide. "I'm not sure what role I could play in anyone's administration. I do have a knack for ticking people off, but aside from that, I don't think I'm cut out for politics."

Arthur Woo smiled as paternally as anyone under age 30 could hope to smile. "We know that. We're more interested in having you lead our security force. Be in charge of Justin's detail. Keep him safe. We know you spent quite a few years with the LAPD. And you have a reputation for getting things done."

I sat back for a moment and pondered this. The Woos wanted me to be the new Bill Thorn, the guy who protects the governor and potentially puts his life on the line for him. That wasn't quite how I saw my future. But I also knew the future wasn't always going to unfold the way you envisioned it.

"That type of job takes a lot of patriotism, Arthur," I said slowly. "Yes, I was on the police force and there were times I needed to put my life on the line to protect others. But I'm not so sure I could jump in the path of a speeding bullet to protect a political leader."

"It's not the Secret Service, Mr. Burnside. We don't expect you to die for your governor."

"But these things can happen."

"Very unusual. And unlikely. We are planning to make Justin's administration a very popular one. We have lots of plans for how to improve the state. In fact, by the time he's done, I'd be surprised if there isn't talk of a national candidacy."

Now it was my turn to smile paternally. "I may be a little rusty in my political science, but if I recall, you have to born in the United States to become president. Justin was born in Seoul. There's a little thing called the Constitution."

"I am quite aware, Mr. Burnside. I learned that in Middle School. But there's also the ability to amend the Constitution. You see, our Founding Fathers were incredibly smart. They knew the world would change and America would need to change along with it. After Justin proves himself in this job, we can advance a constitutional amendment which would allow a naturalized citizen to run for higher office, regardless of where they were born. So a presidency is not out of the question."

I let out a low whistle. "You've really thought this through. You haven't even won the election yet and you're thinking 10 years down the road. Impressive."

"I'm a planner, Mr. Burnside."

"Apparently. I understand your brother went to Harvard. How about you?"

"No, I was a rebel," he said, without smiling. "I went to Columbia."

"Ah."

"I like to think of myself as a visionary," he continued. "And I think I can see greatness in people. I see greatness in Justin. And I think I see some greatness in you, too."

"That's very flattering," I said. "Really, it is. You've done more than your share of homework on me. But it doesn't alter a basic tenet here. I'm still working for Governor Palmer."

"I know. But things change very quickly once an election is over. Your enemies become your friends. It's the way of the world."

"You're aware I've never done this type of work before."

"Of course I am. But that doesn't mean you wouldn't be good at it."

"Why not Bill Thorn? He might be looking for a new job after next week. And he certainly has relevant experience in this area."

"We're quite aware of Mr. Thorn. And to be completely transparent with you, Mr. Thorn has already contacted us about a job after the election."

Hmmm. Now that was very interesting indeed. "Who is Justin's detail man now?" I asked.

"Ken Sang. A friend of a friend. But we're looking for someone better. And we'd like to expand to include, um, those with more diversity."

I didn't exactly see myself as a model for racial equality, but politics does make for some strange doings. "You know, of course, I don't speak Korean."

"Of course, Mr. Burnside," he smiled, this time a little more broadly. "That is, in fact, rather an asset, not a liability."

I nodded and began wondering what conversations might happen right in front of me, ones I would be completely unable to understand.

I told Arthur I would think carefully about his offer. As he rose to leave, he made a final pitch about public service and the need to give back. It was not a speech I needed to hear. After 13 years with the LAPD, I knew all about public service. I also knew how brutal it could get when things went south. But his offer was flattering, albeit a great surprise. I hadn't considered anything like this before, so I didn't have a ready answer for him. There's an old axiom that says you should never turn down an opportunity right away, that sleeping on it might yield some added insight.

Arthur Woo departed, and I looked out the window a little more, sipping on what was now lukewarm coffee. Yesterday, Johnny Cleary was musing about bringing me on as an assistant coach of the SC football team. Today, I was being considered for a high profile job working directly for the governor of the largest state in the country. Maybe tomorrow I'd be offered a job as an executive with the Walt Disney Studios. I didn't want to think too much about the future, the present was still providing me with ample complexities. And as I started to ponder what the rest of my day would look like, this vision was quickly altered.

The person who quietly entered my office was wearing a black hoodie. It was pulled tightly over their head. They moved slowly but purposefully. They were wearing sunglasses. Their hands were tucked snugly inside their sweatshirt pockets, holding something lumpy. They turned toward me and I quickly opened the top drawer of my desk and grabbed my .38.

"It's not what you think," the person said in a surprisingly high-pitched voice, and stopped moving.

"Then what is it?" I countered, aiming the gun at their abdomen.

"Would you mind pointing that thing somewhere else?"

"Would you mind taking your hands out of your pockets?" I directed. "Real slow like."

They went to great effort to present a pair of open palms. Pulling the hood down revealed long piles of curly blonde tresses. The sunglasses came off, and I saw a pair of pale blue eyes.

"Oh, don't tell me," I said, putting the gun down, and leaning back to take in the wonder of it all.

"Yeah," she responded glumly. "I'm Molly."

Eleven

I put the gun down and motioned for her to take a seat. She was tall and slim, just like her father. She had her mother's face and eyes, which is to say she was somewhat pretty. Basically, she didn't look all that different from many other teenagers.

"I'll assume that's not a pistol in your pocket," I started.

"Nope. It's a bagel. Okay if I have breakfast?"

"Sure," I said. "Sorry I can't offer you some cream cheese too."

She didn't respond as she took a folded brown paper bag out of her sweatshirt pocket, and removed a plain bagel. Pulling off small pieces, she ate quietly and stared at the floor, chewing carefully. When she finished, she tried to hand me the paper bag. I made a gesture toward the wastebasket across the room.

"So you're probably wondering what I'm doing here," she said, as she sat back down.

"No, I was just thinking about who to vote for in the election."

She tried to smile, but it came off as more of a grimace. "Good luck with that."

"So you know I've been looking for you."

"Everyone in LA seems to be looking for me."

"But you chose to seek me out," I said.

"Not exactly," she shrugged. "My grandfather told me to come here. Said you'd keep me safe for a little while until this all blows over."

"Oh, he did, did he?" I said, my eyebrows starting to involuntarily arch.

"Yes. That article in the paper this morning started it. Then, word got out that I was at Grandpa's. I guess someone at school posted it on the Internet. There were camera crews and paparazzi all over the street. It was crazy. Grandpa said I couldn't stay. Too risky. He got one of his neighbors to help me climb over their back fence and drive me here."

I wondered just what the risk was in having an 18-year-old girl tucked away inside of a secluded house in the hills above Brentwood. I suppose Buster figured she'd have to come out at some point. Getting her out of the public limelight seemed a pre-eminent concern.

"Why is it risky?" I started.

"Grandpa's afraid I might say the wrong thing to the media."

"Uh-huh. Look, I need more information here. Maybe we can start at the beginning," I suggested. "The part about where you've been the past week. And why."

"I was at my grandfather's," she said, looking down at the linoleum.

"No, you weren't. Not the whole time. Tell me about Diego."

Molly Palmer clasped her hands on top of her head and continued to look at the floor. She didn't cry, but it seemed like she wanted to. She sat this way for a couple of minutes, then she spoke.

"My home life isn't so good."

I shook my head. I thought of my own home life at age 18 and tried to imagine how hers could be worse. Or even as bad. But everyone's pain is different.

"All right. But let's stick with Diego for a minute. What do you think happened?"

"I don't know," she said. "I really don't. I wasn't there."

"Any guesses?"

She shook her head no.

"But you were there last weekend. And someone said they'd kill you if you didn't leave."

She looked up sharply. "How do you know about that?"

"It's what I do. I find out things. Sometimes small things that need to be woven together to see the bigger picture. Tell me about it."

Molly let out a big sigh. "Diego's ex didn't want me around. She threatened me. She threatened Diego. I didn't want to go, but Diego insisted. Said I'd be safer somewhere else for a while."

"So you left. Who came and got you?"

"I drove."

"Stop lying," I said, this time a little more sharply. "You went to the Coliseum on Saturday with your friends. Afterward, you left with Diego. You don't drive. You had no car there."

"Yeah," she said, her mind seemingly racing. "I took one of those ride shares. Uber, Lyft. The one with the pink mustache on the front."

I shook my head. When a person wants to avoid speaking the truth, they'll often conjure up a semi-plausible explanation. When a sheltered teenager wants to avoid speaking the truth, the explanation can range from the doubtful to the ridiculous. But trying to get the whole truth out of Molly wasn't working right now. Time to move the conversation along.

"Okay. How about I take you back home to your mother now?" I suggested.

"Grandpa said no. And I don't want to be there, either."

"Why not?"

"I don't know," she shrugged.

"You've got to do better than that, or back home is where you're going," I told her in a more authoritative tone.

She looked at me, a bit crestfallen. "No. Oh no. Whenever my dad is home, my parents fight. A lot. And when it's just me and my mom, it's crazy weird. I'm tired of it. I want out."

"What do your parents fight about?"

"Mostly what a bad marriage they have. It's the same stuff over and over. They just replay it. One of them thinks the other is cheating. They just take turns making accusations."

"Are they true? Is one of them cheating?"

Molly shrugged and said nothing.

"Are both of them cheating?" I pushed.

She stared down at the ground again. "Like I said, it's

complicated."

I sighed. Such is life, but I acknowledged her life had special complications. I thought of telling her that her father cared enough to hire me to find her, and whatever issues she had with her mother might eventually blow over. The problem was I didn't know if any of that was true. But the concerns that seem huge at 18 frequently have a way of dissipating. Bad things often pass, or at least become manageable. Somehow, I didn't think this approach was going to work with her. Not right now. She had effectively left from home and didn't want to go back. And she didn't have to go back. At 18, she was technically an adult.

"So how is it I can help you?"

"Like I said. Grandpa thought you could find a place for me to stay for a week or so. Maybe a hotel or something. Until the election's over anyway. Then he said we can sort this out in private. He said he can't take care of this because he's a public figure and everyone knows him. Plus he's over 80. He shouldn't have to."

I took a deep breath. This was a high profile case, and this was a girl who needed help. Help that went beyond just having a place to stay for a while. And then I thought back to a case from more than five years ago, a case which ultimately cost me my LAPD badge. It was another young woman who needed help, a girl actually, a 17 year-old teenager. Her name was Judy Atkin and she was deeply lost, deeply troubled, and desperate in more ways than anyone should ever have to be.

Judy had been an orphan, had run away from an

abusive relative, and was arrested on prostitution charges. I did what no cop should ever do. I took her in with me, provided her a place to live and tried to give her a second chance. It didn't work. Judy went back to turning tricks, and when she was arrested again, she panicked. She lied and said she was working for me. The only reason I got out from under that nightmare was because she skipped town and never testified. But things couldn't go back to normal. My life and my career were forever altered.

I looked across my desk at Molly Palmer. She was the scion of a powerful political family, and had a secret she wasn't ready to share. The family wanted to use me, and I wasn't so comfortable with that. There were things I didn't know, and I didn't like not knowing things. Especially when I was being asked to hide the daughter of a sitting governor, who may or may not have played a role in two murders. I would need to inform Lally about her whereabouts. It was just a question of when.

"So your Grandfather thought I'd just take you in," I mused.

"Yeah," she shrugged.

I thought about options. I could put her up in a hotel, but that was a public venue and some enterprising employee would surely notify the media in exchange for a few dollars and a few seconds of face time on TV. I thought for a brief moment of bringing her home to our apartment in Santa Monica and quickly dismissed that idea. As kindhearted as my wife was, she was also an attorney, very smart, and able to smell an ethical problem a mile away. On top of that, Gail was pregnant, we were buying a house, and she had a lot on her plate. I certainly wasn't going to add another significant burden.

"Grandpa told me to give you this." Molly said, interrupting my thoughts as she reached into her pocket and handed me an envelope. Inside was a check made out to me for $10,000, signed by Buster Palmer. I reviewed it carefully. Everything seemed like it was on the level, and yet I knew there were big pieces of this story that were missing. I also knew it was just a matter of time before a few hard-nosed journalists started sniffing around my office.

And then I thought of someone. Someone I had known for years, a person who might be well suited to look out for the daughter of a politician. I hadn't talked with her in some time, but I had a feeling she might welcome the challenge. She had a lot of free time, and she knew something about politics and public personas. And while there weren't many people who could match the financial wherewithal of a Buster Palmer, I thought it was quite possible Crystal Fairborn could come close. Before entering politics, Crystal's husband had inherited a massive real estate empire. I picked up my phone and walked into the hallway to make the call. I was pleased to find her phone number was still stored in my contact list. I was even more pleased when she answered on the first ring.

"Crystal, good morning," I mustered in my most pleasant voice. "This is a voice from the past."

"How mysterious. Go on."

"It's Burnside. Detective extraordinaire. I hope you

remember me."

"Remember you? I don't think I'll ever forget you. And that's a compliment. Sincerely it is. How are you?"

I had come to know Crystal a few years ago, when my friend Wayne Fairborn, her husband, was running for mayor in our small coastal city. In the heat of that election, Wayne was murdered in his office. That crime proved to be one of the most traumatic and difficult cases I've ever investigated. The more I uncovered, the less I seemed to have known about the real Wayne. And the outcome was as unsettling as the case itself.

"I'm doing well," I said. "Very well."

"And Gail?"

"Even better. You know, we're expecting."

"Oh my! How marvelous. Congratulations. Please give her my love. She's such a wonderful person. I'll bet you're both thrilled."

"We are. I admit this was not a planned pregnancy, but I'm all in. Can't wait."

"That's so nice to hear. That just makes my day. You're going to be a great father."

"I hope so. I can't say as I've had much of a role model. Some stuff I'm going to have to make up as I go."

"You'll do fine," she said. "But I have a funny feeling you didn't just call to tell me that."

"Uh, no," I said. "Actually, Crystal, I need a favor. And if it's an imposition, please tell me. No worries if you're not up for this."

"All right," she said a little tepidly. "But it sounds a little intriguing. Everything you do seems to have a lot of excitement to it. And my life could use some right now."

"This will be exciting," I promised as I began to share the details. "I can assure you of that."

*

At one time, Crystal Fairborn lived right on the beach, in a house along Pacific Coast Highway. But it came as no surprise she now had a new address. I doubted she could go on living in the home she and Wayne had shared. Too many painful memories. She had since moved into a Craftsman home on Adelaide Drive in Santa Monica, across the street from the bluffs that overlooked the blue Pacific.

The homes on Adelaide Drive are a throwback to another era. Many were built before World War II, but subsequently remodeled and expanded. They were set back from the street and had large front lawns. They faced northwest, so they were treated to both a spectacular ocean view and a glorious look at the Santa Monica mountains. Years ago, I used to exercise on the 4th Street Stairs down the block from her. This involved running up and down a few hundred wooden steps that led into and out of Santa Monica Canyon. Back then, this was a hidden gem, tucked away on what was once a quiet street. Over the years however, the stairs became a workout hot spot, with dozens of people often lined up to partake. And it was not unusual to see a few celebrities mixed in with the crowd.

Crystal's home was actually a bit modest for the

neighborhood, meaning it was less than 5,000 square feet and did not have a swimming pool in the backyard. While Adelaide only stretched a few blocks from Ocean Avenue to 7th street, it was among the most expensive streets to live on.

We entered the property through a wrought iron gate, and walked up a winding pathway to the front door. I was about to ring the bell, but the door opened before I could push the button. Crystal had been expecting us and as we were quickly whisked inside. She glanced out front to see if there was anyone lurking. No one was. I had checked, too.

"It's been a while since we've seen each other," I said, giving Crystal a kiss on the cheek.

"Too long," she said, and then turned to my companion. "And you must be Molly."

Molly concurred with a cautious nod of the head. We moved across shiny hardwood floors and into a tastefully decorated living room, sitting down on one of two taupe couches that faced each other. A number of David Hockney paintings lined the walls, giving the room a bright splash of color.

"So tell me what the plan is," Crystal asked.

"Elementary, my dear. We keep Molly with you until the publicity starts to cool off and we can sort out what's best here. I'll need to tell her parents she's safe, but I won't tell them where she is. Molly knows she can't leave the premises on her own, which I hope won't pose a problem."

"I'm not going to run off again," Molly protested.

"I believe you. But I'm still keeping your iPhone."

Molly rolled her eyes. "That's my whole life in there."

"This will be a great experience for you. See what the world was like a few years ago. I don't pretend to know much about teenagers, but I do know they give in to temptation. That's why I'm keeping your phone."

"This poses an issue," Crystal said. "I can't spend every minute at home. And I don't want Molly to feel as if she's in prison. I'm not guarding her."

"I don't expect you to. And it's okay for you to go out with her, just be discreet. I'll be around a lot. But it's true, you might need someone else here. Someone who's, um, capable. Just in case."

"Oh. And you were thinking of ...?"

"Well," I said slowly. "I don't think we parted on such wonderful terms last time. But I do recall your father is quite an imposing man."

She gave a small laugh. "Yes and yes. And I'm sure he'd help. I just don't think I'll bring up your name right away."

Crystal's father was named Serge Markovich, a barrel-chested brawler, who laid tile for a living. He was about as quick to get into a fight as I was. He was not someone I wanted to tangle with. He was not someone anybody wanted to tangle with. Which, even at the age of 60, made him well qualified for this assignment.

"All right then," I said. "We have a plan?"

"I'll call my father. There's plenty of room here." Crystal turned to Molly. "Did you bring any clothes, honey?"

Molly shook her head no. "I've been a bit of a nomad this week."

"We'll change that. Gives us an excuse to go to Nordstrom's."

"I'm more of an Old Navy type girl."

We both stared at her. Molly got a little hesitant. "But I'll go wherever you want," she said, looking around. "You seem to have nice taste."

I turned back to Crystal. "Thank you for this. I didn't know who else to turn to."

"You mean you don't have a database full of wealthy women with large homes and time on their hands?" she smiled.

"No," I said. "Maybe I should put that on my to-do list."

I left Molly in the calm hands of Crystal Fairborn, promised to come back later in the day, and drove off. As I cruised down 7th Street, I called Bill Thorn. I thought of driving downtown, but I sensed this would be a short conversation.

"Hey, it's Burnside."

"Yeah?"

"I found that package your boss was looking for."

"Huh?"

I sighed. Maybe this conversation was going to take longer than I thought.

"I found Molly."

"Oh, really?" he said, the rising cadence in his voice indicating a newfound interest. "Where is she?"

"I can confirm she was at her Grandfather's home.

Until this morning."

"Cripes, tell me something I don't know. Half the LA media is parked outside of Buster Palmer's house. Where is she now?"

"Sorry. I can't pass that along yet."

"What?! The hell you can't, you dumbass gumshoe! I want to know where she is now!"

I smiled into the phone. "I want a lot of things."

"Are you kidding me? You're messing with the governor's daughter? You're hiding her? Do you know what kind of hell you're asking for?!"

"Tell me. Please."

"You don't get to hide Rex Palmer's kid!"

"I'm not hiding her. Molly's 18 and she's not a kid. She's doing this of her own volition. Well, sort of. Her grandfather wanted her out of public view. At least until the election is over. But I can assure you she is safe and being looked after."

A long pause permeated the call. Finally he spoke. "We're not done with this."

"No, we're not. There are some pieces to this puzzle still missing. I'll give you an update when I know more."

Another long pause and then a disconnect. Thorn was not pleased and I was sure the governor would not be pleased. I wasn't totally pleased myself, because there was something going on with Molly and with her parents and nobody would talk about it. I drove over to Nicole Palmer's house in Holmby Hills, but no one seemed to be home. I went through my numerous voice mails, but none needed immediate attention. I drove back to Santa

Monica and had a godmother sandwich at Bay Cities Deli. I headed to my office to stare out the window. Nothing caught my attention and nothing spurred my thinking. I debated the benefits of taking a nap. And then, just as I was starting to drift off, my phone rang.

"Mr. Burnside? It's Kristy. From Robinson Gardens? On Ellendale?"

"Ah, yes," I said, scrambling to think back to what was only yesterday. It seemed like much longer. "How's your screenplay coming?"

"Oh, fine. But I wanted to tell you something. Desiree is home right now. I heard her moving around in her apartment. This might be a good opportunity to catch her. If you have time."

Right now I had nothing but time. I told her I'd be right over. I went to the men's room, slapped a handful of cold water on my face, and headed downstairs to my Pathfinder. It was early afternoon and traffic on the 10 Freeway was light. I made it in 17 minutes. Not a record, but close.

I buzzed Kristy's number and she let me into the building. Walking up the two flights of stairs, everything seemed very quiet, as most students were in class. I walked by Kristy's apartment, which was open a crack. She peered out. I motioned for her to close the door. No sense letting Desiree know who was keeping tabs on her.

I tapped lightly on the door and a very pretty young African-American woman answered. She was shapely and looked every bit like she could be the hot girlfriend of a soon-to-be millionaire.

"Desiree. Hi. My name's Burnside. Can we talk for a minute?"

She frowned. "About what?"

"About Xavier. I was hired by the university," I said, handing her my card and knowing I was stretching the truth a little. Jeremy Hoffman wasn't exactly representing the university and I wasn't exactly hired by him.

"Oh," she said, hesitating.

"Can I come inside? This isn't something you'll want everyone to hear," I said, knowing at least one neighbor would take steps to hear everything.

"All right," she said and led me into her apartment. The living room was furnished with a blue couch, matching love seat, and a pecan and glass coffee table. Certainly nicer than the furniture I had as a student. I sat down on the soft couch and sunk a few inches. Hopefully I wouldn't need to jump up at a moment's notice.

"So you've filed charges against Xavier," I said. "For assault."

She pointed to her jaw which still had a few dark marks on it. "Hit me right there."

"Why did he hit you?"

She stared at me. "Xavier's a violent man who plays a violent sport. He also has trouble controlling himself."

That much was probably true. I knew from experience, football players were a different breed. They were quick to flame and many had anger issues. If not for football, some of them would be in regular trouble with the law. Some still were, but football gave them a socially acceptable outlet for their rage. The brutal actions a player took on the gridiron could earn them praise and plaudits. If they did the same thing on the streets they would surely wind up in jail.

"I had a friend in high school," I said, "who was a really good athlete. Ran track. But he said the worst week of his life was the one week he spent trying out for the football team."

"It's not for everyone," she agreed, definitively. "Thank goodness for that."

"There are players who have trouble separating their emotions when they're off the field. When things get tough for them on a personal level, they sometimes revert to warrior mode. It's what they know."

"That's Xavier. No control over himself."

"How long have you gone out with him?" I asked.

"Two years. We met during freshman orientation."

"He ever hit you before?"

She gave me a funny look. "Um, no."

"So what was different about this time?"

Her mouth opened slightly. "I don't know. Maybe something else was bothering him and he took it out on me. But he can't do that. It's just wrong to hit a woman."

"I agree," I said, and then tossed out a zinger to see where it landed. "But Xavier wasn't the one who gave you that swollen jaw, was he?"

"Whaaaa ..." she exclaimed, mouth open. "What do you mean?"

"I mean someone else hit you," I said, watching her carefully.

"No, no, it wasn't like that ... I mean, how would you

know? You weren't here."

"I know you and Xavier started arguing right when he came in the door. Wouldn't that be unusual if Xavier were having some other problem?"

She shook her head. "I don't know. Are you saying you don't believe me?"

"Look, I do know Xavier threw a punch or two."

"He sure did," she said, nodding her head vociferously.

"And Xavier left after he threw those punches," I said.

Desiree Brown stared at me. Her eyes grew wide, and I sensed there were tears forming. Getting caught in a lie is tough, and the more I saw, the more I was convinced she was not telling the truth. I had a vague idea what the truth might be, but I could only present a scenario and see how she reacted to it.

"Someone else was in the apartment with you," I continued.

"How do you know this?" she asked in a bit of a whiny voice, some of her defiance faltering, as a tear slid down her cheek.

"I just know," I lied, feeling the bravado start to turn into confidence. "You were hit all right. But someone else hit you. It wasn't Xavier."

Desiree lowered her head and walked away. Going into the kitchen for a moment, she returned with a tissue and dabbed her eyes. Her mouth was twisted into a weird angle as she tried to choke back more tears.

"What really happened?" I pushed.

"I ... I told you."

"No, you didn't. What really happened?"

"He ... Oh ... Xavier walked in on us. It was ... it was nothing, really. Just a guy who lived upstairs. His name's DeMarcus. But Xavier saw him and started making accusations. The guy stood up to Xavier. I knew that was a mistake. Xavier hit him. Knocked him down with one punch. DeMarcus got up and Xavier knocked him down again. Then Xavier turned to me and said we're done. And he walked out."

"So then you started arguing with DeMarcus about something."

"He said he was going to get Xavier. I didn't know what he meant. But when a guy gets punched in front of a woman, it's humiliating. I was afraid he would go after Xavier with a gun or something."

"Do you know whether DeMarcus owns a gun?" I asked.

"No, but look they're not hard to get. Least not in this neighborhood."

"Okay. Then what?"

"I said I was afraid he was going to get himself killed. Xavier has friends. Some really bad people. Anything happens to Xavier, they would take care of DeMarcus. That's how it works."

"So you tried to stop DeMarcus. And then he hit you."

Desiree looked down at the ground and the tears started to flow more freely. "I'm really ashamed," she sobbed in a halting voice. "I just didn't know what else to do."

"But why sign a complaint against Xavier? Why not

tell the truth about DeMarcus? In addition to breaking the law by filing a false police report, you could ruin Xavier's life. These are very damaging charges."

She took a few breaths. "I thought Xavier was gone for good," she managed, her voice quivering intermittently. "After this, I didn't think he'd want anything to do with me. I thought this was my one shot at getting him back in my life. I knew I could always drop the charges against Xavier."

This time it was my turn to take a few breaths. Xavier could go to jail, his career plans could go up in smoke, and all because his girlfriend didn't want him to leave her. Even if Desiree dropped the charges, anything besides a full and candid *mea culpa* would keep a stigma around Xavier forever, and could still jeopardize his pro football career. The NFL had different views on different infractions, not all of them fair. If a football player gets into a fight with another man, the actions are more lenient than if he punches a woman.

"You need to tell the truth," I told her. "There are serious consequences if you don't."

"I'd have to tell the police I lied to them," she whimpered.

"At this point, it's not about what you did. It's about what you do next."

"Do I have to press charges against DeMarcus?"

I considered this. "Not necessarily," I pondered. "He hit you, but there's no law that says you have to file charges. It's your choice. You have to decide if you want to pursue that."

"What if DeMarcus wants to go after Xavier?"

"I don't know. It's been more than a week without an incident, so that's a good thing. Nothing's happened to Xavier yet, but there's still some risk. And I have an idea about how we can keep a lid on this. But you have to promise to tell the police the truth about you and Xavier."

Desiree sat down. She had stopped crying and started thinking. A long minute passed. "If I do this, it probably means Xavier and I are over."

"Maybe so," I agreed, rising to my feet. "But you two could have been over anyway."

"I just don't understand all this," she shook her head. "How did you know?"

I shrugged. "I can sense when things don't seem to fit right. And I also had a little help here."

"I guess my life isn't going to turn out the way I had planned," she finally said.

"No one's life does," I said, suddenly remembering something Ms. Linzmeier's preacher had said the other morning. "You want to make God laugh? Just tell him your plans."

She gave a small chuckle, but it was attached to a painful wince. "I guess," she murmured.

"But you know, I can guarantee you something, and I promise you it's true. Coming clean is the best path to go down. Living a lie will eat you up inside."

I walked out of her apartment and the cool air hit me right away. I felt strangely sad at the turn of events. I wanted to dislike Desiree for what she did, but all I could do was feel sorry for her. She was young and naive and didn't know that every action could cause a reaction. Newton's laws went way beyond physics. I turned and headed down the hallway when a door opened and I saw another unhappy face. Kristy looked disappointed.

"I take it you heard everything," I said.

"Yes," she said, glumly. "I was hoping my movie would have more of a slam-bang ending."

I shrugged. That's show biz. Every day another heartbreak.

Twelve

The drive up to Hollywood took about 40 minutes in stop-and-go traffic. I arrived at Cliff Roper's office and allowed his cupcake receptionist to escort me into her boss's office. As usual he was on the phone. What was unusual was that he seemed glad to see me.

"Yeah, yeah," he barked into a headset as he nodded happily at me and motioned for me to sit down. "I know all about Dion and his drinking ... hey, who hasn't been pulled over for a DUI once or twice? Look, there's a first time for everything. And we all deserve a second chance, right ... yeah, that's what America's all about, second chances, the NFL should be about that too, my friend."

I sat down and swiveled on a comfy office chair facing a circular table. Roper sat behind his desk, drumming his fingers, waiting for the other party to finish their thought, so he could get on with his monologue.

"I think the league needs to be very careful how they handle these things ... no, I'm not telling you how to run your business. Hey, I'm just an agent, I wouldn't dream of it! ... Look, I once got nabbed for a DUI a long time ago. My father was an alcoholic, so it wasn't my fault ... I'll tell you something. I swore to my mother I wouldn't so much as look at another drink after that ... Yeah, of course it's true. I just want Dion to put this behind him. I think the League should too ... Okay, you let me know."

Roper flipped a button and took off the headset. "What a bunch of dopes," he said. "A guy can't even have a drink without risking his career these days."

"One of your clients, I take it."

"Yeah, guy's been a lush since he was 14. If he wasn't 6'8" and 320 pounds he'd be living under a freeway. Dion's 25 years old and this is his only shot to make a ton of cash. Most coaches would have given up on him by now. But his team is thin on O-linemen. And when you can pile protoplasm that high, it translates into money. I just need to convince the NFL to go easy on him."

"Sounds like it's not his first offense," I commented.

"Everyone deserves a second chance. In his case, he deserves a few of them."

"Ah. I forgot for a moment who I was speaking with."

"Don't get too cute," he warned, pointing a finger at me.

I laughed. Cliff Roper stood all of 5'3" but carried himself like he was a foot taller than anyone else.

"It's my nature," I said. "But I'm here with some news you'll probably like."

"My favorite kind of news," he replied, getting up from his desk and taking a seat next to me. "I'm clearing my calendar for the next 10 minutes. Go."

"That's big of you. And you'll pleased to know Xavier Bishop didn't hit his girlfriend."

"Tell me something I'm not aware of."

"I can tell you he did punch someone else."

Roper took a breath. "Did he now?"

"Upstairs neighbor was with Desiree. Xavier walked in

on them. The guy made the mistake of taking on a football player who can bench press 300 pounds. Xavier put him on the floor a few times and walked out. He never touched Desiree."

Roper processed this. "But someone hit Desiree. So it had to have been the neighbor."

"That's what she told me."

"And is that what she's going to tell the police?" he asked.

"I think I got her to the point where she'll admit her mistake. But this is where it gets tricky. The neighbor was assaulted by Xavier. He could press charges."

"Yeah, but the neighbor also assaulted Desiree. Which means if he files a complaint against X, Desiree could go file a complaint against him. Case closed."

"Not so fast," I said. "We haven't even talked to the neighbor. And from Desiree's description, he may still be upset about what happened. It's been over a week, but you never know about human nature. Some people stew in their own juices for a while before taking action."

"Okay, I'll buy that," Roper said, looking up at the ceiling. "Anyone taking on Xavier Bishop *mano a mano* can't have their head screwed on straight."

"He's a kid. Barely out of his teens. Their frontal lobes aren't fully developed yet. They don't always do the smart thing."

"And you want me to make sure he does the smart thing here," Roper said slowly, probably counting the amount of money he'd need to fork over.

"That's your call," I said. "I wouldn't dream of telling

you what to do. I just don't want you sending your goons around to threaten him. I'm just advising you there's a smart play here. Something that will make everyone happy."

Roper pondered this. "Making people happy. That's what I live for. How much do you think it's going to cost me to make everyone happy?"

"I have no idea. You're the expert on this," I said.

"Don't insinuate things," Roper warned. "So what's this guy's name?"

"You need to promise no one else gets roughed up."

"Sure," he sniffed. "I promise. With sugar on top. Now what's his name?"

"You know," I said, looking him in the eye, "if I tell you who he is, and anything goes haywire, your name may get dropped in the media here. And you know the NFL takes a dim view of agents tampering with college football players before they relinquish their eligibility."

"What?!" he snarled in outrage, leaning forward. "You're threatening me again? Let me tell you something. Nobody threatens me. I threaten other people. That's how it works."

"I'm trembling. You got anything else, besides bluster?"

He stared at me. "Why does everything have to be so hard with you? Everyone else thinks I'm a nice guy."

"I spent 13 years on the police force. I tend to see the worst in people," I said.

"Okay. Wonderful. I'll just talk to the guy. Maybe give him a warm handshake. That good enough for you? You want me to swear on a stack of bibles? On the eyes of my child?"

I nodded appreciatively. "His name's DeMarcus. Glad you're willing to cooperate."

Roper pulled out his iPhone and typed something into it. "So have you said anything to Jeremy yet?"

"Not yet. This type of arrangement falls outside the margins. I think you're better equipped to handle it. And more motivated. If Xavier goes pro after this year, you'll stand to make a lot of money as his agent."

"I'm not his agent," Roper said. "That's against the rules."

"Right. I keep forgetting who I'm talking to," I said and got up to leave.

*

As I walked through the building's subterranean garage, I called Crystal to check in. Molly had decided she needed to exercise, which of course necessitated a quick shopping run to buy workout clothes. The two of them then walked down the street to run the 4th Street Stairs. They had done two circuits and were about to do a third. They hadn't been recognized, but had wisely taken the precaution of wearing baseball caps, sunglasses and scarves. Crystal's father, Serge, was on the way, so things seemed in control. I told them I'd stop by later before I headed home.

There was still something bothering me about Molly's situation. Something she wasn't saying. I couldn't get much out of her, got nothing from her grandfather, and her father was too engrossed in a bitter political campaign to even return phone calls. Her friends were unlikely to talk to me. That left her mother, so I decided to head over to Holmby Hills for another surprise visit.

It was rush hour by now and the freeways were bound to be packed. I took Sunset the whole way, and even that route snaked slowly across the L.A. basin. After decades of delay, the city had finally started to build a light rail system throughout the region to ease the traffic burden. Millions of people had moved to Southern California over the years, many of them deciding to do so while watching USC play in the Rose Bowl game. When it's 70 degrees and sunny on January 1st, there are few places on earth that could be more appealing. The downside was that since so many people had moved here, the region's infrastructure was now being stretched to capacity. I shuddered to think that as a college football player, I had played a small role in all of this.

The last traces of a pink and gold sunset were still visible as I pulled onto the Palmers' street. It was mostly empty and very quiet. Soon, the crickets would be chirping. I was about to push the buzzer when I noticed the iron gate had not been fully closed. I slipped inside and saw a few squirrels playing with each other across the wide front lawn. They were cute, and it looked like they were having fun; it would have been nice if I could have gone over and petted them. But I recalled a nugget my Big Brother, the retired LAPD officer, had once uttered. That a squirrel is nothing more than a rat with nice packaging.

I rang the doorbell but there was no answer. A light was on upstairs, but that didn't guarantee anyone was there. There were, however, flood lights on in the backyard, and that was normally a good indication someone was home. I walked over to the side fence and stood on my tippy toes to see if I could attract anyone's attention. I heard voices and laughter. And I also saw some steam rising from the Jacuzzi. Trying the handle on the redwood fence door, it opened easily and I walked down a narrow stone path leading to the backyard. And that's when I saw them.

They were standing in the middle of the Jacuzzi, their arms wrapped tightly around each other. Their hands caressed each other's back and stroked the other's hair. The two of them were in the midst of a long, deep kiss, and completely unaware someone was watching. Their mouths separated and the two of them gazed into each other's eyes. They continued to touch and stroke each other and their breathing was heavy. They were also buck naked.

There are moments when a private investigator should step back from his job, and give people their privacy. I was not hired to investigate anyone's love life, and I generally didn't like playing the role of *voyeur*. And yet in this particular instance I had some trouble diverting my eyes from the couple. It was surprising in so many ways and also quite mesmerizing. Unfortunately I had stared at this scene for too long. Had I turned away and departed right when I saw them, they never would have noticed me.

I suddenly thought back to something from the other day, something ancillary to this case, something that perhaps only a red-blooded American guy might have remembered. It was trivial at the time, but not any longer. I had been correct in my assessment, although I didn't think I'd get to observe it in quite this way. And while Nicole Palmer was certainly attractive enough without any clothes on, I could now confirm, without any doubt, that Loretta Moss had one hell of a body.

"Who's there?!" Nicole Palmer called out loudly and climbed out of the steaming water.

I turned to leave but heard her call again, demanding that I wait. I gave myself two seconds before looking back. By then she had wrapped a towel around her torso and was walking quickly toward me.

"Hey!" she said as she approached me. "Who is it?"

I took a deep breath myself. "Sorry," I said. "I just came in to read the gas meter."

She stopped about 10 feet away from me. "You're that private detective Rex hired. Bernstein, was it?"

"Burnside. You were close."

"How did you get in here? And what the hell are you doing on my patio?!"

"You got me. I'm a Peeping Tom. But a word to the wise. If you're going to engage in a carnal embrace, you should really keep the gate locked."

"That's none of your damn business," she said. "It's my property. And it's my life, I'll do whatever the hell I like. And I don't need any of my husband's lackeys telling me what I should or shouldn't do."

And suddenly things became clear. Through the hazy steam and the surprising romance came the answer I had been wondering about. Rex Palmer was in a tight election and Molly Palmer had moved out of the house. Why would the governor's wife, a person with such a high public profile, allow herself to be found in such a wildly compromising position? The media had been camping outside Buster Palmer's house today, it was only a matter of time before they descended on Nicole's. She wouldn't have known how, she wouldn't have known when, but Mrs. Rex Palmer clearly wanted to be found out, caught, and placed squarely in the public eye. A politician's wife who drank too much and showed off too much was someone who wanted her husband to lose an election. I didn't know why and it probably didn't matter much. Nicole Palmer's prime concern was most likely that I wasn't from TMZ or the National Enquirer, and that I hadn't shown up with a video camera.

"So this is the secret Molly didn't want to share," I said. "And the one Buster wanted to hide."

"Yeah, so what? Are you homophobic? Or do you just like getting your rocks off watching two women?"

"I don't really care who your lovers are," I said, and this was true. Whether she liked men or women was a non-issue. As was my momentary fascination with them. The issue was what to do next. I was hired by Rex, overseen by his campaign staff, paid extra by Buster, and now in possession of some explosive scuttlebutt which could determine the next governor of California. And yet deep inside me, I knew the one person I needed to look out for here was a very troubled 18 year-old girl. Through no fault of her own, Molly Palmer was embroiled in this unusual episode.

"So then what are you going to do?" she demanded as Loretta Moss, now draped in a similar towel, quietly moved over to join us.

"I'm not totally sure," I said. "I feel as if I have multiple clients, and they're all part of your family. Your husband, your daughter, your father-in-law. Not to mention your husband's campaign staff. And they all have their own agendas. As do you."

"Oh, and what's my agenda?"

"To wreck your husband's political career," I said.

Nicole looked up at the early evening sky which was starting to get dark. Loretta Moss's eyes, however, were locked straight on me.

"That's quite an accusation," Loretta said.

"Thank you. It took a while to stitch it together. I obviously didn't think I'd be seeing you here. But now it makes sense why you were so unconcerned about Molly's absence. You knew she wasn't missing. Everyone knew she wasn't missing. Except maybe her father, who seems to have other problems to concern himself with."

"What are you going to do?" Loretta asked.

"Right now, I think Molly's grandfather had the best idea. Keep Molly out of public view until after the election, and then sort all this out. And the one thing I keep coming back to is that Molly is an adult now and can make decisions for herself. And one of those decisions is where she lives and who she lives with."

"She may be of age," Loretta said, "but I can assure you she is still a child. It's not healthy for a child to have to make that sort of decision."

"I know what's *not* a healthy situation for her to be in. It would be nice if Molly had two parents who wanted to be involved in her life. But that's not the case here. And that's why she was attracted to Diego. He didn't have much, but he had a loving family that wanted to protect him. They couldn't. I don't know who killed Diego or Sofia. But somehow Molly was connected."

"And just what are you saying?" Nicole demanded. "That she was involved in murder? That's outrageous."

"I'm not saying she did it. Just that there's a connection."

"You're insane."

"You wouldn't be the first to suggest that," I said. "But you're hardly a poster child for sane behavior."

Nicole's mouth twisted in rage. "I've had enough of this. And with you. Get out. Get off of my property or I'll have you arrested and jailed for trespassing. I can do that, you know. I'm still the first lady of California."

"All right," I said, knowing she could very easily follow up on that threat. "I'll leave. But one thing still bothers me. Neither of you have even asked if I know where Molly is. Or how she's doing."

Nicole shook her head. "She's with her grandfather. I'm sure she's fine."

At this point, I thought it might be best to let her believe that. It didn't appear her mother was worried, and I had a funny feeling she didn't really care.

I walked back to my Pathfinder and decided this would be a good time to check in on the women of Adelaide Drive. The traffic eased up on the way to Santa Monica, and I parked down the street from Crystal's house. Nobody answered the doorbell so I walked down the block to the 4th Street Stairs. I found them there, Crystal and Molly, sweaty, exhausted and smiling. They were neatly disguised, and had it not been for Molly's pink Old Navy baseball cap, I might have missed them entirely.

"Now there's two healthy-looking girls," I smiled. Both of them smiled back. It was the first real smile I had seen from Molly. It looked good on her.

Crystal spoke in halting words as she struggled to catch her breath. "Molly insisted we do five trips. Up and down. It's been a while since I've done this. My legs are going to be hurting tomorrow."

"Hate to tell you something."

"What?"

"No matter how much they hurt tomorrow, the second day's the worst."

"Lovely," she said. "I'll keep a bottle of Advil handy."

We walked back to Crystal's house. As we approached the gate, I noticed a light blue sedan parked in front of her house. No one was at the wheel. But the license plates clearly spelled out it was a Government vehicle. We quickly moved up the pathway and Crystal unlocked the door. As she did, a figure stepped out from the shadows. He was wearing a dark suit and tie, and holding a gun in his right hand. Bill Thorn motioned to the door.

"Let's take this inside," he said.

Thirteen

We moved slowly into the plush living room. Thorn relieved me of my .38 and we sat down on the two facing couches, Thorn on one, Crystal, Molly and I facing him on the other. Thorn put my gun in his suit pocket and tucked his own firearm away into a holster clipped to his belt.

"You must be pretty good at tailing," I started. "Didn't see you in my rear view mirror."

"One of my boys slapped a GPS device under your fender earlier today. At first I thought Molly was hiding out in that apartment building down by USC. I'll have to pull my surveillance team off of that detail."

"Unrelated case," I remarked.

"Yeah. But your visit to Nicole sure wasn't. She probably gave you quite a show."

"It wasn't what I had expected."

Thorn laughed. "I remember the first time I saw those two. They were going at it like weasels."

"You've known about this tryst for a while?" I asked, taking an awkward glance at Molly, who was paying no attention to our conversation, her eyes seemingly glazed over. "How widespread is this?"

"Not many people know," Thorn said. "Just a few. But they're close to Rex. Obviously we need to keep it that way."

"So what's the play here?" I asked. "Are you going to

take the governor's daughter by force?"

"No. It'll be just like the last time."

"Last time?"

"What? You think she hasn't done this before?" Thorn sniffed. "We usually pick her up at a classmate's house after she overstays her welcome. This time was different, she took off with that Diego kid and we couldn't find her."

"And that's why you hired me," I said.

"That's right, peeper. We've got more important things to do, in case you hadn't noticed."

"And that was you and Shelly who were talking to Diego down at Langer's."

Thorn stared at me. "What do you know about that?"

"Just that some suits were trying to twist Diego's arm into doing something he didn't want to do. It's starting to make sense now, although you guys were there about a week before Molly disappeared. So you weren't trying to find her then."

"What?" Molly suddenly exclaimed, staring at Thorn. "What were you doing talking to Diego? What were you talking to him about?"

Thorn shook his head. "It was nothing, kiddo. We were just trying to help things along."

"Helping things? How?"

"Look," he said, "your father's always had trouble courting the Latino vote. Shelly figured a high profile romance might make that constituency more *simpatico* toward him. Ever since Prop. 178 got passed, Latinos have hated Republicans in this state. Can't blame them really, it was a racist law. We were just trying to move them past that."

"By doing what?!" Molly shrieked. "Pushing me into a relationship with someone?! So it might help my father get re-elected? How stupid are you guys?!"

Those were my sentiments also. Every group has its share of people with boneheaded ideas they can't wait to implement. In most organizations, saner heads prevail, and these ideas never see the light of day. But in a tough election, throwing a Hail Mary pass like this one sometimes becomes an option.

"Look kiddo, your father's in an election ..." Thorn said.

"I don't care about my absentee father! Or my poor excuse for a mother! You had no business butting your nose into my personal life. This is such crap. I can't believe what I'm hearing. Your actions may have led to Diego being killed!"

Thorn shook his head. "That had nothing to do with us."

"You idiots! That had everything to do with you!" she screamed, and then threw her head in her hands and began sobbing. Crystal put her arms around her and stroked her hair. I got the feeling it might have been the first maternal touch she had experienced in quite some time.

I looked at Thorn. "Nice going there."

"Hey, bud, I just work for the governor and his staff. They decide this stuff," he said.

"And he brought his security chief in to talk with Diego?"

Thorn shrugged. "It's a bad neighborhood at night. Not so good during the day either."

At that moment, the sound of "America the Beautiful" went off. We all looked around. Sheepishly, Thorn pulled out his cell phone, slid his finger across it and spoke. "Yes, sir. Right. We've got her ... no sir, I can bring her in. All right, if you insist, sir ... yes, the house on Adelaide. I know. You have that rally tonight at the Javelin Club ... yes, it's nearby ... All right. See you in a few."

"Don't tell me," I said.

"Yes. The governor will be here soon. He wants to pick up Molly personally."

I turned to Crystal. "Well, you said you wanted something to perk up your life."

She nodded. "That old chestnut. Be careful what you wish for."

We sat in silence for a few minutes, Thorn looking at us, Crystal and I looking at Molly, and Molly looking down at the polished hardwood floors. The doorbell finally rang and Crystal got up to answer it. When she returned, Governor Rex Palmer was in tow. A somber look hung on his otherwise tanned and handsome face.

"Molly," he said, kneeling down next to her. "I'm glad you're okay."

"Get away from me," she hissed, not bothering to look up.

"Listen. Everything's going to be all right."

"It's not going to be all right," she said in a quivering voice. "It's never been all right. This can't be how life is supposed to be."

"I'll take you home."

"I'd rather be dead."

"You shouldn't say that."

"I wish I'd never been born then," she said, her voice rising a little. "I think Mom wishes I'd never been born, too."

"You don't mean that," he said.

"How do you know what I mean?!" she exploded. "How can you possibly know anything about me?! You've never been around! You just had me because you wanted to show everyone what a great family man you were. I'm not a prop that's put there to help you win an election!"

"I think we should go," Rex decided, taking Molly's hand. "We'll work all this out later."

"No!" she recoiled, jerking her hand away.

I stood up. "I'm sorry. This can't continue."

Thorn stood up, too. "You don't decide that."

"Let me get something straight," I said. "The governor wants Molly back with him. So he can show the world she's no longer missing, and what a great father he is, and how he can use her in the campaign. Photo ops, that kind of stuff?"

Rex Palmer shook his head. "That's a little extreme. The media has been camped out at her grandfather's house today. The world is looking for her. She has to make an appearance."

"The positive impact on your political campaign notwithstanding," I said, starting to seethe.

"I won't force her to do what she doesn't want to do. But we need to show the world she's all right "

"Won't force me?" Molly screamed. "That's what you said last time! And the time before that!"

I looked at Palmer. "I don't get this. You want her in the campaign. You want her to look happy. You want the world to see a loving father and daughter."

"What's wrong with that?"

"It's bull for one thing. But your own father wants her away from the campaign. He doesn't want the world to know anything. Your father's afraid she'll say the wrong thing in public. Maybe let something slip about Nicole's private life."

Rex's square jaw dropped. "Just what do you know about that?"

"Pretty much everything."

"And who do you plan to tell?" he demanded, placing his hands on his hips.

"I don't plan to tell anyone," I said evenly. "Unless an 18 year-old girl is forced to do something against her will. I don't care whether or not you're the governor, but my sixth sense tells me this isn't the way to be a father."

Rex Palmer glared at me. "I don't pretend to have a perfect marriage. And Buster and I often disagree on things. But one thing should be perfectly clear. I'm her father and you're not. You don't get to decide where she goes."

"That's right," I said, and then pointed to Molly. "She does."

Palmer glanced over at Thorn and made a small motion with his head as if to say it was time to end this conversation. Thorn walked over to me without hesitation.

"She doesn't get to decide this one," Thorn said. "Not now."

Molly didn't move. I stared at Thorn and thought back to an old, old saying. If not now, then when. If not us, then whom. I didn't like how this was going. I didn't like that the governor was sending his staff in to spark a teen romance for their own benefit. I didn't like that a young woman was being used as a pawn to help pimp her father's re-election campaign. I didn't like that I was now working for two members of the Palmer family, each with a different agenda, and demanding different things. And I really didn't like Bill Thorn.

"Molly's not going anywhere," I said. I might not be governor of the state, but I could control my little corner of it. I looked Thorn up and down. He was older than me, but he was about my size and struck me as very fit. And as a former cop, he was not someone to take lightly. All the more reason to get this over with quickly.

Bill Thorn sighed as he started to reach back into his holster. For some reason he thought I wouldn't anticipate it. I reared back and launched an overhand right that landed flush on his jaw. The punch spun him around and sent him down on one knee. For an odd moment I thought of Xavier Bishop and wondered if I could still hit as hard as an all-American cornerback. Thorn started to rise, so I took a step and delivered a solid left to his nose and heard him yelp in pain. He shook his head and looked like he was struggling to maintain consciousness. I stood back for a moment, something you should never do until a conflict has been fully and conclusively decided.

Seemingly out of nowhere, Thorn sprung forward and slammed his fist into my abdomen. He had done a good job of playing possum and it caught me by surprise. The blow knocked the wind out of me and I went down on one knee. I ducked my head and he clubbed me a few times around the neck and shoulders, not doing any real damage, but it was certainly not something I relished. It did give me a moment to plan my next move. I gathered my strength, took a deep breath and shoved my fist deep into his groin area. This time his yelp wasn't cagey, but rather tinged with agony. Mouth open, he fell to the ground, holding his private parts and writhing on the ground.

He stayed that way for a few seconds, which gave me more time to gather myself. But then his hand began to slowly move toward his holster. Either Thorn was a great actor or one tough *hombre*. Maybe both. He drew his service revolver before I could get to him. Still laying on the ground, he pointed the weapon at me in a shaky hand, his teeth clenched, his breath coming in spurts. But before I could decide my next move, a large, hulking figure came up behind him. With a fist the size of a country ham, Serge Markovich hit Thorn viciously on his forearm. The gun fell from Thorn's hand and clattered on the floor. Thorn rolled over in pain and I was fairly certain he wasn't faking this time. I reached down and quickly grabbed the weapon. With my other hand, I reached into his suit pocket and retrieved my .38.

"Nice to see you again," I said to Markovich. It had been three years since our last encounter, but Crystal's father appeared to be every bit as vibrant and bulky.

Markovich looked back at me. "You throw big punch," he boomed, nodding appreciatively.

"Coming from you, I'll take that as a compliment."

"No person being should enter someone's home and behave like this," he said, and pointed at Palmer and Thorn. "You two have poor manners."

Rex Palmer's mouth was wide open. Clearly, this wasn't how he figured things would go. Finally he spoke, attempting to assert his control over a situation that had gone far beyond what he had anticipated.

"This doesn't change anything," Palmer snarled.

"No, it doesn't," I agreed. "The girl stays."

"You won't get away with this," Palmer said. "I can have a dozen Santa Monica police officers here in a matter of minutes."

"That would make a good story," I said. "The cops try and take a young woman against her will. The *Times* will put that one on the front page."

Molly glared at her father and spoke in a low but controlled voice. "Dad, if you go through with that, I swear to God I will tell the world everything I know and everything I've seen. About you and about mom. I'm sick of this shit and I want out."

Palmer surveyed the scene, looking at Molly, looking at me and looking down at Thorn. There was nothing he could really say at this point, nothing he could do to mollify his daughter's anger. Reality seemed to be dawning on him. He had lost his wife to a woman, he was losing an election to an immigrant, and he'd quite possibly lost the love of his daughter. As wealthy as he was, I wouldn't want to be in his shoes right now. But we do reap what we sow. And Rex Palmer's decisions, from marrying a woman he didn't love, to having a child because some people thought that was the right thing to do, to listening to bad advice from ambitious campaign consultants, were now coming back to haunt him.

Crystal walked over to me. "So what happens now? I gather this wasn't exactly part of the plan."

"He won't bring the police. But I think I'll need to call my guy at the *Times*. Just to be safe. In case I need to get our side of the story out."

"Don't worry," she said. "I have a few contacts in the media, too. I have Wayne to thank for that."

"Are you okay with looking after Molly for a few more days, maybe a week or so?"

"Sure," she said. "I like her. She needs someone to talk to and I might be someone who could help. At the very least I can listen, and that's a start. And after what I went through, I know a number of very good professionals who can help her."

"I appreciate that," I said. "And I wish I had called you more. Life, work, it adds up to busy days."

Crystal waved her hand. "Don't even think about it. But it does get a little lonely here. Wayne and I kept talking about starting a family, but, you know, that never happened. Spending some time with Molly will be fine. In fact, this might be good therapy for both of us."

"I do feel the need to apologize," I said to her. "I had no clue these guys would turn up, or a brawl would ensue in the middle of your home. I wouldn't have brought you in on this if I thought it would be dangerous."

"That's all right," she remarked with a slight smile. "Life is always exciting when you're around. I will say that."

*

Rex Palmer strode silently out the door, and I followed him to make sure he didn't come back. But there was no hesitation in his gait. He went directly into one of the light blue sedans now double-parked on Adelaide. The car sped off and I went back to tend to Thorn. Helping him up, I escorted him to the door and asked him if he needed any medical attention. He told me to go fuck myself. I took that as a no.

Leaving Molly and Crystal in the massive, capable hands of Serge Markovich, I drove back home. It was less than half a mile away, but it felt like another world. There was nothing wrong with my neighborhood. Living at 4th and Montana was a very desirable place, the apartment buildings were kept up nicely, the neighbors were friendly. And we were a mere three blocks from the bluffs overlooking one of four oceans in the world. But it was not Adelaide Drive. I thought of the house Gail and I were buying. It was a modest house in a middle-class neighborhood. But it's where we'd start raising a family, and I've always believed a home is what you make of it.

It was a little past 8:00 p.m. when I walked into our apartment. Gail glanced at her watch and joked I was home early for a change. She was about to give me a kiss when Chewy jumped up and beat her to it.

"My two favorite girls," I said and gave Gail's belly a soft rub. "I wonder what will happen if there's a third girl on the way."

"You will be seriously outnumbered, my dear," Gail told me. "Tread carefully."

"I've learned a lot about young women this week. Young men, too. Some of it good, some not. And I've learned a lot about parenting. Mostly what you shouldn't do."

"I can't wait to hear," she said, and we sat down on the couch. Chewy tried to jump in between us, but I pushed her away. She glared at me, walked to the edge of the couch and curled up into a ball.

"Looks like I'll need to make amends with someone," I said, looking over at the furriest member of our family.

"She'll be fine, she lives in the moment. Doesn't harbor grudges."

"Good to know."

"So tell me about your day."

"Oh, my," I started and detailed my past two days. My encounters with Desiree Brown and Xavier Bishop. And Kristy the screenwriter. With Riley Joyner and Connor Pierce and Alex Gateley. And of course, the elusive Molly Palmer. I talked about how they handled things when the pressure got cranked up. And I thought of my own experience when I was 18. This was a topic I had always skated around with Gail, but after my chat with Buster, it was now about to surface. Gail had never pushed me to talk about it, I guess she figured I'd tell her when the time felt right. And that time was now.

It wasn't a surprise to Gail that my youth was radically different than the kids I was investigating this week. Molly and her friends were children of privilege, sent to fine schools, raised by parents who could afford luxuries. But adversity touches everyone. It is like an invisible cloud that floats nearby, wafting in and enveloping you every now and then. You can't avoid it, you can only deal with it. Life makes sure of that.

Gail knew my father had died before I was born, and my mother went back to school to become a nurse. I had told her that my mother had later died, but I didn't tell her how or when. I didn't like to talk about it. I didn't like to think about it. But this was a week where I was dealing with teenagers, schools, parenting and death. And it all just crystallized when I thought back to the summer right before I enrolled at USC.

Everything had started off so nicely. I graduated from high school in early June, the weather was warm and life was easy. I had been granted a full scholarship to play football at USC that fall, so my future seemed secure. A few times a week I went onto the SC campus to hit the weight room and run on the track. I met a few other incoming freshmen and we became friends. I worked a few times a week at Dodger Stadium to earn spending money. It was an easy job and a fun job. I got to see baseball games for free, and what could be better than serving people soda and ice cream on a warm night. It was good exercise and I made some new friends there, too.

But then everything changed. My mother had been feeling unwell for a few months, mostly fatigue and some body aches. In the beginning of July, she began to complain about a pain in her back when she breathed deeply. She thought it was a virus and assumed it would go away. But one morning I woke to see her lying on the floor, struggling to breathe. I called paramedics and they rushed her to the hospital. After she was stabilized, doctors did a chest X-ray and identified a mass on her lung. They ran a PET scan to determine how widespread the cancer was and it lit up like a Christmas tree. There were tumors riddled throughout her body. The doctors said her only option was chemotherapy, something my mother chose to decline. Having spent many years as a nurse, she had seen that chemo wasn't a cure. She felt it was too barbaric, that it didn't prolong life, it only prolonged pain. I spent the next few weeks at her side, helping her and comforting her, but she went quickly. She died during the second week of August.

I talked some more about my mother, as Gail sat next to me and stroked my hand. "Was there any other family nearby?"

"No. My mother was an only child, just like me. My grandparents had passed away a few years earlier. My father had a couple of sisters, they lived back in Nebraska. They offered to let me come live with them. They were very kind. I actually went back to visit during Christmas that year, but I knew I didn't belong there. The people were nice. Salt of the earth. But the climate was very cold in the winter and it struck me as a bit desolate. And I didn't know anyone. I had a few friends whose families moved here from Nebraska. They told me the water flowed just one way; nobody moved back there once they lived in California. I figured there was a reason."

"So you started college right after your mother died."

"Yes. The timing was odd. My life was at a crossroads. One door closing and another opening. But once classes started and football practice began, I had a means to channel my thoughts away from my pain. I could focus on something else. And in a sense, USC became my surrogate family."

"That can make for a strong bond."

"It did. And I knew that as bad as it had been for me, I was being blessed with an opportunity. And I made sure I didn't mess it up. I had a full scholarship, which meant my tuition, room and board were covered. When I wasn't practicing, I was studying, working out, or sitting in the film room, trying to figure out how to be a better player. I avoided trouble like the plague. I don't think I went to a single party my freshman year. I chose my friends carefully. But it paid off. I was a four-year starter and earned my degree. And maybe just as importantly, I learned the value of hard work and stick-to-itiveness. I learned that through adversity can come strength. And hard work really can be its own reward."

"Wow," Gail said. "You never shared that story about your mom with me. I'm glad you finally did."

"This week taught me a few things. It's easy to become a parent. But it takes some doing to become a good one. There's a lot of things that can go wrong."

"It sounds like you did right by Molly Palmer. And it sounds like you got Desiree Brown pointed in the proper direction."

"Yeah. Molly will be okay in the long run. She's at least facing her pain. Maybe Desiree, too. I think I got through to her. But it's not like everything I've been working on is cleared up."

"How's that?"

"Diego Garcia. And his girlfriend Sofia. Two teenage kids are dead and the people who did it are nowhere to be found. The police have nothing to go on. No leads, no clues. If Molly hadn't had an involvement with Diego, their deaths wouldn't have even made the newspaper. It just feels wrong."

"Sometimes you can't solve every case," Gail said. "There's only so much you can do."

"I know. But I think about the parents. Their lives are shattered. I know what it's like to lose a parent, as a teenager. I can't imagine being a parent and losing your child. I don't know how a parent could possibly recover from that. It scares me."

"Because we'll be parents soon?"

"Yes. I worry about things. Being on the job, I saw the bad side of life. I know that's not the reality for everyone. Or even for most people. But it's hard to put aside those thoughts and fears. Juan Saavedra moved his family down to Orange County, hoping for a better life for his kids."

"That's always an option," Gail said. "But let's give Mar Vista a shot. It's nice there. Maybe one day we can afford to own in Santa Monica."

"Sure," I said. "And maybe one day you might become governor."

"Well," she answered, "It sounds like that job has some room for improvement."

*

I slept fitfully that night. Nothing seemed to relax me, and my abdomen still hurt from Bill Thorn's punch. At 5:00 a.m. I gave up and got out of bed, went to my desk and combed through the news on the internet. No one had actually seen Molly Palmer, but reports from her grandfather said she was doing just fine. The latest polls were out and Justin Woo now had a six-point lead over Rex Palmer. USC's football team had arrived in Seattle to play the University of Washington later that evening. Nothing about Xavier Bishop or Desiree Brown was in the papers. I texted Virgil Hairston and told him I had a few things I wanted to discuss with him. And then at 5:30 a.m. I heard the voice of the preacher with the Southern twang. He talked about how if you were honorable, and took care of the ordinary things in life, God would take care of the extraordinary. I listened for a while, and wondered how people could maintain that type of faith. Having seen some of the truly ugly parts of our society, I had difficulty being a true believer.

I spent the weekend at home, cocooning with Gail and playing with Chewy. I had finally been able to teach our puppy how to fetch. When we first got her, I would throw a tennis ball across the living room and she would just turn and look at it. Then she would look quizzically back at me. Finally, after numerous demonstrations, the process began to sink in. I tossed the tennis ball to the other side of the room, she ran over and picked it up with her mouth and ran back to me. Except she stopped about three feet away. When I got up to take it from her, she began to trot over to the other side of the living room. She understood the game of fetch, but hadn't learned to give the ball back. Instead, we had a new game; she would hold the ball and I would get to chase her around the apartment. It was clear who was running the show here.

Gail went off to have tea with a friend, and Chewy and I spent Saturday afternoon watching the USC game. It was an offensive display, as both teams moved the ball effortlessly up and down the field. Washington uncorked pass after pass downfield, torching the depleted USC secondary and picking on Xavier Bishop's replacement mercilessly. Norris Colby was only a freshman and he'd hopefully get better. But today was a rough outing for him as the receiver he was covering caught three touchdown passes. In the end, USC couldn't hold on to a 38-34 lead late in the game. A Washington touchdown pass with 30 seconds left wound up sending the Trojans down to a 41-38 defeat.

The cameras panned Johnny Cleary throughout the game, and vividly captured the frustration on his face. As a former star cornerback, Johnny knew what his defense needed to do, but they just couldn't respond. He tried double coverage but the Washington quarterback simply found a receiver being covered one-on-one. Johnny tried to blitz the linebackers but the Washington offense was ready with a safety valve. He tried having his defensive ends run stunts where they moved laterally before rushing the quarterback through the A-Gap between the guard and the center. Nothing worked. Some days the deck seems stacked against you. A great team can overcome this, but numerous injuries, and Xavier's suspension had taken its toll on USC today. Stanford would be coming to the Coliseum next week, and the winner of that game would likely wind up playing in the Rose Bowl game on New Year's Day.

I flicked the remote and the TV went off. Chewy, who had dozed off at the start of the 4th quarter, jerked her head up, suddenly alert. I tossed a tennis ball across the living room, but she just watched it sail by and then looked back at me. Even my cocker spaniel wasn't up for playing today.

Gail offered to buy me a consolation dinner, but I wasn't really in the mood to go out and I knew a crowded restaurant would be difficult for her. We ordered a pizza, stayed home and talked about the logistics of moving once our escrow closed in the coming week. We planned out where we'd put the furniture, developed a checklist of all the things we'd need for the nursery, and I had my to-do list for the next day. Gail's colleagues had thrown her a shower but there was still a lot we needed. There was a local baby store in West LA, and I filled the Pathfinder to the limit with a bassinette, stroller, glider, car seats, diapers and things I had never heard of before. Fortunately, Gail seemed quite knowledgeable about this area. As I paid the enormous bill with a credit card, I thought of the $10,000 check from Buster Palmer sitting in my wallet. It didn't feel right to cash it, but I wasn't ready to give it back yet. Thankfully, the due date for the credit card bill would be a few weeks away.

I unloaded everything into what used to be my home office and was now a cluttered storage bin. There was still room for me to sit at my desk, but just barely. I called Crystal, and everything was fine on Adelaide Drive. There had been no further contact from the Palmer family or the Palmer campaign since our confrontation on Friday night. And Crystal and Molly were starting to connect. They spent the weekend binge-watching the first two seasons of *The Big Bang Theory*, and taking a few walks in the neighborhood. Carefully dressed, Molly went unrecognized. Maybe by this point, people had the good sense not to care.

I wondered why I hadn't heard back from Virgil Hairston. I texted him again before dinner and then left a message on his voice mail a few hours later. But it wasn't until the next morning that he returned my call.

"Burnside. I'm sorry I haven't gotten back to you. I should have, but my cell phone battery ran out and I had no way to charge it."

"Are you away for the weekend?" I asked.

"No," he said, his voice the epitome of seriousness. "I've been in town, but I've spent most of my time in the hospital."

I frowned. "I'm sorry. Did you get sick?"

"No, no, it's not me. I guess I'm surprised no one from

the police department called you about this."

"What do you mean?" I asked.

"There was a hit-and-run yesterday. Broad daylight, too. It wasn't an accident."

"Wait a minute. Who was hit?"

"It was Adam Lazar. Someone ran him over with an SUV. Just plowed right into him and kept going. He's here at Saint John's. Arizona and 21st. He's stable now, but he was in critical condition for most of the weekend."

Fourteen

There are few hospitals as beautiful as Saint John's Health Center in Santa Monica. The complex is an architectural masterpiece. The main building showcases a curvilinear shape from the outside and a spectacular atrium on the inside. During daytime hours it is flooded with light, and numerous pieces of art hang from the wood-paneled walls. As you walk through the patient section, the curved hallways only allow you to see a few rooms at a time. It is an interesting design and it must have cost a fortune to build.

Adam Lazar was sitting up in bed by the time I arrived. His right arm was in a sling, and his face had bruises. His right leg was bandaged and raised upward. The TV was on, tuned to the local news. He was awake and he was alert.

"Good morning," I said.

Lazar nodded in recognition. "Burnside. Nice of you to come."

"How are you feeling?"

"Oh, wonderful," he answered. "After breakfast, I'm going to run a marathon."

"Glad you haven't lost your caustic wit."

"It'll take more than this," he said. "I always knew I would tick a few people off with my work. Comes with the territory."

"I spoke to Virgil this morning."

"Yeah, he was a real trooper. Nurses said he spent the better part of the weekend with me. I was out of it until last night, though."

"Where did this happen?" I asked.

"Outside my house. I live near Echo Park, not too far from downtown."

"I know where it is," I said. Echo Park was an area I drove through regularly when I worked at Dodger Stadium. It was also close to the LAPD Academy. Echo Park was an eclectic neighborhood that included hiking trails and shooting ranges, upscale coffee houses and bars that served craft beers. There was a nice, man-made reservoir lined with palm trees, perfectly safe during the day, less so at night. It was a community where hipsters and artists coexisted with gang members and working class folk. Realtors had been calling this a transitional neighborhood for as long as I could remember, and they didn't know which direction it would ultimately pivot. Quite possibly, Echo Park would simply stay the way it was.

"Why'd they take you all the way over here?"

Lazar shrugged. "I don't know. Something to do with the insurance, I guess."

"Were you targeted?"

"Was I targeted?" he asked incredulously. "Of course I was targeted. Why else would anyone go out of their way to hit me at 8:00 a.m. on a Saturday morning?"

"Okay, I'm sure you're right" I said, trying to be sympathetic while playing devil's advocate. "But how do you know it wasn't an accident?"

Lazar gave an exasperated sigh and hit the mute button on his remote. "Look," he said, turning to me. "I walked out of my apartment and crossed the street. Looked both ways, just like they teach you in 1st grade. Maybe I should have been holding an adult's hand."

I showed him two palms face up. "I didn't mean to upset you," I said.

"You can't upset me any more than I already am. When I was in the middle of the street, I heard someone gun their engine, and I heard tires squeal. I think I saw it out of the corner of my eye and then *ka-boom*. Witnesses said it was an SUV. The only person I know who owns one of those gas hogs is you. And I don't think you hate me that much to run me down."

"No, certainly not."

"I just had no time to react. Couldn't jump out of the way. The one saving grace was they didn't have much time to build steam, so they weren't going all that fast. They must have been parked there, waiting for me."

"Any thoughts on who did it? Anyone at all?"

"Lazar shrugged. "Like I say, I'm a journalist and I've ticked off a lot of people. Could have been anyone. I know the people who work for Governor Palmer weren't happy with me. Wouldn't be the first time a political leader tried to silence a critic."

"Probably not," I mused. "What were you wearing?"

"Gray hoodie and jeans. Why?'

"Might mean something. You mentioned there were witnesses."

"Just a couple of local *cholos* hanging out on the street corner. They corroborated my story."

"They said it was an SUV?"

"Yeah, that's what they said. An SUV. A black one. Didn't mean much. Gotta be thousands of black SUVs in L.A. I mean cripes, you've got one."

"Yeah," I said, thinking this through. "But I might have an idea who did this."

Lazar stared at me for a long moment. "Wow. Do SUV owners have some sort of a freaking club you all belong to?"

*

I approached the entrance to the Stone Canyon School and came upon the same security guard who was at the post last week. But instead of smiling and graciously waving me in, he held up his hand and took off the wire-rimmed sunglasses. He was not smiling.

"Dropping something off for your daughter, are you?" he asked in a snotty manner that told me my cover had somehow been blown.

"Not exactly."

"State your business," he ordered.

"So you think I was lying to you last week?" I asked.

"What's your daughter's name?" he demanded.

I watched him and decided to see how far I could push the envelope. "Riley Joyner. If she's not in class, she's usually practicing volleyball."

"Riley Joyner" he parroted. "That's a good one. It

worked for a while, huh?"

"All right. What gave me away?"

"Nothing really. Just that article in the *Times* the other day. Ms. Moss told us to be on high alert for outsiders. Everyone has to show ID."

"I left my driver's license at home."

"Sure. Only problem is Riley's dad just dropped her off a little while ago. Dr. Joyner didn't forget his driver's license. He also had Riley sitting next to him. Dead giveaway."

"I guess you're not going to let me in today."

"Scram," he sneered and jerked his thumb towards the road. "I don't know what crap you're trying to pull here, but I better not see you around this place again."

I gave him a small salute as I turned my vehicle around and headed back down the narrow canyon road. I pulled off at the first intersection and parked in front of a house, shrouded in the front by bright red bougainvillea.

I wasn't entirely certain which trail Adam Lazar had taken to enter the school grounds, but I sensed it couldn't be too far away. I walked up the street and saw a small dirt pathway that led into a wooded area. I was sure I was trespassing on someone's property, but that hadn't stopped Lazar. And like Lazar, I slipped on a wet patch of grass and ensured my pants would be making an appearance at the dry cleaner's this week.

After a 10 minute hike, I reached the back end of the Stone Canyon campus. I moved purposefully across the grounds, acting like I was just another parent or teacher with a specific place to go. And I did have a destination, I just didn't know how to get there. I finally came across another middle-aged man and I stopped him with a wave and a smile.

"Hello," I beamed in my best rich dad voice. He gave me the once-over and offered a puzzled expression in return. "I'm looking for the parking lot," I said. "My daughter's new here and I'm a bit lost."

"Oh, certainly," he said and pointed across the soccer field. "Just past the west goal."

"Thanks."

"Say, you must have taken quite a wrong turn," he said, looking at my pants.

"Um, yes," I said, my mind racing. "Actually that happened earlier this morning. Helping the gardener plant some trees on my property. We hired a landscape architect, and well, he thought the bonsai trees would look good next to the deck."

"Oh," he laughed. "Of course."

We parted and I headed across the soccer field. I started feeling good. This rich dad thing wasn't too difficult if you knew the right line to deliver. I reached the parking lot and began walking up and down the rows, keeping one eye out for a black SUV and the other for any security personnel who might be surveying the premises. With video cameras omnipresent, I needed to work fast.

There were over a hundred vehicles in the parking lot, but it only took a couple of minutes before I found the one I was looking for. The black Escalade was parked near the back of the lot. I went to the front end of the vehicle and inspected the grill. Sure enough, the grill was badly scratched and there were small dents in both the front bumper and the hood. I looked underneath and saw a piece of blue denim attached to the underside of the vehicle. This all but confirmed it. Alex Gateley had been in Echo Park on Saturday morning.

As I walked around the vehicle, I saw something else. Something I did not expect to find. I wasn't sure what to make of it at first. Parked next to the Escalade was a silver Toyota Prius. Nothing unusual about that, there had to have been six or seven in this parking lot alone. But this Prius had something a little different. A smashed tail light. And while that alone didn't make it special, there was more. Just underneath the tail light, and not easily seen unless you were looking, were three bullet holes.

I pulled out my phone and quickly found Dennis Lally's number. Fortunately, he picked up.

"Lally."

"Good morning, detective. This is Burnside. Remember me?"

"Oh, of course. I always remember P.I.'s that ask lots of questions and don't provide any answers. I'm sure you're probably looking for more favors, right? Best to call Juan for that. I'm fresh out."

"Nope. I'm actually calling to help you. I'm pretty sure I can lead you to who killed Diego Garcia. And probably Sofia too. Interested?"

"Keep talking."

"I'm here at the Stone Canyon School. In the parking lot. The shooter's car is sitting here. A Toyota Prius, silver, license plate 6XYY661. That's six, x-ray, young, young, six,

six, one. Has a smashed right tail light and at least three bullet holes underneath it."

"Let me run the plates and I'll come down. I guess you really were on the job. You know the lingo."

I laughed. "Just don't take a Code Seven on me right now."

"Geez. Always with the smart remarks. You sit tight over there."

The parking lot was next to an area with a few trees and benches. I sat down and tried to make myself as inconspicuous as possible, while keeping an eagle eye on the area. A few more vehicles pulled in. But after 15 minutes, a tall, lanky student approached the Prius and unlocked it. Trotting over quickly, I yelled out his name. Connor Pierce turned to face me.

"Classes over for the day?" I asked.

He looked at me quizzically. "You're that private detective guy."

"Good memory. Where you going?"

Connor shrugged. "Getting a caffeine buzz over at Starbucks. Want anything?"

"Nice of you to offer," I said, drawing my weapon and pointing it at him. "But you can't leave the campus."

He stared at me. "You're pulling a gun on me again? What is this?"

"I think you know. Those bullet holes in the back of your car. The smashed tail light. You were the one who killed Diego Garcia. And my guess is Sofia, too. The only unanswered question is why."

"I ... I didn't do anything," he managed.

"That line doesn't work, kid. We have evidence."

"It ... it was Alex. I was just the driver. He pulled the trigger."

"Nope. Nice try. I give you credit for creativity, even if it means throwing your friend under the bus. But the eyewitnesses were very consistent on something. Only one person was in the car. And the driver was the one who did the shooting."

"This ... this is crazy," he choked.

"It sure is, kid. But why did you do it? I'm not the police," I said, wondering what he'd do with the next line. "You can tell me."

Connor Pierce leaned against his car and stared off into the distance.

"Was it about Molly?" I asked.

He nodded yes, his mouth drawn very tight.

"Diego was seeing her," I continued.

Another affirmative nod.

"And you didn't like it."

Conner Pierce's breathing grew deeper and more uneven. His chest heaved.

"Why did you do it, Conner?"

A few more deep breaths. Finally he started to speak. "That little prick. He didn't belong here."

"At this school?"

"This school, this city, this country. None of them do. Why don't they just go back to where they fucking came from? This is our country. They're taking spots in our schools, taking jobs. Now they want to take our girls, too? Fuck him. Fuck all of them."

I took this in. "And Sofia? Diego's old girlfriend? Why'd you have to shoot her, too?"

More deep breathing. Connor's chest was beginning to heave. I wasn't sure if he was going to cry or maybe run. I stepped back in case he decided to bull rush me. Even with a gun in their face, I've seen desperate people do desperate things. I hoped I wouldn't need to fire my weapon. But I also needed some answers.

"Do you really have so much hate in you? So much that you would shoot an unarmed girl? And it wasn't like you pulled the trigger just once. Sofia was shot multiple times. She was shot out of anger."

His eyes looked a little wild as he gave me a piercing glare. "Diego was asking for it. And that girl? She actually said she'd kill Molly. I wasn't going to let that twat get away with threatening her. Not here, not now. Not ever. This is still America."

I didn't say anything more. Nothing more was needed. I ordered him to get down on his knees and clasp his hands behind his neck. I continued to point my gun at him, and said I really would shoot him if he tried anything. About five more minutes went by before a dark sedan pulled up, followed by four LAPD patrol cars. Detective Lally popped out of the sedan and I quickly holstered my weapon. I approached and spoke with him briefly, before leading him to the silver Prius. He directed a pair of uniforms to take hold of Connor Pierce.

"This is it," I said and pointed to the rear of the vehicle. He stooped over and examined it for a moment, rose back up, and motioned to the uniforms. They put the handcuffs on Connor and led him to the back of one of the cruisers. The other officers got out of their cars and milled about. Lally put gloves on and went through the Prius. A few minutes later, he emerged with a 9 mm handgun.

"Looks like we got something here," he crowed. "The two victims were shot by a nine. We'll run this through ballistics but I think we found us a murder weapon."

"There's something else I uncovered here, detective," I said.

"What? More crimes being solved by the local private police force?"

"Uh, well, yeah. There was a hit-and-run in Echo Park on Saturday morning. A *Times* reporter was targeted. Adam Lazar. He's stable now, but the vehicle plowed right into him."

"Didn't look like the Prius had any front-end damage."

"No," I said, gesturing to the black Escalade. I showed him the grill and pointed to the denim I had found on the underside of the car. Lally crawled under and looked for himself.

"Something's there all right," he said, slapping his hands together as he got up. "I'll run the plates and get some tow trucks up here."

"This one belongs to a friend of Pierce. Big guy named Alex Gateley."

"Okay," he said, and then barked instructions to the uniforms, who went off in search of the school's administrative offices. He turned back to me. "So how did you know about the Prius?"

"I actually came up looking for a black SUV. I knew

Gateley drove an Escalade. The Prius? I stumbled on it. But you know, sometimes the things you're looking for are hiding in plain sight."

"In other words, you got lucky," he said.

"Luck is where preparation meets opportunity," I pointed out.

Lally shook his head. "Some great philosopher say that?"

"I don't know. I think I got it from a fortune cookie. I'm just glad this case is done with."

"Yeah, me too," he said. "I'll be back in a little while. Need to drop off a package."

Lally climbed back into his sedan and for the first time I noticed a figure in the back seat. He wore a uniform but it wasn't an LAPD blue. It was dark green and the man wearing it didn't look happy. His hands looked like they had been cuffed behind his back.

"Hey, Dennis," I called out.

"Yeah?" he asked, rolling down the window.

"What'd that security guard do?"

Lally shook his head. "The dope tried to prevent me from entering the grounds. Said it was private property. Like this is some foreign country that law enforcement can't enter. Some assholes think they can do whatever they want. If they've got enough clout, maybe they can. This one doesn't. We'll see if a few days in the can doesn't change his attitude."

I gave a quick wave to Lally and smiled at the security guard. He didn't smile back.

Fifteen

I spent most of the day at Stone Canyon, talking to the police, and perhaps as importantly, not talking with any students or school administrators. Loretta Moss tried to implore the investigators to hurry things along, but she was strongly admonished to be quiet, stay out of the way, and speak when she was spoken to. Riley Joyner made a wry comment, referring to me as "Dad," and sending a number of dirty looks my way. I shrugged them off. One day I'd be the parent of a teenager. Hopefully one who wouldn't feel so entitled.

The sun had just set as I drove onto Adelaide Drive to check on Crystal and Molly. When I told them about Connor's role in the murders of Diego and Sofia, Molly nodded her head in acknowledgement, albeit without a look of surprise. Despite Buster Palmer's assurances of keeping the police at bay for a while, I told Molly they would be here soon to question her. Tears streamed down her face, although I wasn't entirely sure who she was crying for.

In an unexpected move, Rex Palmer had taken time out of his campaign schedule that morning to visit Molly again, and to apologize for his behavior. He told her he wanted to make things up to her, to try and make things right, knowing he might be a little late. He said that regardless of the outcome of the election, he would be making more time for her in his life. Rex also told her he planned to file for a divorce from Nicole. Once the election was over, of course.

The next morning I waited until the rush-hour traffic had eased and then drove downtown. I pulled into the subterranean parking lot at One Wilshire and handed my keys to a valet. I assumed Jeremy Hoffman would validate.

"Good morning," I said, as Jeremy's assistant led me into his plush office. The view from the 22nd floor was clear today, and I could see all the way to the ocean. I could even see Catalina Island, jutting out ever so slightly on the distant horizon.

"Oh, if it isn't the super sleuth," he said, rising and shaking my hand. "I've had quite an interesting time reading the newspapers this morning. Although your name was conspicuously missing, I have a feeling you were actively involved in the investigation."

I rubbed my abdomen, which was still sore from where Bill Thorn had slugged me. "Very active. But I'm happy to have my name kept out of it. Clients tend to shy away from publicity-seeking P.I.s."

"Yes. And I do need to apologize to you. I wasn't aware Molly really hadn't gone missing. I told Rex I didn't appreciate him using me here. And I certainly didn't like the way a supposed missing girl wound up getting embroiled in a double murder."

"I doubt the governor had that one planned. Hard to believe, but he may actually have been out of the loop. His father is another story."

"Ah yes, Buster. The man behind the man. It would have been nice if the two of them were on the same page. But Rex doesn't share Buster's right-wing views. And he has good reason, California's not going to elect a conservative Republican again for a long time, if ever. The state's changed. The demographics are different. Rex can't navigate those waters. And the people he chose to run his campaign, they were just a bunch of old college cronies who didn't know what they were doing. His joke about Justin Woo's accent came from his campaign advisors. Bush League stuff. I know Rex is still within a few points of Woo, but winning this election now won't be easy."

"Could it be that's what Buster really wanted?" I asked.

Jeremy thought about this for a moment. "I don't know. I'm sure Buster has his own agenda. It's hard to imagine he'd want his own son to lose. But stranger things have happened."

"You know anything about Connor Pierce?"

"Sure. The family is old money. I'm certain the parents are devastated. I didn't think Connor would ever go and shoot anyone. Especially not over a girl. And I was especially surprised to hear about the racism. He never struck me as a bad egg. But people will always surprise you."

"What do you think he's looking at?"

"If he were a typical defendant, maybe 25-to-life. But he's not typical. Look for a plea bargain down the road. He might do 10 years. Maybe. And depending upon who's governor, there may even be a pardon one day. I've seen people walk on crimes even more egregious than this one."

"Not exactly fair, is it," I remarked. "And I'm sure the victims' parents wouldn't be happy with that."

"Absolutely not," Jeremy agreed. "But crimes of passion elicit sympathy among judges and jurors alike. There's different rules for different people. And like it or not, it's the world in which we live."

"The senseless of all this still bothers me. The racism, the hate."

"You can travel to the four corners of the world," Jeremy sighed. "And still not escape any of that."

"I suppose."

"You just do the best you can do. That's all there is. But I have something positive to share."

"Oh? what's that" I asked.

"You heard about Xavier Bishop?"

"No. What happened?"

"Some very good news," he said, his face brightening."Xavier called me last night. Desiree recanted. Said she was too consumed with emotion and couldn't get her story straight. I assume you played a role in that."

I smiled, shrugged and said nothing.

"All right, well, however it got done. Johnny's going to make an announcement reinstating Xavier to the team. He'll be playing on Saturday against Stanford. And boy, do we need him."

"Sure do. And I imagine a Mr. Cliff Roper may have had a hand in getting everyone to play nicely. I believe you're acquainted with this gentleman."

"Um, yes," Jeremy coughed. "You know, we don't always get to choose our allies. And as unsavory as Cliff might be at times, this is a scenario that's tailor made for his, um, skills. It's not perfect, it's not neat. And I imagine it cost Cliff some money to keep that other kid from pressing charges against Xavier. But I think the outcome was the best we could hope for."

"So everything worked out. Sort of."

"We live in an imperfect world."

"Say, Jeremy. Speaking of the Stanford game on Saturday."

"Yes?" he said, a slight smile crossing his face as if he knew what was coming.

"Would it be an imposition to get me four tickets to the game? I have a friend who's a big fan. And he also provided some help on this case."

Jeremy made a note on a piece of paper. "I'm sure I can arrange something. And it's not an imposition to do this for you. Trust me, people who I barely know think nothing of asking for 50 yard-line seats."

"Nervy."

"Perhaps," he said. "But I can assure you many people want things from me. And they come from all walks of life. Sometimes they come out of the woodwork. Let me take care of this. I'll have something delivered to you later in the week. I think you'll be pleased with the seats. And I may arrange for some added company for you at the game."

"Oh? A new client wouldn't be bad. My schedule has opened up now."

Jeremy smiled more broadly, and didn't say anything more.

*

The rest of the week went by quietly, although not uneventfully. The mortgage people finished gathering documents, and Gail and I closed escrow on our new home in Mar Vista. We started the arduous process of packing, or I should say Gail directed and I followed her instructions.

On Saturday, I told Gail I was going to invoke my day of rest. I half-heartedly offered her a ticket to accompany me to the USC-Stanford game, knowing what her response would be.

"If I have trouble moving in and out of a restaurant, the last place I'm going is the Coliseum. And as you know, football was never one of my passions. Go. Enjoy it with Juan and his kids."

I called Juan and told him if he and his sons could make the drive up from Mission Viejo today, I'd have a nice surprise. Provided he wasn't working, of course. Juan laughed into the phone. "I'm a captain, remember? I control my schedule now."

We met early, outside of the Coliseum, in front of the headless statues that were unveiled right before the '84 Olympic Games. Juan's sons were 13 and 16 and looked just like him, save for the silver hair and pot belly. I was pleased to see that Juan's kids seemed genuinely thrilled to be at the game. It was reassuring to see teenagers who were appreciative of getting something nice. Jeremy Hoffman came through with great seats on the 40 yard-line, about 30 rows up from the field. These were seats that typically were only available to big donors or people willing to spend a lot of money with a scalper. And as we settled in to enjoy the pre-game festivities, another group moved into the row in front of us. One of them looked quite familiar. And I shouldn't have been surprised.

"Now just what are you doing in seats like this?" exclaimed Cliff Roper. "Pretty far above your pay grade, I'd say. I just can't imagine where you got them from!"

"Yes," I said, "same place you got yours, I suspect. Our friend on the 22nd floor is quite generous. If not very discerning."

"Hey, hey, hey. Remember what I told you about trying to be a nicer guy?"

"Coming from you, I considered the source."

"You need to turn off that acid wit," Roper said and pointed to his two companions, a pair of very lean, muscular young men, both of whom appeared to be extremely fit. "Especially if you'll be coaching these fellas next year."

Juan gave me a look. "You're doing what?"

"Nothing's been decided," I said and turned back to Roper. "How do you know anything about this?"

"I know about a lot of things," Roper said. "I heard you might be picking up the whistle. With a kid on the way and your wife stuck on a government salary, you need to earn a grown man's living. Coaching's a gold mine these days."

"You're getting ahead of yourself," I said. "And aren't you going to introduce me to your friends?"

Roper put his hands up. "These young men? Just met 'em. They had seats up in the nosebleed section, probably where you usually sit. So I invited them down here with me. I had a few extra tickets. Turns out they're defensive backs. Seniors in high school. Martin Domfort, Jordan Solomon, meet Burnside. Good guy to have around if you need to rough someone up."

We shook hands. "I take it you fellas play football somewhere in the region?" I asked.

"Yeah," one of them said. "Up in Ventura. We've been offered full rides here. Coach Cleary's been pushing us to decide early."

"Coach is a great guy, known him forever. And this is a great university," I said, knowing anyone who has a relationship with the school needs to be very careful when speaking with recruits. I turned to Roper. "And you just met these fellas?"

"Would I lie to you?" he said, not bothering to answer and providing only a wink instead. "How about you introduce me to your pals. Couple of them look like they're ready to go out for their high school team. Don't know about the pudgy one, though."

Juan Saavedra laughed and introduced himself and his two sons. "My older kid may go out for varsity football next year. Need to work on his mom. She's worried about concussions."

"Women," Roper said, "that's why we love 'em. You a coach?"

"Nope. I'm a captain with the LAPD. Rampart Division."

Roper eyed him carefully. "You got a card? We should talk sometime."

I shook my head. "You have any outstanding warrants you need him to fix?" I asked. "Or just a pile of speeding tickets?"

"Always with the wise cracks, this one," Roper said, his comments interrupted by the stunning young blonde who slipped past him and turned to smile at me. I looked at her with surprise, and probably with a measure of awe. A few other guys were looking too, and not bothering to sneak glances, but rather staring extensively. Honey Roper had that affect on men.

"Well, hello there, Mr. Burnside," she beamed. "It's been a while, hasn't it?"

"It has indeed," I said and watched for her father's reaction. "Too long."

"How is Gail? I spoke with her a few weeks ago. I've been meaning to stop by."

"She's good. And I'm sure she'd love to see you."

"So," she said, the radiant smile still pasted on her gorgeous face. "How are you doing with all of this?"

"With impending fatherhood? Scared to death. People say I'll do fine, but in my line of work, I usually see the parents who messed up somehow. Or maybe just had bad luck. Either path makes me nervous."

"You know, I think you're going to be a good dad."

"Aw, you're just saying that," I teased her.

"Nope," she shook her head definitively. "I know you

well enough. And believe it or not, I actually know what a good dad is."

"Really?" I said, eyebrows arched. When your father's been arrested numerous times for major felonies, it doesn't set the best example. The fact that Cliff Roper had never been convicted didn't change the fact that he was not up for any Father of the Year award.

"I know what you're thinking," she said. "My dad has, um, an unusual background. But in the end it comes down to how your dad treats you, how he looks after you, whether he puts your needs first. Believe it or not, my dad has been pretty good. Not perfect, but pretty good. I know others may think differently, but he's not their dad. He treats me as if I'm special. And as a result, I think I am. Can't ask for too much more than that."

I glanced at Cliff Roper, who was nodding intently as he listened to his daughter lavish praise on him. He had a pleased look on his face and slipped an arm around his daughter. I looked over at Juan, who was pointing to the eternal flame at the top of the peristyle end of the Coliseum, and explaining that USC always lit the flame in the 4th quarter to commemorate the Coliseum's two Olympiads. I thought about my own father who I never knew, and I wondered what he had been like. My mother had rarely spoken about him, the subject had just been too painful for her.

My thoughts were interrupted by the Trojan Marching Band beginning their rendition of the national anthem. A few minutes later, the teams lined up for the opening kickoff. Both USC and Stanford were cautious at first, neither team taking many chances, each one scoring a touchdown after long, time-consuming drives. Xavier Bishop started at cornerback for USC and played exceptionally well. On one play, Xavier's receiver got behind him and was about to reel in a long pass, but Xavier recovered and surged forward at the last moment to tap the ball away. The defenses dug in and the first half ended with the score tied 7-7. It may not have been the most exciting first half, but I enjoyed watching the strategy unfold, and seeing good defense played by both teams.

Stanford received the kickoff to open the 2nd half and started on their 20 yard-line. After a pair of running plays garnered only a couple of yards, they were faced with a 3rd down and long. They needed to gain 8 yards for a first down, or else they'd have to punt the ball to USC. The Stanford offense lined up with five wide receivers, which meant there were no runners in the backfield to pass block. In fact, the only player in the backfield was the Stanford quarterback, who was lined up in a shotgun formation, five yards in back of the center. I usually watched the defensive backs, this was my position, and I probably did it more out of habit. On this play I was glad I did.

Xavier Bishop wore jersey number 1, so he was easy to spot. He was lined up on the right side. As the quarterback barked signals, Xavier began to creep closer to the middle of the field. He shuffled away from the receiver he was supposed to guard and danced closer to the quarterback. When the ball was snapped back to the quarterback,

Xavier exploded toward him at a dead sprint. Johnny had called for a corner blitz. This meant Xavier's receiver would be covered by a slower defender, if he was even being covered at all. The entire play was predicated on Xavier getting to the QB before he could throw the pass.

A blitz in football has its roots in the German war tactic called the *blitzkrieg*. It involves a quick, powerful, unexpected attack that uses speed and might to disable an opponent and unhinge them. It is a commonly used play in football, but normally employed with linebackers rushing the quarterback. Occasionally a safety will blitz, but it's rare that a cornerback would be sent in this way. The element of surprise was a key component.

The Stanford quarterback caught the snap from center and began going through his progressions downfield. He saw an open receiver and began to move his arm back into a throwing position. But the quarterback couldn't see Xavier Bishop flying toward him from his blind side. And when Xavier Bishop crashed into him, the ball popped out of his hand and shot straight up into the air.

Xavier fell on top of the quarterback but then looked around wildly for the football. It took him a second, but he picked up the arc of the ball and saw where it was going to come down. Without even getting up, he launched his body, twisted around and stretched out his right arm. In a prone position, falling on his back, the ball landed in his hand, but you could see it bobble as he tried to maintain control of it. Xavier pulled the football into his belly and pressed it there tightly with his right hand. He then wrapped his left hand around the ball as the referees blew the whistle. The ref closest to him signaled USC had gained possession. It was one of the most unique and brilliant interceptions I had ever seen.

The crowd cheered wildly and Xavier's teammates raced over to celebrate with him. They slapped his helmet joyously as they ran off the field. The entire USC team was jumping up and down and the Coliseum felt like it was shaking. It literally felt like an earthquake was happening. Fans in our section, people who never met each other before, were high-fiving and hugging. Juan grabbed my shoulder and yelled into my ear. It was a spectacular interception and it was a true game-changer.

USC scored on the next play, their tailback taking a handoff and running up the middle, untouched, into the end zone. It was as if the Stanford team was too stunned to respond. They did regain their composure, but the 2nd half was similar to the 1st half. It was a defensive struggle, and neither team scored again. USC came away with the win, 14-7.

As the seconds ticked down on the scoreboard, I bade goodbye to the Ropers and to Cliff's new friends. I brought Juan and his sons down into the Trojan locker room to meet Johnny and a few players. Xavier Bishop, drenched in sweat and smiling expansively, saw me and gave me a big hug.

"I owe you, man," he whispered into my ear. "I don't know what you said to Desiree, but she did the right thing. Told me all she wanted was what's best for me. By the end of our talk, I had tears in my eyes."

I looked at him. "Does that mean you're getting back

together?"

Xavier Bishop answered me with a little shrug. But he was still smiling as he did it.

Sixteen

California's gubernatorial election was held on the Tuesday following the USC-Stanford game. Rex Palmer, like his Stanford alma mater, went down to defeat. Unlike his alma mater, the election wasn't even close. While the polls showed Rex to be trailing by five or six points prior to the election, the results were nowhere near that. Justin Woo won by almost 20 points and was elected governor in a landslide. It was the most lopsided win over a sitting governor in this state since Ronald Reagan was elected many, many years ago.

I waited a few weeks for the dust to settle before going and talking to the one person who might provide closure on some lingering issues. I knew from experience that certain cases simply end and you don't always get resolution on things. But I generally tried to unearth whatever details I could before moving on to the next case. My natural curiosity had led me into this field, and had served to help me become successful at it. Leaving questions unanswered was not something I liked to do.

It was a Friday around 10:00 a.m., sunny and lazy. It was the type of day that makes being outside a joy. I lowered the windows of my Pathfinder as I drove up Tigertail Road, enjoying the warm breeze lapping softly on my face. I approached Buster Palmer's home and was reassured to see the street fairly empty. No media, no paparazzi. Just a couple of gardeners, one mowing a small lawn, the other using a leaf blower to corral leaves from a nearby silver maple tree.

The housekeeper remembered me and escorted me through the house, past the parlor and onto an outdoor porch overlooking a rustic canyon.

"Come on over, young man," Buster boomed. "Have a seat. Take a load off."

I sat down on a bentwood rocking chair. "Thank you for seeing me again, sir. Much appreciated."

"Oh, I figured you'd be back. You struck me as the type. And I figured you had a few more questions for me. Your kind always does."

"You seem to have figured me out," I smiled. "Glad you're in the mood to talk."

"Talk. That's about all I do these days," he responded. "But I like to think I'm quite adept at it."

"Yes. I'm sorry to hear about Rex. Tough to lose an election in such a big way."

"Disappointing, I would agree," Buster said. "But you take the good with the bad in politics. I've been around long enough to know most people can make a comeback. I just don't know if Rex should bother."

"Why's that?"

Buster shook his head, maybe a little sadly. "He's not cut out for politics. Doesn't have that instinct. You have to know when to compromise and when to dig your heels in. He was too quick to cut deals with the legislature. And sometimes you have to ask for a favor without promising anything in return. Offering merely the thanks of a grateful governor may not sound like much, but it demonstrates strength."

"Seems like sound advice. Why didn't Rex follow this?"

"Ah, Mr. Burnside. You've yet to have children. They have their own constitutions and they are their own people. As much as you want to help them, they have to carve out their own path. There are times that will lead them straight into a ditch."

"Speaking of children," I said. "I wanted to ask you about Molly. That whole situation confounded me. I was hired by Rex to find a daughter that wasn't really missing. Can you shed some light on what happened?"

"Yes sir, I believe I can. Now anyways," he said. "I was the one who suggested Molly go stay with her friends, although I certainly didn't suggest she go into the *barrio*. She needed to be away from the campaign and away from that poor excuse of a mother. Nicole was a huge liability in this campaign. Carrying on with a woman was just one example. The lack of discretion was even worse. Throw in the drinking and you have a toxic stew. Thankfully, the media didn't focus on Nicole. The *Times* tried to, but I was able to quash it."

"Oh? So much for freedom of the press."

"Yes, you'd be surprised at how little freedom there really is in America. And I know I'm old, but I know about social media and how things can get out. But I also know that if you pay enough money, you can keep many things quiet. And secret. Everyone has their price, Mr. Burnside. Everyone."

"So how is it that Rex seemed to think Molly was missing?" I asked.

"Oh, that was Nicole. For whatever her crazy reasons, she and Rex had grown estranged to the point where they despised each other terribly. So when Molly went off with that Mexican kid after the football game, she told her mother. But Nicole told Rex that Molly had gone missing. Guess she wanted to mess with Rex's head during the final throes of the election. Evil woman, that one. I tried to tell Rex that things were being handled, but as I said, some kids don't like to listen to their parents. You'd think they'd grow out of it when they become adults."

"So why didn't Molly let her father know? Or is this more of the kids-and-parents thing."

"No need to be smart with me, Mr. Burnside. Molly hadn't been happy with Rex for quite a while. Didn't fully understand the important position he had. She felt he had one job and one job only. To be her father."

"So all of this came down to a bunch of important people not liking their family members, and not talking honestly to one another. Sheesh."

"I can see how it might sound dysfunctional to an outsider," Buster Palmer sighed. "And I can't say as I'm proud of it all. I'm the patriarch of this clan and I bear some responsibility. But you know, the world does what the world does. Hopefully Rex will find his way. Maybe one day he'll hold the world in the palm of his hand. Like I used to."

"All right," I said. "I can't say as I fully understand the inner machinations of being a parent yet. Maybe one day.

But I do have another matter to discuss with you."

"Oh?"

I reached into my pocket and pulled out the $10,000 check Molly had handed to me. "This was your payment to provide Molly with a safe place for a while. I didn't really need to spend it. I'm sure you know, she's been staying with a friend of mine."

"Yes, yes, Mrs. Fairborn," he said, nodding approvingly. "Quite an impressive woman. Molly loves her. And I might add, I think Rex may, too."

I stared at him. "You're kidding."

"I'm afraid not, Mr. Burnside. Apparently since the election, Rex and Crystal have been seeing a lot of one another. And for once in her life, I think Molly actually approves of what her father is doing."

"If that don't beat all," I said, shaking my head.

"I'll bet you never thought of yourself as Cupid, now did you?" he smiled.

"No, sir. Never, to be quite honest."

"I know that wasn't your intent. But you showed remarkably good judgment in placing Molly with Crystal Fairborn. So if you're all right with this, I'd like you to keep the check. I'm sure with a child on the way, you'll be able to put it to good use. Lord knows, I have plenty of money. Consider this a bonus for a job well done. Even if much of it was earned being a matchmaker."

"That's quite generous of you," I said. "Sincerely, it is."

Buster waved a hand. "It's nothing, really. And if things work out the way I expect them to, we'll invite you and your wife to the wedding."

"Rex may not be too crazy about that idea."

"I'll insist. I still have some juice around here."

"Well, if they do wind up tying the knot, I'm sure you'll be relieved about one thing."

"What's that?" Buster asked.

"She won't be marrying Rex for his money."

*

Gail and I moved into our new home the Sunday after Thanksgiving. We spent much of December setting up the nursery, painting, wallpapering, figuring out where to put furniture and on which walls to hang pictures. Or I should say, Gail decided and I followed her suggestions. And oddly, while my sleep was no longer being interrupted by Ms. Linzmeier, I still found myself waking up at 5:00 a.m.

I took on a few small cases, mostly insurance fraud I could handle without much incident. Our next-door neighbors, The Conways, welcomed us during our first week with a homemade apple cake. They invited us over for dinner the following week and they were a friendly couple. They also had a dog, a feisty little dachshund who would yap occasionally, so a few play dates were arranged with Chewy. And it didn't take long for our quiet puppy to begin picking up some new, and less-than-delightful habits. While we were convinced that back in Santa Monica she didn't even know how, after two weeks in Mar Vista, our little dog had finally learned how to bark.

USC made it to the Rose Bowl game and was scheduled to play Michigan State on New Year's Day. One of the oddities of Southern California weather was that we normally get a lot of fog this time of year, and an occasional rainstorm. But it rarely ever rained during a Rose Bowl game, and it looked like this year would be no exception; the forecast was for sunny skies and warm temperatures. I visited Johnny during one of the team's practices and wished them good luck. Johnny didn't bring up his casual offer of a coaching job again and I didn't ask him. I still hadn't settled on an answer for that. I did have an answer for Arthur Woo, however. I provided him with a polite and gracious decline of his offer to head up security for his brother, now the governor-elect. While the job had a certain appeal, I had more important responsibilities now, and flying back and forth to Sacramento wasn't going to be one of them.

While the doctor had told Gail that her due date would be right around Christmas, Shelly Busch had proved to be a better prognosticator. It was New Year's Eve and we were still expecting. Shelly herself would remain busy with politics; her husband, Landon Busch, had announced the formation of an exploratory committee for his candidacy to become the next U. S. Senator from California. The election was almost two years away, but I imagined Shelly would already be knee-deep in fund raising. And after badly mismanaging Rex Palmer's re-election campaign, working for her husband was most likely the only job in politics she could get.

Gail and I celebrated New Year's Eve with takeout from a local Chinese restaurant. She said she had a craving for roast duck, but I had a sense she was using that as an excuse. In her condition though, I felt she had every right to get something special. And whether it was the duck, the fried rice, or the fortune cookie that hinted something amazing was about to happen, Gail woke me at 4:30 a.m. to tell me her water had broken. It took me about two minutes to get ready and we were on our way to Santa Monica Hospital. Even though I drove slowly and not many cars were on the road at this hour, I still needed to swerve to avoid a few intoxicated drivers who were veering all over the road. Some things never change.

Gail spent 12 hours in labor. They applied an epidural right away, but it could only minimize the pain so much. Time moved slowly. The Rose Bowl game was on TV, but in what was probably a first for me, I paid little attention to how SC's football team was doing. The nurses told us some women wound up spending over 24 hours in labor, and I shuddered to even imagine that. We were fortunate. Gail gave birth to a healthy 8-pound baby boy at a few minutes before 5:00 p.m.. I smiled through my tears as she made the final push, and out came our son. The medical staff took over and handed him to Gail a few minutes later. I watched her positively glow as she gazed into his eyes. After a few minutes, she handed him to me and I started to take him over to a seat by the window.

And then it happened. Hospital rooms should never have wires on the floor. There should never be a dangerous place in which to step. They should never afford opportunities for people to trip. Especially in a delivery room where new parents are sleep-deprived and not paying attention to basic, everyday matters. As I cradled our new little package, my foot got caught on a wire and I felt myself losing my balance. A horrible coldness took shape in the pit of my stomach.

This wasn't supposed to happen. You don't carry a child safely for nine months only to have something catastrophic happen a few minutes after they enter our world. A whirlwind of bad thoughts spun instantly through my mind as I felt myself lose my footing. In a split second, I focused my energies and tried to let my instincts take over. I twisted my body around so I would land on my back and not on the baby. I could absorb a blow; our newborn could not. I clutched the baby to my chest, and for the strangest moment I thought of Xavier Bishop cradling the football against his body so it would not touch the ground. You do what you have to do.

And then, as quickly as I lost my balance, I somehow regained it. Whether it was through the years of athletic training or simply divine intervention, I felt my body stabilize and both my feet landed flat on the ground. My breathing was deep and erratic. I looked around to see if anyone else noticed, but no one had. The doctor was taking care of Gail, the nurses were reviewing paperwork, and no one had seen a thing. I certainly wasn't about to say anything. I looked down at our son, my heart pounding furiously. This would have to be our little secret for a while.

I caught a glimpse of the TV, saw the final score of the Rose Bowl and that USC had won. I realized, seemingly for the first time, that January 1st would be my son's birthday. I had a feeling we would be spending many New

Year's Days together, probably some of them up in Pasadena, attending the Rose Bowl game. My son and I just had our first exciting moment together. I knew there would be many more.

The End

About The Author

David Chill was born and raised in New York City and educated in the public schools. After receiving his undergraduate degree from SUNY-Oswego, he moved to Los Angeles where he earned a Masters degree from the University of Southern California. David Chill is the author of seven novels: *Post Pattern, Fade Route, Bubble Screen, Safety Valve, Corner Blitz, Nickel Package* and *Double Pass*, all featuring Burnside, a private investigator and former LAPD officer and college football star.

Post Pattern was a finalist in the St. Martin's Press contest for New Private Eye Mystery Writers. The Burnside series has received much critical acclaim, and all of his novels have spent time on the Amazon.com best seller lists. David Chill currently lives in Los Angeles with his wife and son. If you would like to contact David Chill directly, please email him at: davidchill3214@gmail.com

If you enjoyed Corner Blitz, then
don't miss David Chill's sixth
Burnside novel....

Nickel Package

Here is a sample chapter of this
terrific mystery...

NICKEL PACKAGE PREVIEW

It was supposed to have been a routine background investigation. Just gather some information on a high-profile job candidate. No one was supposed to die.

"We're looking for a new CEO," declared the wily executive.

"Too bad for me," I said, with a wink. "I just signed a 12-month lease for office space."

The wily executive smiled patiently, but it was not a genuine smile, it was one which could be switched on and off at will. His name was Nick Roche, and he had a handsome office. The carpet was thick and the couch was soft. The walls held real artwork that looked expensive and probably was. The view from his office reached the Pacific ocean. It had rained over the weekend, our first storm in over one month, so the sky was sun-washed and pristine. I could almost see Catalina Island.

 "Jay told me you had a wise guy streak in you," Roche said.

I smiled back at him. We were both smiling. It was a pleasant, cordial meeting. "Glad you've been put on notice," I said. "According to Jay, you need a background check done."

"Yes, Mr. Burnside. We need someone good. My brother-in-law told me you're very astute."

"Jay's astute as well," I remarked. Anyone who calls me astute deserves to be repaid in kind.

"I suppose. He makes pretty good money, anyway."

I continued to smile, although the last comment gave me pause. For the past three years, I had taken a career detour, a lucrative move that had earned me a boatload of money. Gobs of money. More money than a P.I. like me could ever make, and ridiculously more than the salary I earned as an LAPD officer, many moons ago.

"Money isn't everything," I said, hoping he wouldn't counter by telling me that, no, in fact, money was the only thing. Thankfully, he did not.

"You're right."

The past few years had indeed been lucrative for me, but the process had taken its toll. The hundred-hour work weeks were the proof. And even if USC's new head coach had asked me to stay on as a well-heeled assistant, I wouldn't have done so. I had even rejected the opportunity to join my old friend Johnny Cleary in the NFL. My son was now three years old, and I had missed so much. I didn't hear him say his first words, and I didn't see him take his first steps. There were some things money could not buy, and some jobs that were not worth the personal cost. I needed to make a course correction.

"So tell me how I can help you," I asked.

"We're looking for a new CEO," he said. "Chief Executive Officer."

"They used to call that guy the President. I gather that's *passé now*."

"Very much so. Especially here at BMB. We have a lot of Presidents."

"Uh-huh. And you're the President of Finance. Has a nice ring to it."

"Finance and Operations," he pointed out, holding a clarifying index finger in the air. "But it's not that unusual within the entertainment industry."

I nodded. Big egos need big titles. And it was never more true than in show biz. When you've grown up in Los Angeles, you can't help but rub up against the ostentatious demeanors and outsized demonstrations of wealth and power. They are everywhere. It's not unusual to be driving down the street and notice you're surrounded on all sides by BMWs and Mercedes. And an occasional Maserati or Rolls Royce.

"Who are your CEO candidates?" I asked.

Roche pulled a pack of cigarettes from his drawer, slid one out and lit it. I thought of reminding him smoking, even inside private office buildings, was illegal in California. I also thought of my fee going up in smoke and decided to exercise some discretion.

"We have a number of people," he said, blowing a plume of

smoke up at the ceiling. "But there's one in particular who excites the Board. His name is Eric Starr. You might have heard the name."

I shook my head. "Sorry. Unless he's good at knocking down passes -- or wide receivers -- I probably wouldn't have paid much attention. At least not for the past three years."

"I understand," he said. "Coaching is more than a full-time job. Jay filled me in on your background. Quite a career you've had. College football star, LAPD officer, private detective, coaching football at your alma mater. You've certainly had a marvelous life."

"It's far from over," I pointed out. "I'm just shifting gears."

"Sorry," he said. "No offense intended."

"None taken."

As marvelous as it may have seemed, my decision to accept Johnny's offer to coach defensive backs at USC led me into the hardest job I had ever undertaken. Johnny's teams had been enormously successful, so the school gave him latitude on hiring decisions. I had played college football for the Trojans many years ago, but had no experience whatsoever as a coach, so my learning curve was steep. As I discovered though, I was good at it. I liked working with young athletes, but I took the most pride in using football to prepare them for the real world.

All of my players were extraordinary athletes who knew the fundamentals of how to play cornerback and safety. I taught them the intangibles, the little pointers that would give them an edge in a high profile game. But I also emphasized the metaphors that winning can be applied to all aspects of life. And I made sure they were keenly aware that most college players don't go on to star in pro football. The NFL is hyper-competitive, and it can take just one injury to end an athletic career. The kids needed a road map for going forward, if their dreams of a pro football career never materialized. From my own painful experience, I could certainly share how the random wind of fate could derail anyone's plans.

"So tell me about this Eric Starr," I said, changing the subject.

"You can read his full bio online," Roche said. "But I'll give you the nickel tour. He grew up in Orange County, father's a high-level executive with a tech firm. Eric spent a couple of years working there, met a colleague and they went out on their own. They started the Laputa Company. You've heard of that, haven't you?"

"I have."

"A few years later, it's one of the biggest internet companies in the world. It's got everything. It's a media company that provides news and content. It's a search engine, an ISP, a social media site and an online retailer. Billion dollar business. Eric didn't create the technology, but he grabbed the reins and made it a success. He's more of a marketing guy."

"And he's willing to give up his baby to come work for BMB?"

"We're in discussions. BMB's 20 times bigger than Laputa, and he'd oversee a movie studio, TV networks, theme parks and video games. We're a huge business. This could be a good next step for him."

"So he'd be your boss."

"I've got a contract. I'm not concerned about my future."

"Okay. And you think Eric's the guy to run BMB."

Roche shrugged and held up his palms. "Some people on the Board think so. He's got a track record of success. And he can bring fresh thinking to a 75 year-old company."

"But there are concerns about Eric," I remarked.

"There are."

"Tell me about them."

Roche leaned back in his leather chair and stopped the dialogue. He seemed like he might have been deep in thought. Taking a long drag on his cigarette, he let the smoke slowly waft out through his nostrils.

"Eric has a history," he began, an air of drama filling the room. "He makes quick decisions, usually based on his gut. He's sometimes right, mind you, but he flies by the seat of his pants. In the tech world, you can get away with that, everything moves so quickly. Over here, when we make a decision to green light a movie or build a new theme park, we're investing what might end up being hundreds of millions of dollars. Being wrong can cost the company a lot of money."

"Seems like you've studied Laputa."

"I know a few people. A few of our former execs moved over there. They talk."

"Okay, fine," I said. "But I know as much about corporate life as you do about football schemes. Just what are you really after?"

Roche took a glance out the window, his appearance of deep pondering starting to morph into a look of annoyance. My comments often had that effect on people.

"Eric's got a history. Big partier, bad behavior with women, not using good judgment. You name it."

I raised my eyebrows. "Well that never happens in show biz, does it?"

"You have to understand," he said, his voice rising along with his impatience, "that we've gone through three CEOs in the past four years. We're a publicly traded company. Fortune 500. This isn't just about hiring another yahoo in to run a movie studio. We need a seasoned professional, but also someone who's a visionary. Someone who can lead us into the future."

"Okay. I can dig into his personal background. But let me ask you something. Three CEOs in four years? This place sounds like a revolving door. Why is that?"

"A few reasons," he said tersely. " Four years ago, our CEO retired. He had spent 25 years at the helm. We replaced him with someone internal, but they didn't deliver results. Some bad investment decisions. These days, a CEO is judged every quarter on his financial results. A few bad quarters and they're out. Simple as that. Same with the next CEO, he had a number of movies flop at the box office. Our most recent CEO, Malcolm Taylor, he was only here for a year before he resigned. There were some personal issues. But he wasn't cutting it either."

"Sounds like it's easy to fail here."

"It's easy to fail everywhere these days. And all of the past CEOs came up through the ranks at BMB. Our core business is the movie studio and that's where these guys made their bones. Production Execs. Entertainment types. But it hasn't worked out. So the Board's looking for something different. Can't keep doing the same thing and expect different results. You know. Sisyphus rolling the rock uphill and all. "

"Why don't they bring in a finance guy. Maybe someone like you."

He smiled again. "Our roots are still in show biz. I have an MBA. From Harvard. But people look at me as a suit. The Board doesn't think suits have the creative vision. I'm not complaining, mind you. I'm very well compensated for what I do. But moving up isn't going to be an option for someone like me."

"All right. You mentioned a few internal candidates. You want me to look into them too?"

"No. We probably know enough about our internal people. But it's unusual that outsiders are even considered, so the Board is being meticulous here. This is new terrain for us. So we want you to look into Eric's background, talk to whoever you think might provide any insight."

"What about my talking to Eric himself?" I asked.

"No," he shook his head definitively. "The Board doesn't want any footprints."

"That's going to be difficult," I pointed out. "When you start talking with friends and colleagues, word spreads. It can't help but get back to the person."

"Jay said you were good. You'll figure it out."

I decided to leave this one alone for the time being. "Just who is this Board you're referring to?"

"Board of Directors. They oversee the company, provide guidance, advice. It's stacked with people who have diverse backgrounds. CEOs from other companies, a few politicians, dignitaries, couple of academics. There's even a USC professor on our Board. Dr. Ethan Kanter, maybe you know him. He teaches at the Film School there. Cinematic Arts."

"Don't know him. I didn't mingle much with professors. But I'm surprised you didn't pick someone from the Marshall School. USC's Business program is one of the best in the country."

"The Board is largely selected by the CEOs," he shrugged. "They bring in people they know and trust. Usually it makes sense. Occasionally they bring in their friends. Some CEO from Disney once added the principal from his son's grade school to his Board. Then he added an actor."

"And they both got approved?"

"CEOs are given a lot of leeway on things. They have

enormous power. That's why we're being especially careful up front here. Our stock has been getting hammered. Shareholders want to see results. And fast. We can't afford any more mistakes."

I thought about something. "Do you have a Security Director here?"

"Of course."

"What's his involvement been?"

"Well, Ferris looked into Eric initially. But we need an outsider now. Someone impartial. That's where you come in."

"Ferris. Is that Hector Ferris?"

"Yes, he reports up to me. You know him?"

"Worked briefly with him at the Broadway division of LAPD. Long time ago. Hector made Lieutenant if I recall."

"That's right. He started a couple of years back. Right after he retired from the police department. Thorough guy."

I agreed. Hector Ferris was certainly thorough, maybe too much so. I didn't tell Roche that Ferris's retirement was orchestrated by the Chief, who got tired of him poking his nose into every nook and cranny. The Chief of Police is like any other executive. Appreciative of hard work, but more than willing to jettison anyone if they get under his skin.

"Can I speak with Hector?"

Roche hesitated. "I suppose," he said, thinking about it for a minute. "Sure. I'll take you down to his office."

"So then I'll start today," I said.

"Good."

"You know what my rate is," I said, a bit apprehensively. Normally it was a thousand dollars a day, although that was three years ago. And BMB was my first paying client since hanging out my shingle again. Given the plush corporate surroundings, as well as my newfound high income expectations, I needed to brand myself as a premium investigator. Charging a high fee was one way to accomplish that. So my special rate for BMB would be fifteen hundred a day. Plus expenses.

"I do," Roche agreed, getting to his feet. "And Jay tells me you have a son who's pre-school age. This should help cover part of the cost."

"I guess Jay's been pretty chatty. I'll have to chide him about discretion. I'm having lunch with him later."

Roche smiled. "Southern barbecue is his favorite. Comfort food for him."

"I'm expanding his horizons. We're going old school L.A. He'll like it. So how urgent is this background check?"

"It's for the Board, so everything is urgent. Corporate life, you know. I'll assume this should only take a few days. Today's Monday. I'd like something by the end of the week."

"Fine. So will I get a check today?"

Roche gave me a condescending look. "This is a multi-national corporation, I don't keep a petty cash drawer" he said. "Send me an invoice."

*

The office Hector Ferris occupied was nowhere near as plush as Nick Roche's, nor did it have much of a view. There was a window, but it faced a parking lot. There were pictures hanging on the walls, but these were prints of classic movie posters, not original artwork. There was a black leather chair, but no couch. And the two seats facing the desk were standard issue gray cloth and utilitarian to boot. In one, however, sat an attractive woman, who did not quite seem at home in the drab surroundings.

"Hector," Roche announced, bouncing inside and motioning me to follow him. "This is the fellow I was telling you about. Mr. Burnside has heard of you."

"And I've heard of him, too," he said, rising and shaking my hand. "Mister Private Eye."

"Lieutenant."

"It's no longer Lieutenant," he said. "You can call me Mr. Ferris."

"Sure, Hector. Whatever you say."

Ferris paused. "I remember you now from Broadway

Division. You were a good cop. Then you turned into a smartass."

"I always was. I just hid it well."

The attractive women stood up and extended her hand. She had tawny eyes and a wide-cut mouth, pretty, but in an L.A. sort of way. Slender, mildly buxom, and a well-honed use of cosmetics helped her look good while appearing not to try. She had well-behaved, straight auburn hair that stopped right at her shoulders. From her ears dangled a pair of small, sparkling diamonds.

"Patty Austin," she announced. "President of Production."

I shook her hand. "You have a firm grip," I said, not telling her that it was stronger and less moist than Hector's.

"Why, thank you. I'm flattered," she said, and overtly batted her eyelashes a few times.

"Patty," Roche nodded at her, his smile a bit wary. "I hope everything's all right. Didn't think I'd see you in the Security Director's office today. Someone hitting on you again?"

"Nothing Hector and I can't handle," she grinned. "Don't worry, Nick. It won't cost you any money. I know how you worry about the bottom line."

"Someone around here has to," Roche commented.

"Well my business here is finished for now," she said, and casually handed me her card. "Private Eye, huh? I'll bet you have a lot of good stories."

"More than I can tell."

Patty Austin gave me a final smile and a wink as she walked out. "If you'd ever like to share, I just might want to hear about a few."

Roche looked back at Ferris as the pretty woman walked out into the hallway. "I'll leave you two to talk shop," he said, and hurried out the door to catch up with Patty.

Ferris pointed to a chair as he moved behind his desk and eased himself slowly down into his chair. He was a portly man with a wide girth and black, curly hair. He wore a cheap yellow shirt with a clip on tie, and looked every bit the role of the ex-cop with an office job. Ferris maintained a placid expression, but there were lines of age cutting across the forehead, and jowls forming under his wide jaw. The only feature that struck me as out of place in a corporate environment was the lump under his left armpit. That meant he was prepared for adverse situations. As was I.

"Burnside," he studied me. "Didn't know you very well when you were on the job."

"I knew you though."

Ferris made a small choking sound and said nothing.

"Sounds like you heard some stories about me," I said.

"Sure. Who didn't? Officer Burnside. You were famous. And not in a good way. How did you wind up here on the BMB lot?"

"Friends in high places," I smiled.

"And you're investigating our future CEO."

"That's my assignment. Anything you want to tell me?"

Ferris gave me a long stare. I looked him in the eye for a few moments, got bored, and turned my attention toward his window. Not much was happening outside either.

"Yeah, there's something I want to tell you," Ferris said, and I looked back at him. "This investigation on Eric Starr? It's mine. I started it and I want to finish it. You need to report to me. Whatever you learn, I want to know about it."

"That's nice. Makes sense, too. But, no, sorry."

"No?" he asked, eyebrows arching.

"No. I was hired by Nick Roche. I'm being paid out of Nick Roche's budget. He approves my invoices. I report to him, not you."

"You don't make friends easily, do you?"

"Neither do you, if I recall. Look, Hector," I sighed. "I want to work with you. Not against you. But my rules are pretty straightforward. They're not negotiable. When I find out something, you'll be the second call I make."

Ferris gazed at me some more. Then, as if some magical wand of acceptance had been waved over him, a sense perhaps, that arguing with me would be fruitless, he reached into his desk and came out with a manila file. He put on a pair of gold-framed reading glasses and perused some papers. "Eric Starr. Quite a success story. He built a great fortune over at Laputa."

"As they say, behind every great fortune is a great crime."

Ferris looked up at me again, still maintaining his placid face. I wasn't even sure he had heard me. "Eric does have some history," he finally said. "But nothing that would prevent him from taking the reins here."

"Tell me about his history."

"You know about his partner and the accident?"

"Partner?"

"Business partner," he said frowning. "It was all over the news. Jack Beale. Couple of years ago. Took his boat out one day with some friends, did a booze cruise. Everyone having a good time, just sailing along on the ocean blue. Then someone noticed Jack wasn't there. Not on the boat, nowhere."

"Only one exit," I said.

"Yeah, and the ocean's an awfully big place to search. His body never washed ashore. Probably wound up somewhere in the middle of the Pacific."

"Think he was pushed?"

"Always a possibility. Best anyone could figure is he got drunk and somehow fell in. But there were about 10 people on the boat and their stories all matched. It was finally ruled an accident. Can't have a homicide without a body."

"Was Eric on the boat?"

"Nope, he was actually in New York at the time. Can't beat

that for an alibi. I guess the epilogue is what happened to the Company. The terms of their partner agreement. If one partner wasn't around, the other would assume control. Eric was king of the hill. And his wife got nothing. When someone disappears, they have to wait seven years before the missing person's declared dead."

"You've done your homework. Anything else?"

"Nothing out of the ordinary. I mean, if we were hiring a traditional CEO, he'd be taken out of the consideration pool right away. But not around here. There's been behavioral issues. Drugs, a few fights. You sometimes see this in guys who launch internet startups. Not a lot of boundaries."

"As opposed to the entertainment industry," I observed.

"There are similarities, sure."

"Think there's more?"

"I know there's more," he said, somewhat earnestly. "I just can't pry the details out of anybody. Everyone knows I'm with BMB and won't speak with me. That's why you're here."

"Any suggestions where I should start?"

"How about at the beginning?"

I rolled my eyes. Everyone is just so witty these days. "All right," I said. "I'll poke around. Who've you talked to so far?"

"Mostly colleagues at Laputa. They all say he's brilliant. A little crazy. But they won't go into details."

"A little crazy isn't bad sometimes," I mused. "Can lead you to new things. Ideas you never thought of."

"Right. Maybe you should head up our search committee. I'll go ask the Chairman of the Board to step aside."

"Maybe you should. Say, let me ask you about that Patty Austin."

Ferris raised his eyebrows. "What about her?"

"Roche made a comment about someone hitting on her. Anything to that?"

"What do you care?"

I shrugged. "Just curious. That's why I like P.I. work. Might mean nothing, might mean something."

Ferris looked at me curiously. "Sorry. There are some things I don't talk about."

To purchase the full copy of Nickel Package, please visit www.Amazon.com

Corner Blitz

www.ingramcontent.com/pod-product-compliance
Lightning Source LLC
Chambersburg PA
CBHW020559260626
47157CB00003B/780